Happy Birthday, Caragh!

LIAM'S PROMISE

By John F. Picciano

Enjoy — Uncle John

PAGE PUBLISHING, INC.
New York, NY

First originally published by Page Publishing, Inc. 2014

ISBN 978-1-62838-345-4 (pbk)
ISBN 978-1-62838-346-1 (digital)

Printed in the United States of America

PREFACE

Some will doubtlessly describe this as a book dealing solely with the explosion of Flight 800 while en route from New York to Paris in July 1996. It is not.

Many accounts, theories, and opinions hypothesizing about the true cause of the air disaster that claimed the lives of 230 passengers have been published worldwide. Two polar-opposite camps have been formed: one supporting the official benign government position and the other insisting that a missile, whether domestic or foreign, whether fired intentionally or accidentally, struck the Boeing 747.

The what-if scenario described in this book has been fabricated in order to create a background and literary landscape for a work of fiction about the relationship between a father and his estranged son. While much of the technical information about the aircraft and the crime scene investigation is factually accurate, all of the character portrayals and the causes of the crash itself, as presented in this book, are purely fictional and not intended to represent any particular person or event.

This is, first and foremost, a story of a young man forced to come of age in a hurry. It is a lesson about the limitless reservoir of courage and integrity that can often well up in the human heart when one is faced with seemingly overwhelming fear, dread, and inertia.

I would like to express my deepest thanks to my wife, Suzi, for her inspiring enthusiasm and support for my humble efforts at this, my first attempt to write a novel. Special thanks go to my son, Bill, for his invaluable editing skills and story line insights. I would also like to acknowledge the technical expertise and support of my law associate, Peter J. Caso, captain, US Navy, retired; Thomas J. Baker my Fordham classmate who, as an FBI Special Agent assigned to Paris, coordinated the French side of the TWA 800 investigation; and Ray Becker, retired Special Agent, FBI.

Thank you for reading the book. I hope you enjoy it as much as I enjoyed writing it.

John F. Picciano
Huntington, New York

Boeing 747-400 Fuel Tank Arrangement

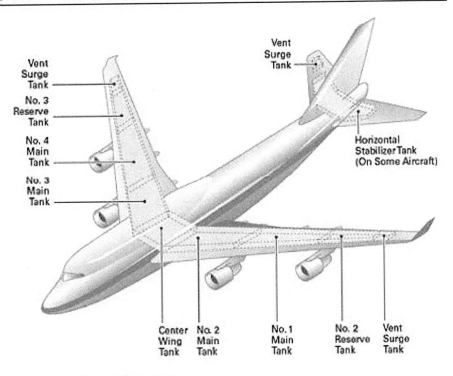

Total Usable Fuel

Airplanes With a Horizontal Stabilizer Fuel Tank	216,389 liters (57,164 U.S. gallons)
Airplanes Without a Horizontal Stabilizer Fuel Tank	203,897 liters (53,864 U.S. gallons)

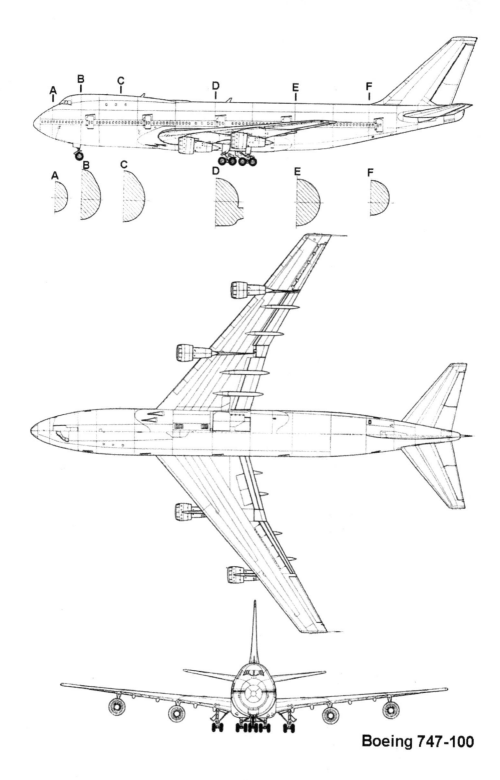

Boeing 747-100

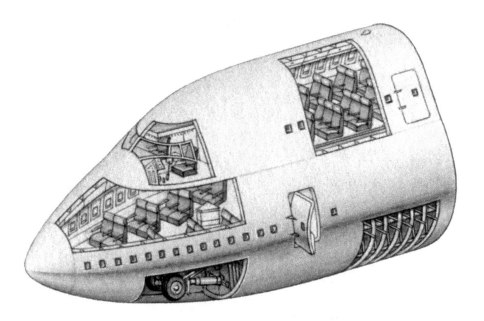

PROLOGUE

The young, weary pilot was thrown back into the seat of his A-6 Intruder as it was catapulted off the deck of the aircraft carrier, both engines roaring at full throttle. A brisk, humid southeast breeze mixed the warm, moist night air with the fumes of spent jet fuel over the towering steel decks of the lumbering sea giant as it plodded through the night and blackness of the South China Sea. Dozens of flight and ordnance crew members were scurrying over the deck, their eerie silhouettes moving purposefully in the now-routine dark, "lights out" launch of yet another bombing raid over North Vietnam. Due to a week of unusually good weather, this was the fourth consecutive night of attacks.

As soon as the pilot gained altitude, he banked left and looked around for his squadron buddies so he could group up in formation, but there was no other aircraft in sight. As he angled the jet toward the northwest, he looked behind and below toward the carrier, but it was gone. There was nothing but a dark, rough-looking ocean below him. As he looked down to his left, he spoke quickly on the intercom to his navigator: "What the hell is going on, Mac? Where are the rest of the guys?" When he didn't get an answer, he turned and saw that the second seat was empty. He was flying alone.

Instantly, a red missile warning light began to flash through the cockpit as the familiar "Ah, shit" alarm started screaming at him. All around him he could see dozens of surface-to-air missiles, with glowing red fire tails lighting up the ocean surface, rushing up at him from all directions. As soon as he tried to roll and dive out of the way of one, three more seemed to hone in on him. He pulled back hard on the stick, but it was nonresponsive, as suddenly all of his controls locked up. He was seized with panic as he realized that he was no longer flying the aircraft. By now his heart was racing. In wild fear and desperation, he hit the eject lever, bracing himself for the canopy to blow and the seat to rocket out of the aircraft. But nothing happened. He was surrounded by stillness and deathly quiet. Suddenly, a roar and a burst of blinding light filled the cockpit.

He screamed out—then sat up abruptly. As his eyes focused on his surroundings, he realized that he was lying in his own bed. His war in Vietnam had come alive again as a bad thirty-year-old dream. John Worthington Mayfair had not had a recurrence of this once-familiar nightmare for many years. His wife, Lee, had already quietly wrapped her arms around him, knowing all too well what was happening.

After several moments of lying in the dark, he spoke softly, trying to conceal his fear. "Lee, this is now two nights in a row. I haven't had this dream for years. This is really unnerving me. I can't stand this sense of dread hanging over me like a big black cloud. Why am I having this feeling of impending doom? Why now?"

"John, you've always taken your dreams way too seriously. Don't overanalyze them. Your war in Vietnam is long over. The only war you're fighting now is with yourself and, at the moment, with Liam. You're safe here on terra firma with me and the kids. In the scheme of the universe, and in the final analysis, you must know that there is nothing in this life that can hurt you. You understand that, don't you? Besides, God is not going to let you move on to the next life while you have major unresolved issues with any of your children. Don't you know that by now, o ye of little faith?"

Lee Mayfair paused. "John, in exactly one week, you'll be flying to Paris to finish up your merger deal. Why don't you take the time you have now to resolve everything with your son? That's probably what's really eating at you."

"Hon, I'm going to be very busy and under a ton of pressure getting ready for this trip. Will you do me a big favor while I'm gone?"

"Sure, what is it?"

"Will you call Liam and invite him and Maggie to stay with us here in New York for a long weekend, when I get back?"

"John, I think you're the one who needs to make that call. You haven't spoken to your son in almost a year. How long are you going to let this feud fester between the two of you?"

"I know. It's been really bugging me. I just don't know what to say to him. I doubt he'll even want to talk with me after all this time."

"Well, I know for a fact that he's very interested in talking to you. He's told me as much. Why don't you call him and invite him down to New York yourself. It will make a big difference coming directly from you."

"Lee, I know you still talk to him on the phone once in a while. This comes a lot easier for you than me. Do really think he'll listen to me?"

Lee propped herself on an elbow to face her husband. "Yes, I do. It's time to fix this estrangement, John. Please call him tomorrow before you leave for Paris."

"I will, as soon as I figure out what to say."

"Excuse me? Since when does the grand orator need to figure out what to say to anyone?"

Lee raised her voice and squeezed his hand. "John, just do it. It will put your mind at ease. You need to resolve this sooner rather than later."

On the other side of the world, the sun was coming up on an arid outcrop of land overlooking the Mediterranean. The Carmelite monastery, with its tiled roof shining atop the hills of Haifa, Israel, was founded in the twelfth century and had survived almost complete destruction by the Turks a hundred years later. There, in the bowels of the centuries-old church, was a cave thought to be the place where the prophet Elijah lived and prayed. Alone, in one of the smaller cells of the monastery at the end a long dark hallway, a small, young Palestinian man was just waking to the morning call to prayer.

Outside the dark, ascetic chamber, a barrel-chested man, armed with an Uzi automatic submachine gun, stood in the doorway and spoke to the young man in Arabic. "Come along now, Ahmed. Let's go down to the kitchen and get some breakfast before the monks come back from Mass."

"Avi, when are you going to tell the prior and the rest of the monks who I really am? Why must there be all this secrecy? I'm sure they already know I'm not a Christian. I never come out of this damned cell except to eat and relieve myself. How long do you intend on keeping me here locked up in a shroud of mystery? I want to be free."

"I've told this you this many times. You're not a prisoner, Ahmed. You're here for your own safety. You're free to leave anytime you want. But think about what you're saying. If you choose to return to the West Bank, without the protection of Israeli security, how long do you think you can survive out in the open before your friends find you? Even with all the money and protection we've already given you, you must know that they will find you. Once they do, and it would only be a matter of time, you'll be a dead man."

Ahmed was growing tense and began to fidget. "When is your country going to fulfill its end of our agreement? I'm tired of being separated from my family. They have no idea where I am. And I'm sure the PLO is wondering the same thing. I've spent more time in the past three months talking with you and your security people than I have with my own family in the last three years. I want to be reunited with my family now, as you've promised, in America."

"Not to worry, Ahmed. You're almost at the end of your journey. You're flying out tomorrow morning from Tel Aviv to New York, where you'll be debriefed extensively by the American FBI. Duplicate originals and a floppy disc of all of your records will be turned over to them there. Once you've been interrogated by their agents in New York, you'll be brought back here to Haifa for just a few days, where you'll be reunited with your family. Don't worry about them. They've also been under our protection and are out of harm's way in a different location. Then, once we've taken care of a few diplomatic details, we'll arrange for new identification for you and your family. You'll all go back to America together to spend the rest of your days in peace and freedom, just as you've requested. Be patient, Ahmed. It will all be over soon.

"And by the way, yesterday I noticed you were speaking in Arabic to that young Palestinian boy who works in the kitchen. You must not engage him or anyone else in any conversation, whether in Arabic, Hebrew, or English. Don't speak at all—to anyone. It's too dangerous. If word gets out about who you are, why you're here, or when and where you'll be traveling over the next week, you may not survive your planned trip to America. Do you understand that?"

"I may not survive this night, my friend. The PLO is not stupid. They know that when their business manager and bookkeeper disappears, without explanation, there is a good possibility that their records have been compromised. And because my family has also disappeared, I'm sure that has created a heightened urgency to track me down and kill me. You may have the upper hand for the moment, Avi. But they are relentless, as you will see."

"Ahmed, you overestimate the PLO's abilities. Trust me, they will not locate you or your family. That is, if you learn to keep your mouth shut."

"I've read of this so-called American witness protection program. The FBI can hide people from the Italian Mafia, but they're no match for our people. Even though all our original records are still in their proper files at our headquarters, I'm sure they know by now that I'm a major liability to them. In the end, I think they'll probably find me and my family. When that happens, I'll be a very rich, but a very dead man."

"You exaggerate, Ahmed. And remember this . . . we've never lost anyone who was under our protection. And by the way, you have it turned around. It is the PLO that is no match for the FBI, as you will soon discover."

Ahmed looked up and saw the contrails of a jet airliner heading west high above the deep blue water of the Mediterranean. *Perhaps it's en route to New York*, he thought. Still staring into the sky, he spoke, as in a whisper. "Avi, I had a dream last night that you weren't able to protect me. Someone had tied up your hands and put tape over your mouth. I dreamed that a Hamas missile blew up this monastery. No one was left alive. Among the corpses they found, while digging through all the rubble, they even came upon the preserved body of the prophet Elijah."

A subtle grin crept over Ahmed's face. "I wonder, Avi, do you see the irony in my dream?"

Avi was growing impatient with his unwilling guest and rolled his eyes. "No, why don't you tell me?"

"Why would our Hamas brothers waste their time in murdering the great Jewish prophet when all they need to do is wait for the Jews to do it themselves? After all, you have become experts at it."

Avi glared at Ahmed. "I have remained silent on this subject up till now, Ahmed. But make no mistake about your own history. Islam was founded on the scimitar of Mohammed, not on any noble idea or philosophy. Nothing has changed for all these centuries. There is nothing peaceful about your faith. You have turned violence into an art form."

Ahmed fired back instantly. "Really? And what was the weapon Moses used to kill the Egyptian slave master in cold blood? Or the weapon Abraham held poised over the heart of his son Isaac on Mount Moriah? Or the weapons used by Joshua to kill and conquer our ancestors and occupy the lands of the Canaanites and the Philistines? And you dare to call Islam a faith of violence?"

The two men stared at each other for several quiet seconds. Finally, Ahmed lowered his eyes and heaved a heavy sigh. "Avi, you asked me the other day why I am defecting to the West and betraying the PLO. I avoided your question then, but I will answer it now. Our cultures share very few things in common. But the one thing we share most intimately is violence. It is, throughout the many centuries of our conflict, our greatest and most enduring bond. Our culture permits us to murder to achieve justice and conversion of the infidel. Yours uses the excuses of self-defense and preservation as you dominate and suppress our people."

Ahmed grew very quiet and looked directly into Avi's eyes. "So you want to know why I am running away from my people? It is because, even though I am still young, I feel like a tired, hopeless old man. I cannot and will no longer justify murder, for any reason, especially in the name of religion. Therefore, I will not associate with those who do. I am finished."

Avi responded slowly. "Yes, it's true. The Jews, God forgive us, have killed their own prophets. Even, some would argue, their own Messiah, the one who taught the world to forgive those who kill and maim. But Islam has kept pace every murderous step of the way. As soon as we put down the rifle, your rockets rain down on our heads. There is no solution, Ahmed. It is hopeless."

"Avi, I have read the Koran and both the Old and New Testament from cover to cover. I am beginning to believe that Jesus, my fellow Palestinian, is the only rational man among us. And that his teachings are the only true solution." Ahmed threw his hands in the air. "But then, I am not permitted to have these thoughts. To speak them aloud would get me killed. At least until now."

Ahmed put his hand on Avi's shoulder. "Perhaps I dreamed about Elijah because he is our common link. Did you know that both our faiths believe that his return will signal the end of times? All the signs are there, Avi. I am now convinced that you and I are witnessing that end . . . and the final wrath of Allah."

"Stop, Ahmed! You are speaking nonsense. It was only a silly dream. Don't turn prophet on me now. Come, let's go down to the kitchen. I can smell the bread baking."

A week later, J. W. Mayfair finally cleared the long security line at JFK International Airport, ready to board a Boeing 747 flight to Paris. As he hurried to the gate, he ran to a pay phone. He tried to place a credit card call to his son Liam in Boston just as the last boarding call announcement echoed over the PA system. He gave up the attempt, resolving to call him once he arrived in Paris. As he got settled into his starboard-sided window seat, he noticed a thin, young, well-dressed, Arab-looking man walking down the aisle toward him. He watched as the man paused, squeezed past a heavyset older woman who was standing in the aisle, and sat down next to JW. The man immediately opened a copy of the Koran, adjusted his wire-rimmed glasses, and began to read.

JW extended his hand, smiled, and introduced himself to the young man.

"Hello there, nice to meet you. J. W. Mayfair is my name. So what brings you to Paris?"

The young man looked up, returned the smile, and spoke in broken but understandable English. "My name is Ahmed. I'm pleased to meet you as well. I'm going home to gather my family and bring them back with me to America."

"So are they in Paris?"

"No, in Jerusalem."

"Really? What do you do for a living there?"

After some nervous hesitation, the young man said, "I'm an accountant." He quickly tried to change the subject. "Do you have a family here in New York?"

JW reached into his wallet and took out a photograph. "This is my beautiful wife, Lee, my three sons, and my equally beautiful daughter," he beamed.

"What a wonderful coincidence! I too have a wife, three sons, and a daughter! Unfortunately, I haven't seen them for many months now."

"That's too bad. But why so long? Have you been away on business?"

Again, the young man hesitated, glancing over his right shoulder: "It is very complicated and difficult to explain. However, I will try to do so if you like."

Suddenly, a big, swarthy man seated directly behind them jumped up, leaned over the seat, and shoved a finger into the young man's face. He spoke sternly under his breath with obvious anger, in what sounded to JW like Arabic. "Shut the hell up, Ahmed, before you get us both killed, goddammit!"

Shocked at the abrupt interruption, and not understanding a word of what was just said, JW decided to withdraw his polite overture. "If you don't mind, I'd like to use the opportunity, as soon as we get airborne, to use this to call my son," he said, pointing to the phone built into the back of the seat in front of him. "I hope I don't disturb you. I'm trying to make peace with my youngest son and end our long estrangement. We haven't spoken in almost a year now."

"Peace. Yes. There is nothing more critical and sacred, especially within the family. I hope that you and your son settle your differences very soon, my friend."

As soon as the plane gained altitude, JW leaned his head toward the window, turned his back to the other passengers, and could barely be heard speaking softly into the phone. Twelve minutes later, just as the passengers had begun to quietly settle in for the long night flight to Paris, JW suddenly began to scream into the phone.

"What . . . the . . . fuck? Oh, my God! That's a SAM! Liam, I don't know what the hell's going on here! I'm looking out a starboard window, and I'm staring at a goddamn rocket with a white plume coming right up toward us from the bow of a freighter. I gotta go, son . . . pray for me."

In one horrible split second, J. W. Mayfair was thrust back in time. His mind's eye saw himself behind the controls of his A-6 Intruder. He could hear the shrill sound and see the red light of the cockpit missile warning system in his head. His heart began to race as he envisioned the dim lighting of the cockpit and that dreaded red light, the foreboding of radar-guided missiles streaking up from the dark surface toward his Intruder. His eyes cringed at the bright flashes of white light illuminating the cockpit and the night sky around him. The bursts of flak. The huge fireballs from direct hits on the B-52 bombers he was assigned to protect. In his momentary fantasy, he saw the silent firestorm of ignited munitions on the ground. He could sense the rumbling vibration of the five-hundred-pound bombs exploding thousands of feet below and filling the air around him.

Finally realizing where he was, JW looked down again and saw it clearly. There, twelve thousand feet below him in the fading light of dusk, he could see the unmistakable shape and running lights of a large oil tanker below to his right, steaming out to sea in the dark. Streaking off what appeared to be its forward deck was the familiar profile of a small surface-to-air missile, its gray-white trail sharply contrasted against the indigo of the ocean surface. It was the same horrible vision he had encountered so many times in nighttime bombing raids over Haiphong and Hanoi. His hands instinctively went to the stick, to pull back, climb, and roll over sharply to the left away from this mindless dragon of death. Suddenly realizing that he was still holding the portable phone and not the controls of his Intruder, he threw it down at his feet. He stumbled over the small man to his left and barreled into a flight attendant, knocking her to the floor. He bolted up the aisle, startling all those seated in front of him. As he muscled his way past another stewardess and charged toward the cockpit, he screamed, "Roll it over, roll it over . . . There's a missile coming up our ass on the right at five o'clock!"

Several women seated in the front rows panicked and began to scream hysterically.

Meanwhile, far below on the ocean surface, three men ran feverishly around the foredeck of a large supertanker, screaming and yelling at each other in Farsi. One of the men ran to the port side of the gray behemoth carrying a large, heavy-looking object on his back. High above them in the night sky, the 747 exploded in a giant ball of fire and began to fall silently to the sea, broken in two. All that could be heard on the deck of the ship was the slow, plodding drone of the diesel engine screws driving the dark freighter forward into the night.

Two minutes later, both J. W. Mayfair and his new Arab acquaintance lay dead, entombed in one hundred feet of water.

SILENCE OF THE DRAGON

A dark, primeval death mask lay over the face of the man lying deep in sleep. Hovering motionless over the man was a red dragon, its cold, unblinking eyes staring impassively, as though patiently waiting to devour a woman's newborn child. In a blinding flash of lightning and deafening thunder, the man was bolted upright. Billows of black, acrid smoke quickly filled the forward cabin. Straining to see through the darkness to his left, Liam could barely make out the facial features of the man to his left. He sickened as he realized that this man, still strapped into the seat, now engulfed in flames, was his father. The man flailed his arms toward him, hands outstretched like a blind man groping for a lifeline. His mouth was contorted into a slow-motion pantomime of a silent scream, unheard in the din and confusion of the shrieks of other disembodied faces being devoured randomly by the dragon. Suddenly, the surge of a cold, howling wind filled his senses, a momentary relief from the exquisite surge of terror that had seized him. In an instant, the man's face had become a charred, featureless mass of burned flesh. His father grabbed Liam's left arm with a vise grip, his lips still quivering, urgent, begging to be heard, yet mute, as the hand slowly slipped away into the blackness below, trapped in the descending fuselage slowly spinning downward into the sea. Suddenly, a loud voice from a distance bellowed through the darkness.

"Liam! Open your eyes. Look at me!"

Liam was suddenly aware of Maggie's soft presence gently tugging at his left arm, trying to ease him out of what appeared to be yet another of his recurring nightmares. Sweat poured over his face. His T-shirt was soaked. His heart raced and skipped till he thought he would pass out. Finally, after what seemed like minutes, he opened his eyes with a blank stare. His face was drawn and colorless. After a few more long seconds of silence, he took in a long deep breath and spoke slowly and deliberately.

"Maggie, I can't take this anymore. This was the worst one yet. I'm losing it. This is too much."

"Your father again?" Maggie knew the answer before he nodded.

"You've got to see someone, Liam, a professional. This is getting way out of control. I heard that some of the other families have started counseling. Please, Liam, what have you got to lose? These dreams are taking over your life. It's time to take charge of this!"

It had been nearly two years since the crash and the start of his dreams. He started having them once every two weeks or so in the beginning and now suffered with them almost every other night. On some nights, the stricken plane was filled with panic and flames. On others, it was suspended in an eerie, quiet free fall, like a wounded hawk in an out-of-control death spiral, plunging into a smooth, moonlit sea. Always constant, however, was the ghoulish face of his father, mouthing words that Liam could never hear or understand.

Liam Mayfair had known in his heart for many months that it was time to pay the piper—to face the demon down. Liam's father, John W. Mayfair, had been killed in the crash of TWA Airlines Flight 800 over the eastern end of Long Island. His dreams, his memories, his every thought had become morbidly obsessed with the death of his father.

Once again, his mind raced back to that late evening. At first the news was surreal. It was no more than a ten-second radio sound bite as he was getting out of his car. Disjointed words about a flight to Paris out of New York's JFK falling off radar, an explosion seen by fishermen and other eyewitnesses. The next few days and weeks were filled with a flurry of speculation coming from all quarters: the talking TV heads, the ratings-starved talk radio show hosts, the sullen-faced politicians hungry for a headline and a photo op, the reporters climbing over each other, ruthlessly competing for an edge. The story rocked Washington and the foreign news desks for weeks, out of proportion to the reality—or at least, so it seemed at the time.

Liam recalled that as he drove alone through the night from Boston to his parents' home in Manhattan, his mind had been flooded with images of his father. His thoughts drifted back through all the fights and harsh words spoken to one another. He began to panic at the repercussions of the horrible news. For the first time in years, he prayed aloud. "Please, God, don't let him be aboard that flight! Please, Lord, not now" Liam longed to be greeted by his mother with the news that his father had somehow missed his flight and was sitting in the airport lounge, arguing with a ticket clerk trying to get aboard the next available plane to Paris. As he approached the FDR Drive, he saw the sun's first rays reflect off the towers of steel and glass standing sentry over the East River. Liam reached his mother's condo, parked his Jeep, ran to the building, and took the elevator to the penthouse floor. He opened the door and found his mother standing alone quietly at the large windows facing the sun coming up in the east. He embraced her and immediately broke into uncontrollable sobs. His mother, Lee Mayfair, said nothing and simply held her son tightly in her arms.

At that very moment, less than seventy miles to the east, coast guard vessels, Suffolk County Marine Police crews and FBI crime scene investigators had already converged on the crash site in the waters of the Atlantic about five miles off Moriches, Long Island. Many of them had been on the water all night, slowly and purposefully weaving their way through the devastation and carnage spread out over the ocean surface. The only sources of light on this moonless night were the crews' flashlights and Air National Guard parachute lights that would flare then burn out and fade into darkness. Chief Petty Officer Steve Gross, who had grown up on the waters of his native Long Island, had been working without a break all night, operating an inflatable Zodiac launched from the command ship *The Bainbridge Island*. The only sounds on the calm waters came from the low-throttled engines of the ship and the gentle clanging of the ship's hull against the plane's fuselage and tail section as it moved slowly through the wreckage field.

As they struggled in the dark to locate and recover bodies, Steve and his crewmates shared an unspoken dread of the rising sun. They knew the horror it would expose. Finally, as the sun's first rays filled the horizon with hues of pink and purple and blue, they got their first daylight view of the hellish scene spread before them. The sea was covered with floating corpses, plane seats, cushions, papers, cups, clothing, infant formula bottles, the orange waterlogged sacks of Airmail, the diplomatic pouches, and the bizarre coating of gold glitter that had been blown out of boxes and now covered the hair and clothing and faces of the dead. The scene before them was surreal as they pulled more mutilated passengers and detached body parts out of the water and lifted them up to the fantail of the ship to be bagged and tagged.

Steve was a twenty-five-year veteran of the coast guard and had recovered many bodies at sea, most of them drowning victims. But he had never seen anything resembling this horror. He and his crew would work for nearly thirty six hours without sleep and had become dehydrated while laboring throughout the following day in the hot sun in their white protective suits. The foul aroma of spent diesel fuel, which had been burning uncontrollably just a few hours earlier, now created a glimmering sheen on the water surface. The sickening smell filled their nostrils and permeated every pore of their bodies and every fabric of their clothing. That, and the slow, tedious recovery of mutilated body parts, which were stored in bio bags and buckets, began to take its toll on the crew. Finally, as Steve had anticipated, several of the younger crew members grew nauseous and faint and had to board the command ship and go below to get some water and bottled oxygen.

On the way back to port, huddled on the aft deck, Steve lapsed into a brief, fitful sleep. His disjointed dream images were scattered and nonsensical. He saw the faces of the bodies he had pulled out of the water come to life as their mouths tried in vain to form words that were unintelligible. He wondered how many of his dreams over the next few weeks or months would replay these images as he tried to shake the though from his mind.

As the cutter pulled into its berth at the Moriches Coast Guard Station, Steve leaned over the rail to catch some fresh air and was struck by the mass of humanity assembled before him. Hundreds of reporters, cameramen, and satellite dishes from every news agency in the world were now occupying a marine base usually manned, at most, by only a few dozen men and women. These news services were already reporting that of the 230 souls who took off aboard the Paris-bound 747 that beautiful July evening, there was not one survivor. Barely half of the bodies were recovered and identified in the immediate aftermath of the crash. Eventually, Steve and his crew would help recover and tag at least some remains of all the passengers aboard the flight. Dozens of bodies pulled out of the water by the coast guard in the early dawn were not recognizable, as many of their faces had been burned, crushed, and distorted. Of the remaining bodies found during the deep-water salvage operation over the next few weeks, the added mutilation of the sea made many appear to be nonhuman, almost alien.

As Steve slowly disembarked, he spotted his commander, who was walking hurriedly toward him. "Are you OK, Steve? You've been on duty now for over thirty-six hours. I'm ordering you and your crew to get some food and sleep now. Is that clear?"

"Yes, sir. It's been pretty rough out there. It's only just beginning to hit me."

"Yeah, I know. Try to get some sleep though. We're going to be at this for days and weeks to come."

"Excuse me, sir, but do you happen to know the name of the guy who's heading up the FBI forensic team?"

"Not yet. But I know the name of the New York SAC. It's Merle Jones. I've already spoken to him. He's the big guy standing over there in the shirt and tie, talking with some reporters. Why do you ask?"

"Oh, no reason. I was just wondering who was in charge."

As Chief Petty Officer Gross turned and walked toward the crowd of media, he pulled a small, opaque, water-filled plastic bag out from under his protective suit. He held it up to the sunlight, squinted into it, and then lowered it down to his side. For the first time since he retrieved it from the ocean surface during the night, Steve thought he noticed something small and dark moving slowly in the bag.

JOHNNY, WE HARDLY KNEW YE

Liam Mayfair, recently turned twenty-three, had just graduated from Northeastern University with a double degree in English literature and journalism, just the June before his father's death. The featured obituary piece in the *New York Times* had referred to him simply as the youngest of four surviving children of John Worthington Mayfair, Esq., who, it was duly noted, was executive vice president and general counsel for Internet Data Solutions Inc., a computer software company with offices in New York, Chicago, and Dallas. The brief article reported that John Mayfair was in fact flying to Europe that night to put the finishing touches on the acquisition of a French-based company. *What useless, inane pieces of information*, thought Liam. As an aspiring writer and journalist himself, he recognized these factoids as nothing more than weak, amateurish attempts to put flesh, color, and dimension, however mundane, on the bones of a man few knew well—least of all the obit reporter who submitted the story to the *Times*.

Liam Mayfair, like many sons of overachieving fathers, did not really know anything about his father's business or, for that matter, the private person behind the public persona. John Worthington Mayfair was an enigma to his son, someone best suited for study and objective analysis from a safe distance, like an abstract work of art hanging lifelessly in a museum. JW, as his friends called him, was trained as a trial lawyer. He had built up a thriving trial litigation practice and had finally taken on partners, eventually hiring over fifty associate attorneys. He had expanded his practice into Internet commerce and finance and its far-flung network of opportunities. And according to his few close friends, he had found a rare niche for himself in the high-tech Internet world of electronic data transfer, along with all the endless spin-off applications of the technology. He was, some thought, that rare, counterintuitive kind of traditional conservative who openly embraced every change and advance in technology he could wrap his brain around. JW was like a boy pressing his face up to a candy-store window, bringing home every state of-the-art piece of electronic gadgetry known to mankind. His three sons and only daughter were typically bemused at the display of all of their father's "toys." His wife, Lee, was somewhat less so. JW would boast that his five-acre retreat home on Shelter Island was the first on Long Island with a solar-powered flagpole. A former US Navy pilot, JW would stand barefoot out on his redwood deck at dawn, even on cold, subfreezing mornings, to watch Old Glory slowly rise at the end of a clanging bronze halyard, while listening to a prerecorded audiotape bugle rendition of "Reveille" playing in the background. All this was done, as he would proudly announce to the world, without drawing a single watt of electricity from that "god-awful power grid" to which he had always felt enslaved.

"Now ain't this the cat's meow?" he would murmur to himself with a smug grin on his face, as he saluted the high-tech start of each new day.

Liam's girlfriend, Maggie McAdams, a tall, lean, striking redhead from Quincy, Massachusetts, had met Liam's father only once, one cold December evening when JW and Lee visited them in Boston. She remembered that the dinner was arranged by Liam's mother, Lee Mayfair, on what she described as "neutral ground," at a popular Italian restaurant in the North End—well away from the apartment he and Maggie had just begun occupying together on Beacon Street on the other side of town. The evening was marred by tension and awkwardness, filled with his father's many familiar and unspoken signs of disapproval. Every long moment of strained silence screamed a message that Liam heard loud and clear. His mother, Lee Mayfair, in the run-up to the evening, had been referring to JW in her phone calls to Boston as "your father" rather than "Dad"— an unmistakable sign that JW was in his "preacher" mode. This sermon, intended for both Liam and Maggie, was painfully plain and uncomplicated. Theirs was an arrangement that, although tolerated for the sake of family peace, was not one which would ever be blessed or acknowledged. Fair enough, resolved both Liam and Maggie. They knew that John Mayfair was painfully outspoken and candid in his core beliefs and opinions and not at all timid in voicing disapproval. Yet despite his blunt and rough edges, he was hopelessly honest and well-intentioned. What they saw in JW was the same unabridged version of what they got from JW. What they heard in his words was nothing less than what he honestly believed in his heart.

Since his father's death, Liam had spent countless hours, usually in those short, still moments before dawn, when the soul is most exposed to the power of subliminal fear, staring at the ceiling, despairing of sleep, as he recalled the years of sparring with his father. They had fought over the profound and the mundane, from sports to music, from politics to sexual mores. Words, it seemed, were never merely spoken between them; rather, they were hurled at each other. Usually it was JW, the trial lawyer, the skilled cross-examiner, who did the talking. Liam, on the witness stand, tried to field the rapid-fire questions, like a juggler with too many balls in the air at once, hearing each yet unable to answer any one before the assault of the next. And so it all went on for years. With too many words tossed into the air at once, all falling to the floor, unheard, tangled, and meaningless. Never, it seemed, did either of them muster the courage to look beneath the words, to peer down into the dark wellspring of their conflict. Neither would dare speak of the essence of what each truly felt about the other or about any of the stuff of which fathers and sons are naturally made.

Yet in spite of the wall of silence that separated them, Liam had only just begun to sense in his gut, at the moment his father was ripped away from his family, that something good and comfortable was beginning to emerge from the rancorous cloud hovering over them. He had begun to perceive some momentary thaw, a warming sense of peace and mutual acceptance that most fathers and sons don't usually enjoy until much later in life. Usually not until long after all the dues of life have been paid and sons beget sons of their own. Perhaps it was a simple maturation, a chronological passage of time. Maybe it was just the balancing of male hormones that had enabled Liam in the past year to recognize the vague profile of someone good and noble behind the gruff facade that enveloped John W. and set him apart as a caricature of himself. Liam's view of his father reminded him of rose petals, barely peeking out from under their prickly calyx, rising high above the thorns and ready to unfold on the first warm day of spring.

After several minutes lying silently in Maggie's arms, Liam's sweat-covered body grew cold. His heart returned to its quiet normal rhythm. He suddenly became aware of an acute, overpowering sense of sadness brought on by some indescribable loss and lost opportunity. His father had lived and died by the word—the "currency of his trade," as he was fond of saying. Yet JW could not, or would not, spend any of it to breach the wall of ice that had grown between him and his youngest son. Liam knew there was a king's ransom of that currency left on that poker table, unspent. Words that were never spoken in life were now locked away forever in death. The melancholy went down deep into the marrow of his bones. The urge to sob aloud had been trembling at the edge of his soul, ready to erupt for a long time. But like his father, Liam would never allow the boy's passion to rule the man, especially in front of Maggie.

Finally, Liam slipped out of Maggie's embrace and lumbered out of bed. He walked slowly to the window and parted the faded Irish-lace curtains. Another dull, steel gray dawn of March was creeping over the pale, glass-still waters of Gardiner's Bay. A few cat's-paws swirled out on the water near the jetty. His thoughts suddenly drifted to one early foggy morning, many years prior, sitting as a young boy on the beach with his father. He recalled the scene in vivid detail and remembered asking his father if all the deer on Shelter Island had gotten there by taking the ferry along with the people across from Sag Harbor or the North Fork. JW laughed out loud as he pointed to a dark object barely visible in the heavy mist. It looked like a small log, floating out on the water, moving slowly toward them. As it got closer, Liam could make out the head of a very young buck that had become separated from his mother. He was quietly swimming toward the beach, eyes wide, and nostrils flared, breathing hard as he made his tough daily commute from the mainland. "They don't have any money for the ferry, Liam, so they have to swim back and forth across the race every day, even in the cold of winter," was all he got as a chuckled response.

Liam, ever the naive literalist, was momentarily thrown back in time as he relived, in exquisite detail, the feelings of sadness and anger at the apparent injustice of it all. He remembered pleading with JW, "I have some money saved. Can I pay for him to ride the ferry? Please, Dad?" JW's off-the-cuff attempt at humor had been wasted on his young, lofty-minded son. Liam remembered being confused by the welling up of his father's eyes. It was the only time in his life he could ever recall seeing tears fall from his father's face.

Life, to Liam, beginning as a very young boy, seemed to be filled with a series of unpleasant surprises, converging on him from all directions. Like the young deer swimming through the mist, life always seemed to come at him in various disguises and shapes that usually turned out to be nothing as they first appeared to be. Liam was one of those rare individuals who constantly struggle and probe to find the meaning of life rather than allow enough time for life to disclose that meaning on its own terms. He was like the boy who suddenly realizes that the only way he can see the hidden tiger in the 3-D image is not through strained effort, but by simply relaxing and allowing it to reveal itself. Once he could figure out how to master that fine art, he thought, understanding all the complexities of life and death would be his for the taking.

Meanwhile, Maggie had stepped quietly behind him and slowly put her arms around his waist, breaking the silence. "Liam, please, I beg you. Call Dr. Frankel today. He gave you his business card at Allison's a few weeks ago. Do you still have it?"

"So you think your lover is a candidate for the loony bin? I warned you I was damaged goods! Your mother is starting to look like a prophet, isn't she?" A slight grin faded on his face as quickly as it had appeared.

Maggie spoke sternly now, stepping round in front of him, grabbing both arms and looking directly into his dark eyes.

"These nightmares are not going to go away on their own. Not without some professional counseling. If your father hadn't died in that crash, you would have wound up on some shrink's couch a few years down the road anyway. You yourself said there's plenty of old family baggage in that thick head of yours that needs to be claimed and opened. You know, all that unresolved father-son stuff?" She lifted his head to meet his eyes, trying to draw out some nod of recognition for the truth. "Come on, Liam. Tell me you know I'm right!"

"I know, I know. Yes, you're right. I'll be fine though. I just need some more time to work everything . . ." His voice trailed away, collapsing under the weight of his own self-deceit.

"Liam, honey, you're running out of time. You haven't been yourself in over a year. First, locked away in that underground cell of an apartment in Boston and now, cooped up like a hermit crab out here alone all winter in your father's summer house. It's time to snap out of it. Look, I've got to get back to work in Boston. Meanwhile, you should be there too, looking for a job. You haven't done anything about any of those calls from the recruitment office and that headhunter. You know, that old guy with the bad knees who beat you in tennis last year? What's his name, Bob Hirsch? He's got some great leads for you. What about that job opening he mentioned at the Boston Globe?"

"Maggie, I'll call him . . . soon . . . I promise. As far as your shrink friend is concerned, I'll sleep on it." The Freudian slip was no sooner out of his mouth that it raced back to slap him in the face. They both grew suddenly quiet.

"Oh, I almost forgot. Your mom called late last night while you were asleep. She didn't know I was staying out here and was surprised to hear my voice. She asked if you could be at a meeting with her lawyer, Mr. Abrams, and TWA's lawyer tomorrow morning in New York. She asked that you drive into the city today and stay overnight at the family condo. She said it was important."

Liam instantly grew agitated. "What does she need me for? She's got a great lawyer handling her case against TWA. Abrams is a tough old street fighter. He was Dad's former law partner. Besides, I'm the youngest and third in the Mayfair line of succession. I've got two older brothers, God help us, with law degrees. They should be doing this. Not me. I don't want to be involved in any part of this."

"Liam, you know how your mom feels about this lawsuit idea. She doesn't like to discuss it with anyone, probably not even with her own lawyer, unless she absolutely has to. Her wounds are still too fresh. Besides, it's obvious, at least to me, that you're her favorite. She trusts your intuition, your common sense. She probably wants you to help her make the right decisions for the family—from the heart, not just the pocketbook. Didn't you already say that she wants you to be part of the negotiations if and when any offers are made?"

Liam said nothing as he looked over Maggie's shoulder out the window toward the bay.

Maggie slipped her arms away from Liam and turned to walk away. "Well, it's your call. Consider the message delivered. I've got to get on the road if I'm going to catch the ferry. I've got an early dinner meeting tonight with a new client and can't be late. Come on, why don't you shower and let me make you some breakfast."

Liam stood at the window, looking out over the harbor, not hearing a word she said. His mind drifted to his two older brothers and his "baby" sister. How easy their lives were, growing up in a family that was so well provided for. How quickly they all seemed to adjust to their father's sudden death. Sure, they had been shocked, as he was. They each cried and partnered with Mom's every heaving and silent sob, every grieving step of the way. But somehow, each of them moved back into the mainstream and comfortable rhythms of their lives, hardly missing a beat.

Liam, on the other hand, was consumed by a feeling of isolation. Standing alone, hiding from all his friends and family in the darkest corner of the parking lot at the funeral home, drowning in images of his father. Throughout the one-night faux wake and funeral Mass the next morning, he felt nothing. His emotional well had dried up and become a desolate, barren psychic hole. He had somehow conquered the urge to weep and had totally withdrawn from the family. He was partly embarrassed by his inability to bounce back up on his feet, but mostly fearful of the emotional cauldron he knew lay locked up inside him, simmering only millimeters beneath the surface. Instead of getting on with what he had hoped would be a shovel-ready career in journalism, Liam had been languishing in a zombielike state of limbo. His life was stalled, dead in the water, consumed in his reverie of everything and yet nothing.

At the time of the Flight 800 explosion, he had been living with Maggie in her Beacon Street apartment in Boston. Within less than two weeks after the crash, Liam had suddenly moved his things back into his own dark and dank basement apartment on Commonwealth Avenue. He gave no explanation to Maggie, who was surprised, hurt, and confused. He would crawl out of his underground hovel only under the cover of night for some fast food and an occasional rare evening with Maggie at her place. For the next six months, Liam did not respond to his mail or answer his phone. He had suddenly fallen off the face of the earth, becoming truly incommunicado from his family and friends. He would stay up all night reading Kafka and Dostoevsky and Nietzsche. His refrigerator was bright and empty, save for the ever-present bottle of cheap Russian vodka in the freezer. That Christmas was the first Liam would spend utterly alone, refusing to answer dozens of worried calls from his mother, his siblings, and even Maggie. It was the nadir of Liam's heretofore brief existence, and he had no idea how to cry out for help.

Finally, on one frigid, early morning in January, reality caught up with the young recluse. Liam had been awakened by a harsh pounding at his door and, within minutes, found himself standing in his bare feet on the cold Commonwealth Avenue sidewalk, squinting up into the morning sunlight, watching the sheriff's eviction crew move his bed and furnishings to the curb. He would not have accepted his mother's urgings to move into the vacant summer retreat home on Shelter Island had he not found himself dazed and confused and very much panicked by life's latest hard slap to the face. Liam loved his mother. But at that moment, she was no more than an ill-fitting, uncomfortable, yet very convenient life vest. His ingratitude was palpable. Lee Mayfair endured it with the patience of a mother who clearly saw and felt the anguish in her son. Her child was in desperate need of some tender loving care. A small price to pay, she reckoned, as she tried to convince her youngest son that his family was not a crutch but rather an oasis, a bright, steady beacon of light amid the depths of darkness into which he had slipped, unnoticed by the rest of the world. Lee Mayfair had finally come to fully understand an old adage her mother had once used: "A mother can only be as happy as her unhappiest child."

Much of the family's elaborate funeral plans were scuttled when, after several weeks, Lee Mayfair was told by the government that JW's body had not yet been given up by the sea. Liam recalled the eclectic memorial Mass that was hastily orchestrated. It contained the essentials of JW's favorite Latin hymns. But it closed out oddly with an old spiritual, a New Orleans jazz tune JW loved since his childhood. The classic funeral dirge, "Just a Closer Walk with Thee," was wailed by a lone trombonist as the empty casket was wheeled down the church aisle. *What a bizarre musical collage*, Liam remembered thinking at the time. *Funny*, he thought, *how well we all knew his music yet how poorly any of us knew JW the man.*

PRIMOGENITURE

Sitting at the foot of the bed, Liam was startled out of his reverie by the phone. He jumped across the room to grab it, dropping the receiver to the floor. Before he could get it to his ear, he heard the familiar, brash voice. It was Colin, Liam's older brother. His tone was as loud and annoying as the ring of the phone.

"Hey, little brother, got a job yet?"

"Hello yourself, big brother. What's up?" Liam replied, ignoring the sarcasm.

It was already well past 9:00 a.m., and of course, Colin knew the answer before he posed the question. In fact, Liam had not even tried to look for a job since his father's death, quick to offer a lame excuse that the job market in Boston was "too tough at the moment." Colin was always playing the smart-assed lawyer type, thought Liam. Another of the unattractive and dominant genes inherited from their father.

Colin, the firstborn to the Mayfair clan, was, as JW would often say, "to the manor born." Indeed he was, in every sense of the word. From the moment of his heralded arrival, he had been the crown jewel of the family, the fair-haired heir apparent. He went on to graduate cum laude from Princeton, then Yale Law School. He was quickly grabbed up by a white-shoe law firm in Manhattan at some absurdly inflated salary. Colin, the consummate overachiever, also excelled in sports. He played varsity basketball in high school and college and club rugby in the "off season" and was now regularly putting away his Wall Street buddies on the squash court at the New York Athletic Club. And as if his gifted life was not Hollywood scripted enough, he had married second runner-up in the Miss Connecticut Beauty Pageant. He had met his beautiful but slightly airheaded debutante wife while she was an undergrad at Yale.

"Hey, listen, junior. I just got off the phone with Mom. She says she wants you to come into the city tomorrow for a meeting with Frank Abrams. What's that all about?"

"Jesus, why can't they all just leave me out of this?" Liam uttered quietly to himself. He was too tired to betray his annoyance.

"I have no idea, Colin. I guess I'll find out tomorrow."

"Yeah, well, seems to me you should save yourself a trip and let your older brother, the lawyer, handle this one, wouldn't you say?"

"Look, Colin, that's fine with me. You seem to have all the answers on this lawsuit thing anyway. Why don't you call Mom back and get me off the hook. You wanted to fill Dad's lawyer shoes, not me."

Liam's irritation was escalating by the second. Liam waited for Colin's response, long delayed.

"I already suggested that idea to Mom. Didn't fly. I can't figure what she's thinking. I mean, I know about this litigation stuff. It's right up my alley. Look, why don't you go ahead and attend that first meeting with TWA and Mr. Abrams. Let me know what happens, and I'll arrange with both of them to take over for you from that point forward. OK?"

"Sure, whatever you say. I really don't want any part of this anyway. I can't deal with all of this right now. Know what I mean?"

"No problem, little brother. Stay in touch, OK? Gotta go."

Liam hung up the phone without saying a word. He immediately drifted back to one of his earliest and oddest memories of his older brother. It was an overpowering realization that struck him, oddly enough, at his kindergarten graduation. He remembered thinking at the time that no matter what he would do with his life when he "grew up," he would never be able to fill his big brother's shoes, much less have the nerve to try them on. He made a mental note to tell the psychologist,

Dr. Frankel, if he ever got the nerve to make an appointment, about that bellwether moment in the fifth year of his life. How strangely clear and sharp the memory was. He would have used the word "epiphany" to describe it then but didn't know its meaning well enough to use it in a sentence until he was in the second grade. Colin, he was sure, could not properly define the word today if his life depended on it. Colin only used words with six or fewer letters, or at least so it seemed—and then only just enough of them necessary for him to make his point. Somehow, Colin equated words with weakness—an unforgivable state of affairs for a fledgling trial attorney, but one well suited for someone vested in creating an aura of power. Upon his father's death, Colin assumed he had been left with the mantle of control—or so he would have his mother and brothers believe.

Colin was fine-tuned in the art of perception and the outward appearances of people and things. He was especially sensitive to others' opinions of himself and his character. To his friends, he seemed to be overly burdened with an honorable sense of honor and a dutiful sense of duty. There was no doubt that Colin Mayfair could always be counted on to "do the right thing." Yet, like JW, he often proved to be a humorless pain in the ass while doing so. Colin was Machiavellian in his work ethic and occasionally even in the affairs of the heart. Nevertheless, he was loyal to his little brother and family to the death. In short, Liam loved him. Lee Mayfair, as with most mothers, had that certain nondescript soft spot in her heart for her firstborn. Liam, however, whether or not she could ever bring herself to mouth the words, was the most special of her three sons. He was the child with whom she was mind melded, the one whose pain she felt with exquisite anguish, the son for whom she harbored sublime hope and promise.

Suddenly, Liam heard the sound of Maggie's car tires accelerating out of the driveway. He looked at his watch and realized she had been waiting downstairs for him to shower and come down to the kitchen for breakfast and had probably had just about enough of his sullen, introspective mood. He ran to the window to call out to her, regretting the atmosphere of silence and separation he was carelessly creating between them. There, in the dust and flying gravel of Maggie's hasty exit, he spotted another familiar car parked in front of the garage door. Just then he heard his brother Alex's familiar booming voice and the sound of his heavy footsteps bounding up the stairs to the bedroom.

"Oh no, not now, Alex," Liam mumbled to himself.

Alex burst through the bedroom door without knocking. "Hey, Liam, do you realize I've left a dozen phone messages and e-mails for you? What the hell is going on? Are you ever coming out of your little retreat house out here, for Chrissake?"

"Look, Alex, I'm headed into the city this afternoon. Mom wants me to be with her when she meets her lawyer early tomorrow morning. I'm sorry I never got back to you. I'm not in very good shape right now."

"Yeah, I know. Mom told me. Liam, I'm not kidding, I'm really worried about you. This sounds like serious depression. You gotta get out in front of this, as soon as possible. Do you know what I'm talking about?"

"Yeah, I do, and I appreciate your coming all the way out here to see how I'm doing. But it's really not necessary. Everything will be fine. I have to shower and clear out. I can't spend any time with you right now, Alex. I'm sorry."

"OK, not a problem. I understand. But promise me you'll do something about this blue funk you're in. I'll be at Mom's condo for dinner tonight in the city. Can I tell her you'll be there too?"

"Sure, I'll be there. And by the way, tell her she didn't need to send you out here to check up on me. I really can take care of myself, you know."

"Yeah, well, when you don't answer your phone for weeks at a time, can you blame her for worrying? Say, wasn't that Maggie who flew by me out there on the road? Is everything all right between you two?"

"Everything is fine, Alex. I'll tell you all about it tonight. OK?"

Later, as Liam stood under the hot shower, eyes closed, his thoughts drifted to Alex and the realization that he had probably driven out East because he heard panic in his mother's voice. His head swooned at the sudden coordinated contacts from his brothers and the urgent meeting with his mother and Frank Abrams tomorrow in Manhattan. He had actually enjoyed the solitude of his winter retreat out on Shelter Island for the past several months, and this sudden unwelcome attention disrupted his quiet equilibrium. His mother had obviously urged his brothers to make contact with Liam to make sure he wasn't "dead in a ditch" somewhere down by the beach. Anxious pressure began to swell in his mind. That old familiar cloud of guilt and fear began to hover menacingly over him once again.

THE MAYFAIR BOYS

JW had often marveled as to how different from one another each of his three sons turned out to be. Alex, son number two, was nothing like Colin or Liam. Alex smiled, partied, and glad-handed his way through Florida State, getting by with barely passing grades. His fraternity and social obligations consumed so much of his dance card that the considerable damage to his report card was inevitable. Yet old JW had managed to pull some hefty strings and got Alex into Tulane Law School, thanks to the intercession of an old navy buddy, a fellow A-6 Intruder pilot, Charlie ("You can call me Captain, son") Evans. Captain Evans happened to be not only a member of the school's board of trustees, but also former president of the Tulane Law Alumni Association. Liam had met Charlie one

Christmas Eve at the family home on Shelter Island. Evans and JW spent most of the evening absorbed in slow-motion hand reenactments of their nighttime bombing missions over Hanoi. Before either fully realized what was happening, and after having emptied a bottle of expensive twelve-year-old scotch, their reverie and war stories quickly took an abrupt tailspin into a drunken stupor. Neither ever saw, much less tasted, the Christmas turkey or the holiday trimmings Mom had painstakingly put out for the old friend and houseguest. Lee Mayfair, always the proper lady, shot what would normally have been her best death-ray stare at the drunken sailors. Realizing that her gaze had flown past the target unnoticed, she stormed off to bed in a huff, her face flushed, and said nothing. Colin had already gone off to the backseat of his Ford van with Miss Connecticut runner-up and missed most of the excitement. JW and Captain Charlie were conked out on the floor, like two grounded jets, one on either side of the creche at the foot of the Christmas tree. Liam, Alex, and their little sister, Darcy, pretended to ignore the two sailors lying on the floor and quietly enjoyed their dinner with the sound of Bing Crosby's "White Christmas" flowing like honey from the dining room stereo speakers.

That Christmas Eve, Liam was treated to a rare, telling vision of his enigmatic father. He had quietly, carefully, and with great awe and attention witnessed the complex skill and art of persuasion of his disciplined father on a well-defined mission. He and Alex both had a glimpse of JW in real action—mano a mano. No lifeless A-6 combat reports embellished over time, but real action, in real time, with real characters. Old JW had followed the moonlit phosphorescence on the ocean surface and, once again, brought his Intruder safely below to the flight deck, all bombs delivered on the target. Mission accomplished.

Only three months to the day after JW's well-planned Christmas Eve operation, Alex's jaw dropped to the floor as he read his crisply worded acceptance letter into Tulane Law School. *What an odd coincidence,* he thought, *to get the good news so soon after receiving letters of rejection in quick order from eight other law schools.* Liam had confirmed what he had always intuitively suspected about the secret of life's success. Good grades are very good—but schmooze and booze work even greater miracles in the longer haul of life. JW had often later said that Alex got his big break with a "wing and a prayer." Liam later more aptly described it, always under his breath, as a "wink and a pair of asshole drinking buddies."

Nevertheless, to his credit, Alex Mayfair gradually settled into the routine at Tulane, managed to post some decent grades, and graduated literally on the same day in June that Liam was scheduled to graduate from Northeastern. However, given JW's disappointing inability to yet master the gift of bilocation, he elected to attend Alex's graduation ceremony in New Orleans and sent his wife, Lee, to Boston as the official family emissary—with best regards to Liam, of course.

Alex was disoriented, almost like a lost ship at sea, for the first few months after the plane disaster. But after turning down a decent job offer in New Orleans, he had decided to come home. He just didn't have it in him to start his career, virtually alone, in a still-unfamiliar venue. Alex finally landed a job with a small personal injury litigation firm on Court Street in Brooklyn. Not exactly the French Quarter, he thought. But after having just been admitted to the New York and New Jersey Bar, he was anxious to start working and get on with his life. There was nothing white-shoe or genteel about this position. The only skill Alex needed was the art of haggling over the dollar value of "soft-tissue" whiplash injuries inflicted in fender bender auto accident cases.

Liam's two big brothers were now also brothers "at the bar," literally and figuratively. One night while sipping expensive brandy at an upscale downtown Manhattan bar, they had both conspired to impose their hang-tough, "let's take a verdict" strategy on their naive mother in her wrongful death lawsuit against TWA Airlines. Neither arrived at his opinion with the benefit of any particular courtroom experience, as neither had yet stepped foot into one. The only courtroom drama either had ever seen was the kind featured in TV shows like *The Practice* or *LA Law*. As Colin would conveniently put it, he was much too valuable an asset to his firm, writing brilliant legal research rather than merely going to court. He would bill the mandatory sixty- to seventy-hour weeks for corporate clients who, for the most part, dreaded litigation, especially the horrific expense it represented. While in senior partner Preston Smith's office for only a few fleeting seconds one afternoon, waiting for his boss to look up from his paperwork to hand him a FedEx package, he had glanced for a moment about the opulent office. He happened to notice an ornate plaque on one of the mahogany-paneled walls. It read simply "A Trial Is a Fright, and Not a Tea Party." Colin had yet to learn anything of its terrible significance. In fact, he didn't have a clue. His father, JW, however, knew its meaning well, having successfully tried nearly a hundred heavy personal injury cases to verdict over the years. Liam's brothers' opinion of their mother's lawsuit was simple, if not simplistic. They didn't need courtroom experience to predict the outcome of their mother's case.

As Colin would pontificate, "I mean, really . . . what more does Mom need to win?" Wasn't her noble cause lined up perfectly with the stars? Wasn't she on the side of the angels? The facts were indisputable, weren't they? A commercial passenger plane carrying their father fell off the radar screen, blew up, and crashed into the sea. Hundreds of people were killed. Those were all the facts you needed to prove to win a jury verdict. Right?

Little did Colin and Alex realize at the moment that both of these cocky graduates of the TV drama school of law were about to have a rude awakening to the reality of high-stakes litigation.

Liam suddenly became aware of his prolonged reverie. Rather than trying to control it, he embraced it and let it flow over him like the hot water showering his body and mind.

"Who the hell am I? Where the hell am I going?" he said aloud to himself. He had often thought about his tenuous role and position in this larger-than-life family. It was a place marked with unfulfilled expectations and an ominous, dark cloud that always seemed to hover over his head. Self-doubt hounded his every thought, like the pesky presence of a mangy, flea-infested dog. Liam F. X. Mayfair was the third of the male-heir trilogy, born into the already lengthening and imposing shadows of his two older brothers. The sequence of his arrival in this life reminded Liam of the countless times he stood on the basketball court playground as a kid, nervously waiting to be picked, praying it would not go past the third round.

By the time Liam ventured out onto the basketball court and baseball diamond, JW had already paid his dues to Little League and CYO and was finding it harder to devote time away from his burgeoning law practice. Without either of them consciously realizing it, Liam had inadvertently let his father off the hook in his obligatory field appearances. By then, Liam had made a critical, yet subconscious, life decision. Tired of staring every night, while at dinner, at the mantle full of his brothers' sport trophies, Liam resolved that he would break off in his own unique direction. As a result, he grew up as a quiet, nonathletic, lanky kid with a keen, uncanny ability to observe what everyone else considered unobservable. He could see everything visible and hidden in one wide sweeping glance. It seemed that his mind was always running in high gear at full throttle, lapping the field of his peers, not to mention his teachers. Instead of MVP sports awards, Liam won every math and spelling bee on the school's agenda. The only time JW ever had to discipline him was when he tried to get Liam to stop reading under his bed covers with a flashlight late at night and get him to sleep.

In short, young Liam had acquired, very early in life, that most rare of talents—the ability to be content unto himself, in the very private world of his vivid imagination. Whether this skill was a product of design and a reflection of self-confidence or a defense mechanism brought on by the lack of his father's attention, no one could, or would, dare venture an opinion.

For the first fourteen years of his thirty-two year marriage, JW's home had been filled with a rough-and-tumble mix of burgeoning testosterone. Each of the three boys accumulated accolades and honors, vying for the ever-diminishing supply of their father's approval. In fact, however, and largely unbeknownst to his sons, JW was supremely, but reservedly, proud of each and every one of them. He could usually be heard humming the theme to the old TV show *My Three Sons* while standing in the shower. One early Saturday morning, while waiting for a photographer to arrive at the house for a family portrait, as the boys stood, squirming in protest of their new blazers, starched shirt collars, and ties, Lee turned to JW and said, "You're going to have to stop with that stupid TV theme music you hum every morning."

"And why is that, woman?"

The answer made his jaw drop.

"Because you're about to have a daughter, macho man, that's why."

"But I thought . . . But you said . . ."

Lee just grinned like a Cheshire cat, the soft lines about her blue-gray eyes completing the smile.

"This house could use a dose of frilly lace and girl curls—or do you have something against women?"

The birth of beautiful baby Darcy, the family planning oversight, turned the Mayfair household on its ear. Everything suddenly seemed to become organized, purposeful, and balanced overnight. Even the language on the backyard basketball court improved. JW loved every minute of the transformation. To him, his daughter was the hidden jewel of his heart, the Star of India, the Hope Diamond. Recently turned seventeen, Darcy not only had all her mother's natural and inner beauty, she also had a Broadway-quality singing voice. She was the only person in the world who could make JW flush with emotion just by singing the opening aria from *Pagliacci*. Music was their eternal and loving bonding agent. At an early age, Darcy learned to play her willing father like an Irish harp. Even more importantly, she learned how to avoid stepping over that discordant line that often estranges fathers and daughters.

During the heavy litigation years, Lee Mayfair would proclaim JW's weeklong "absences" and lack of family interaction to the children with the simple yet stern words: "Your dad's on trial!" The words were clearly understood and interpreted by the two older two boys to mean "Be quiet! Go to your rooms and get your homework done. Your father is under pressure preparing his trial testimony for tomorrow."

But for Liam, the supreme literalist, his recollection of these words as a young boy conjured up a darker, more sinister image. It spawned a vision of his father standing in shackles in the criminal docket, charged with unspeakable crimes, fighting for his life before a hanging judge. JW would often later recount the first parent-teacher meeting he was able to attend with Liam's third grade teacher, Ms. Applebeck. She was very pleased to finally meet Liam's father and told him she was "very sorry for your troubles." When JW asked which troubles she was referring to, she responded. "Oh, I just assumed, with you having to having to be in court so often, that you were under indictment in some kind of big criminal case. Every time I asked to meet you, Liam would just say, 'My dad's way too stressed right now. He's on trial.'"

Liam and his brothers and sister would soon learn that during their father's "trials," all family life, all baseball and soccer games, all father-son or father-daughter activities at school, every emotional need of the family would go into a deep freeze, a still-life form of suspended animation. JW's life while on trial would become consumed in a constant state of fear, worry, and mind-numbing attention to the minute detail of experts and evidence and strategy. The evenings preparing for the testimony of the next day were often filled with headaches and indigestion, all of which would be hopefully justified by the glorious, albeit fleeting, thrill of victory when the foreman would rise and announce the award of a ridiculously exorbitant sum of money for his client. The sound of the verdict and the money it meant for JW and the firm almost didn't matter to him anymore. It was the vindication of an unspoken promise made to his client that he really craved and for which he fought so hard.

JW, like most trial lawyers and professional baseball players, was more than a little superstitious. He became obsessively habitual in his routines in the last days of a trial. Just before the verdict was read in open court, he would always turn to Bobby Klein, his loyal trial prep man, with a grin and say, "Don't worry, Bobby, if justice prevails, we'll appeal." A few weeks later, the grinding cycle would begin anew. And thus summed up the success or, as some would argue, the ultimate failure of the life of J. W. Mayfair, prominent attorney-at-law.

Yet, while his father's elevated level of stress while on trial was obvious to Liam, it was just as clear to him that JW loved his work and wouldn't have wanted it any other way. JW often made it clear to his children that for all its inherent gamesmanship and cynicism, the legal profession was ultimately a noble one, always to be held in high esteem, even in the face of society's tarnished view of it.

Of the many JW war stories Liam recalled hearing growing up, usually while seated around the family dinner table, there was one in particular that Liam pressed fondly into his memory. It was the time JW, while picking a jury in Manhattan, encountered a young man who was more cavalier and contemptuous than most in trying to worm his way out of jury duty. When asked the pro forma question whether he would be willing and able to focus his attention on the matter at hand for what promised to be a tedious two-week trial, the young man whined in a high-pitched voice. He said something vague about the "enormous personal stress" he was under at that moment and how that might "distract" him from his duty to be open-minded and fair in his analysis of the evidence. Expecting to hear some kind of serious excuse about a parent's terminal disease or some other such catastrophic event, JW was stunned and angered when the young man began to rant about the fact that he was in the process of moving from one apartment to another and that his accumulated "stuff" was "all over the floors in unopened boxes." He complained that this left him with an "overwhelming" feeling of disorganization and personal chaos. JW decided he had had just about enough of this spoiled little wimp and set about to teach him a lesson.

He said to the young man. "Sir, do you know what today is?"

"No, why?' came the limp response.

"Today is June 6. Does the date mean anything to you?"

"Nope. Should it?"

JW stared at him in disbelief and wagged his head in disgust. "On this date in 1944, the Allies landed on the beaches of Normandy to take the war to Hitler on the European mainland. It was only the greatest, most dramatic military enterprise in the history of the world."

The young man just glared back at JW in obvious contempt and said, "Yeah . . . and so what. Is that some kind of national holiday or something?"

"Tell me, junior. Do you think those young men, most of whom were about your age, while they were running up those beaches into a solid wall of machine gun fire and mortar shells, would have been willing to trade the panic and fear of having their heads and guts blown apart in exchange for the 'overwhelming stress' of not knowing which box your fucking CD collection is in?"

At first the rest of the jury pool gasped and then slowly broke into applause.

JW walked solemnly over to the young man whose face had turned a crimson red. JW paused at the rail of the jury box and leaned into his startled face. "Listen, sonny, my gut inclination is to pick you for this jury and force you to sit through this trial from start to finish, whether you want to or not. I'm pretty sure I can significantly add to the level of your 'overwhelming' stress. I'm also sure that my adversary here wouldn't object to having you sit on this jury, especially after my little outburst. But on second thought, I don't want to waste any more time with you. Why don't you just go home? While you're moving and reorganizing your boxes, I suggest you take a moment and think really hard about the responsibilities of being an American citizen. And when you think about the incredible liberty and freedoms you enjoy, why don't you give some thought as well to the ultimate sacrifice that others have paid for it? Grab your hat. You're excused, you little shit!"

JW had spent his entire legal career walking that ever-present fine line between the constant demands of both form and substance in the law. Unlike many attorneys who eventually succumb to the siren sound of their own voices and the stroking of their massive egos, JW fought that temptation tooth and nail. He learned to avoid the nitpicking and haggling over trivia and instead drove relentlessly to the heart of the issue. He always kept his eyes fixed on the big picture—on the goal, the desired outcome of the case. JW's lawyer sons had not yet learned these valuable lessons of the trade. In short, Liam knew that neither Colin nor Alex had the foggiest notion of the anxiety and chaos that was about to come crashing down around them in the case their mother had reluctantly filed against TWA.

Liam knew that his father, if he could only communicate with him somehow from the grave, even if only in his nightmarish appearances, would explain to him exactly how to proceed. He would show him how to guide his widow through the ensuing first round of negotiations with Mutual Casualty Insurance Company. JW would explain how to place a fair value on his life—in death. Liam knew that JW would have given his trial summation with unmatched eloquence. Liam could close his eyes and imagine every word of it. His father would have had the jury in tears as they retired for their verdict. He could picture the foreman having already pulled out a calculator from his coat pocket and looking back for one last scornful glance at the defense counsel table as he led his fellow jurors out of the courtroom in single file to "do the right thing." He also knew that this was, as JW would have called it, one of those "heavy" cases with a potential for millions of dollars. Much would be said, amid the sobbing of the female jurors, about his father's "conscious pain and suffering," about the final moments of horror as the plane fell toward its crushing rendezvous with the sea, about the all-consuming fear of a sure and impending and excruciatingly painful death. He could hear the description of the choking smoke in the cabin, the ignited jet fuel consuming and burning the flesh of his dying father, the banshee screams of the other passengers doomed to the same fate. There would be the long, mundane, yet indispensable testimony of the expert economists as to the amount of the financial support of which his widow and children had been so abruptly and forever deprived.

However, Liam also knew that it would be assumed by everyone outside the family that his father's estate was substantial—of mammoth proportion. He knew that public perception would automatically assume that Lee Mayfair was a woman who didn't need to rely on any money recovery or settlement with TWA to continue in the lifestyle to which she had become so happily accustomed. However, what Liam and the outside world didn't know was that, to the contrary, John W. Mayfair, in the months before his violent death, had leveraged and mortgaged almost all of his estate. He had gambled his sizable wealth in capitalizing the Internet company that he had founded and gotten off the ground. All that now lay comatose, barely hanging on to life support. The merger deal that JW was flying to Paris to wrap up in July on that ill-fated flight was now, according to the *Wall Street Journal*, "on hold"—a clear euphemism among business sophisticates for "dead in the water." Without the merger, his fledgling company, along with the millions that he and several other investors had poured into it, was doomed and destined for the "capital loss" side of the ledger. Despite his tender age, Liam could understand simple economic truths. Lots of brilliant Internet ideas with no working capital, no foreseeable profits, and no financial knight on a white horse meant simply that the company, and his dad's once impressive estate, died along with John W. Mayfair in the crash of Flight 800. The frightening reality was that once the death of the company was finally acknowledged publicly, there would be barely enough to pay the rent of a modest one-bedroom apartment for his mother. The palatial four-bedroom penthouse condo in Manhattan, the summer home on Shelter Island, the beachfront house in Naples Florida, the stock portfolio would all soon have to be sold to satisfy the huge debts that would soon be filed as liens against the properties. To make matters worse, JW had let his two-million-dollar-term life insurance policy lapse.

Liam had only first learned of the financial havoc when his mother had mentioned it, one evening over dinner soon after the funeral. She casually commented that she was thinking of selling their Manhattan condo. Confused at first, he had finally coaxed the tearful truth from her. There was no other option, she lamented. She would have to sue TWA. Lee Mayfair made a weak attempt at self-justification. As she reasoned, the NTSB and the FBI reports of the crash, after twenty months of investigation and over six hundred witnesses interviewed, had attributed the likely cause of the explosion to a spark from a short circuit in the center-wing fuel tank. More importantly, the government had definitively ruled out a bomb or missile strike. Lee Mayfair had absorbed enough negligence law from JW over the years to quickly recognize the likelihood that defective wiring or aircraft design were involved. Lee knew that she had the classic ingredients of a dramatic cause of action for negligence in the wrongful death of her husband. And she went straight to the man who would know better than anyone else.

THE COMMITMENT

Lee's gut instinct was quickly confirmed by Frank Abrams, JW's former law partner. Lee Mayfair wasted no time in consulting him about a lawsuit against the airline, visiting his midtown Manhattan office the very next morning after the funeral service. Like Abrams, Lee got to the point quickly. She was in serious financial trouble. Her family's breadwinning husband had been taken from her and the children by what she intuitively suspected was the gross negligence of a major international airline company. She desperately needed someone to throw her a financial lifeline.

Lee sat upright in one of Abrams's leather office chairs and wasted no time. "Is the case winnable, Frank?" Lee asked.

"Lee, that depends on a lot of factors and information I don't have yet," Frank replied.

"So is that a yes then?"

Frank just grinned and said, "Slow down, Lee. Let's see how my research plays out. These airline cases have a lot of built-in limitations and hurdles I would need to get around first."

"Frank, I know the FBI is taking a major role in the investigation. You wouldn't be placed in a conflict situation with your former employer, would you?"

Frank simply smiled and shook his head.

"Not to worry, Lee. That won't be a problem. In fact, I have good friends still working for the bureau who might be very helpful, depending on what they're free to tell me about their investigation."

Lee had known for years what most of the New York legal profession knew through direct courtroom experience. Frank Abrams, the tall, bald-headed, bullnecked, seasoned attorney with over thirty years of tough trial experience was not one to be easily denied or diverted. His compass was always pointed straight ahead no matter what adverse turns or obstacles he encountered at trial. Frank had mastered the "third and goal yardage" kind of self-disciplined mind-set he had developed as the starting fullback at Columbia University and had later perfected into his superior trial skills. There was probably no better or more feared cross-examiner in the New York metro area than Frank Abrams. And it was because of that skill and confidence that Lee Mayfair had developed a deep admiration and respect for JW's former partner. She trusted his honest and direct mannerisms. When not speaking with that deep and reassuring voice that had become his trademark, Frank Abrams had established another peculiar habit of chewing on unlit cigars. "I don't smoke 'em," he would say. "I just like something to sink my teeth into, something that won't bite back." Frank was one of those few men whose head was meant to be bald. His convenient opinion was that hair would only be a "distraction from my natural, tough, good looks."

Frank had served, before going into private law practice with J. W. Mayfair in New York, as an FBI special agent, working the UFAP (Unlawful Flight to Avoid Prosecution) squads in the Miami and Chicago offices, two of the toughest FBI venues in the country. He served during the political and cultural upheaval of the late '60s and early '70s and the final J. Edgar Hoover years, and soon learned that quick advancement in the bureau was made a lot easier by earning commendations in the fugitive and bank robbery divisions rather than in the dull, white-collar crime units. He had served in both with quiet distinction. In short, Abrams had parlayed the skills he had honed in tracking down, interrogating, and capturing fugitives into an enviable reputation as one of the most feared and respected trial lawyers in New York.

Since the day of the crash of Flight 800, Frank Abrams closely followed the newspaper accounts and media speculations as to the cause of the TWA explosion and kept in close contact with Lee and the children whenever he could grab a free moment. He had his personal theories as to what brought down that commercial jet but kept them to himself. When Lee arranged to meet with Frank again about the lawsuit, once he had become familiar with the NTSB investigation, his first reaction was to try to gently dissuade her from what he knew would be a protracted, expensive, and frustrating battle. He sensed immediately that she may not be emotionally equipped for the fight. He answered her straightforward questions with dull, lawyerlike precision.

"Yes, I can make out a decent case, provided I have the right expert testimony and enough discovery material.

"Yes, I can probably win a successful verdict against the airline and/or the plane manufacturer based on defective wiring, negligent maintenance, and inspection of the aircraft, among other theories."

He went on to explain, in slow and measured words, that the loss of John W.'s projected average income for Lee and the family's support would be considered very substantial. In fact, as he continued to explain, because of the volatile nature of the medical expert testimony about JW's presumed excruciating pain and terror in his dying seconds or minutes before the 747 fell thirteen thousand feet and crashed into the Atlantic in a ball of flames, the verdict could very well be unprecedented.

"Lee, to be blunt, the verdict could be well into seven figures," he answered her. "But it won't be a cakewalk. These kinds of cases never are."

His words were like a life vest thrown to a drowning, panicked woman. Frank Abrams was coming to the realization, as they continued to meet, that it wasn't just Lee Mayfair's financial security, but her emotional stability as well that would be thrown into serious jeopardy without a jury verdict. He tried to remain positive.

"Lee, you know better than most that in this business, there are no guarantees. But for what it's worth, I'm beginning to like our chances."

"I was hoping you would say that, Frank," Lee muttered aloud.

Frank Abrams silently promised himself, once he understood the gravity of his former partner's debt-ridden estate, that he would have to go for the jugular. "Take no prisoners" would be his mantra on this one. He could already begin to feel the familiar knot take shape in the pit of his stomach. He knew that TWA would send wave after wave of paper assaults and dozens of young snotty-nosed associates at him—countless motions, interrogatories, endless out-of-town depositions of witnesses and experts in a high-stakes war of attrition. "Whoever kills the most trees in the paper war wins, Frank," JW used to say to him. Frank had fought the big courtroom battles many times before, had treated the bleeding ulcer and the crushing migraine headaches so often that they seemed like intimate members of his family.

Whatever thoughts he had entertained in the last few years of retiring to his second home in Arizona would be sidetracked for at least another twenty to twenty-four months while he started what he knew would be the last great sensational fight of his long career. Frank and Carol Abrams had few dreams and no children whose dreams they could derivatively enjoy. But they shared a deep desire to escape the shrill sounds and frenetic lifestyle of New York City and move into the beautiful home that they had painstakingly built into the side of a mountain with a deck facing west, toward the pastel sunsets of northern Arizona.

As with many seasoned trial attorneys, Frank knew that his own shelf life was limited and due to run out soon. He had grown terribly weary of the monotony and compromises of the game. Just that morning, he had pathetically complained to Carol that the only variety he had come to look forward to every morning was deciding which side of his face to shave first. However, for at least the present moment, he sensed the thrill of the hunt once again and was growing excited. This fight would not be driven by money. He had accumulated enough wealth to last through many comfortable retirements. It would be motivated by the most personal of reasons—loyalty and pride. This woman sitting across him at his desk was the wife of one of his closest and most intimate friends—a widow who was desperate for not just anyone's help, but his. His teeth clenched down on his wet cigar. He held Lee Mayfair's hands in his own and committed himself for the long haul.

"Lee, however long it takes, I'll see it through. How about you? Do you have the stomach for it? It could really get nasty."

Lee tightened her grip on his hand and spoke quickly: "I'll do whatever it takes, with only one proviso."

"What's that"?

"I want Liam, not my two lawyer sons, to be my spokesman, my personal liaison with you and your team. I want him involved in the discussions and negotiations every step of the way. Are you all right with that?"

Abrams looked puzzled.

"What's this all about, Lee? It makes more sense that Colin and Alex would want to stay in this loop. Why Liam?"

"I'm asking you to trust me on this, Frank. My reasons are very personal. Just tell me you'll agree to it. Please."

"OK. Though I'm not sure Liam will be happy getting in the middle of this. But that's fine with me."

ALEA IACTA SUNT

Frank Abrams sat alongside Lee Mayfair in the massive conference room, bathed in an uncomfortable silence. The only sound came from the click of a swinging pendulum on an antique railroad clock on the far wall. The room was filled with an unsettled air of tension, thick and tangible. The musty smell of old law books wafted off of the shelves. They were clearly on enemy turf, and Lee could almost sense the presence of the proverbial prince of darkness. Rutlers, Canning & Michaelson was one of the premiere defense litigation firms in New York, with satellite offices in Boston, Chicago, and Los Angeles. Abrams referred to them openly as "Ruthless, Cunning, and Machiavelli." Frank was looking for some yellow legal pad in the black leather briefcase opened in front of him on the glass-topped mahogany table. At the other end of the cavernous room was a lone, small, dark-skinned man in a white smock, setting up a tray of coffee and pastries. The sharp clanging of the sterling silver utensils and porcelain cups being laid out on the table created a strange, offensive affront to the cathedral-like silence that enveloped them.

Lee Mayfair was acutely conscious of why she needed to be in this room at this moment in time. As she daydreamed of her dead husband, she suddenly remembered the reaction of her parents and friends when she first announced her sudden plans to marry J. W. Mayfair, a young man just discharged from the navy, a pilot who had flown bombing missions while assigned to the Seventh Fleet aircraft carrier USS *Enterprise*. How improbable and even unwise, everyone seemed to think, was the union of Lee Mary Picard—the pretty, blond, youngest daughter of a Gloucester lobsterman—and this brash, bull-in-the-china-shop, know-it-all, hotshot A6 Intruder pilot. Lee was fun loving yet quiet, unassuming, and all business. JW was tall, dark haired, broad shouldered and full of piss and vinegar. He was loud, cocky, and a little out of control, having grown up fast and furious as a young naval officer whose psyche was twisted by the tension of hundreds of adrenaline-soaked, below-the-radar bombing missions over Hanoi and Haiphong.

JW never spoke of other targets, except one evening over dinner with a navy buddy. He had been plied with too many gin and tonics and finally agreed to explain the mission for which he was awarded the Silver

Star. JW had destroyed some bridge called Hai Duong. Apparently, it was a big deal at the time, at least to those admirals who thought their job was to win a war that no one else in Washington seemed interested in winning.

JW and Lee had hit it off instantly, all pistons firing in perfectly timed unison. Their goals, their values, their common Catholic backgrounds, even their language had a smooth, natural symbiosis—a resonance of pitch that ran deep and rang true like a bronze tuning fork. There was never any doubt, from the first afternoon they met, as part of competing crews in a small Fourth of July sailing club regatta off Nantucket, that each knew exactly where the real finish line was—not out there on the water, but securely berthed and anchored alongside one another. Lee had captained her father's Tartan 27. JW was part of hastily organized cadre of sailing misfits, all former navy friends. From that day forward, she would ruthlessly remind her friends and children that she and her two-man crew soundly beat JW's boat on that windy, sunny afternoon. Her boat had plowed over the finish line, close-hauled, with the rail in the water, almost a full minute ahead of JW. She still smiled at the auditory memory of the wonderful sound of the air horn blasted by the club's commodore, welcoming her to victory as she stood, smiling, at the helm.

It was all smooth sailing from that day on. They were married four months later, to the day. JW was not one to detour from his mission or take his eyes off the top prize. And Lee, who immediately recognized the depth and strength of his personality and character, was not about to let this guy sail away into the sunset without her.

The only troubling sign Lee had seen in JW that wonderful Fourth of July weekend was his odd and troubled reaction to the elaborate Grucci fireworks show fired from the deck of a barge anchored one hundred yards out on the bay. JW suddenly grew very quiet and excused himself, saying he needed to hit the head. He did not reappear until well after the last of the grand finale explosions, almost thirty minutes later. It was not until several years after they were married that Lee finally was able to get JW to talk about his aversion to fireworks. She cried aloud when he told her about the B-52 and A6 crewmen, many of whom were personal friends, whose lives were instantaneously extinguished in all those bright, horrible, nighttime explosions of light he had come to relive in the onset of his postwar nightmares. She realized then, for the first time, that not all the horrors of war were borne by foot soldiers in the muddy trenches of ground combat. Many were suffered in the sky as well. They were married almost twenty years before JW was finally freed of his nightmares. For all that time, and on all those nights, Lee had simply held his trembling body close in her arms, in the dark, and said nothing.

Suddenly Lee heard muffled conversation in the adjoining room. She recognized the irritating voice of the curt and officious secretary who had led them into the conference room forty minutes earlier. The woman had simply said then, "Mr. Canning will be with you shortly. Help yourself to some coffee if you like." Lee saw the blood rising under Frank's starched white collar. Frank kept his cool but added this clearly intended slight in the ledger sorted away in the corner of his brain—the place reserved for dicks like Canning. It wasn't until another ten minutes later, as Frank reached into his pocket to pull out the remains of a cigar, that the French doors finally opened and three men in dark suits walked through, each in lockstep with the other. The man with the well-groomed gray hair spoke first as he entered the room and approached Frank with his hand extended.

"Frank! It's so great to see you again. What has it been, two years or so? How's Carol? I would have thought you would have been well out to pasture by now!" The dig did not slip by unnoticed.

Lee observed quickly that the smile on Canning's face did not extend to the eyes but seemed frozen at the mouth. Frank got up very slowly, without smiling, and likewise extended his hand without saying a word. Bill Canning ignored the body language and pressed on.

"So what brings you into this case, Frank? Wasn't JW your law partner some years ago? I would have guessed that this case would be a little too close to home for you. No conflict of interest issues for you to be concerned about?"

Canning suddenly looked to his left. "Oh, excuse me. You must be JW's widow, Mrs. Mayfair. I apologize for meeting you under these circumstances. Frankly, I didn't expect to see you here today. But then,

Frank is always full of surprises. I knew your husband . . . a great trial lawyer . . . in his day."

The additional slight was as subtle—as JW used to say—"as a fart in a space suit."

Frank Abrams finally spoke, the unlit cigar still clenched in his teeth. "Hello, Bill. Actually, it's been almost three years. I would have thought you would have memorized the date. It was the Allied Chemical suit, as I recall. I believe that was the case where US District Court Judge Wiley was all set to start a contempt proceeding against you right after my plaintiff's verdict. He was really pissed about that hack witness you rushed into court on the last day of trial, without notice. You remember him, don't you? You know, that guy with the bad wig, the one we all were convinced, including the jury, perjured himself? You dodged a huge bullet on that one, wouldn't you agree?"

Canning glared at Abrams for a moment. He threw a quick, self-conscious glance over at his two young associates but recomposed himself quickly.

"You have some memory, Frank, selective as it is."

Abrams plodded forward: "You know, Bill, I've often thought you probably would have won that case if your last-minute eyewitness's story wasn't so obviously full of shit. But hey, that's what makes horse races, right?" Frank's smile widened as he spoke.

Canning looked down at the table and drummed out a nervous beat with his fingers. He quickly remembered why he never liked Frank Abrams. Abrams had cut Canning's "eyewitness" to pieces and had left his perjurious blood all over the courtroom floor. When he finished his cross-examination, Frank had turned dramatically to the jury, looked each in the eye, and said with a smile, "Any resuscitation—er, excuse me, I mean redirect, Mr. Canning?"

Canning changed the subject quickly, noticing out of the corner of his eye that his two young associates had shot a quizzical glance at one another.

"So, Frank, why don't we get right down to the business at hand, shall we? If I may be blunt, do you really think, in your wildest fantasy, you have any kind of case against TWA? You realize of course that the FBI and NTSB preliminary reports aren't based on any hard forensic evidence. It's an interesting theory, this faulty wiring business. But it's only that: a theory. And theories don't make cases, Frank. Experts with lab-tested evidence do. There isn't a single case out there where any commercial plane has ever been brought down by an explosion tied into defective fuel-tank wiring. My guess is we will never know what happened to that plane. As a matter of fact, the NTSB hasn't even been able to replicate the explosion in the way the FBI thinks it may have happened. Were you aware of that, Frank? Or are you just reading the newspaper accounts of the NTSB report?"

"Bill, when I lay out my evidence to the jury, they won't be reading newspapers. They'll be reading and listening to the testimony of qualified—not fabricated—witnesses." Abrams was getting pissed now, and he fired that shot from the hip.

"I've got some former NTSB engineers lined up, Bill. You'll be able to depose them soon enough at your customary rates. Those hundreds of miles of wiring running through and around those five fuel tanks, not to mention the wiring in the AC units directly under those tanks, were old, dried out, exposed, and defective from the get-go. There was trouble going all the way back to the design and manufacture of that plane—right in the blueprint stage. You and I both know there was some kind of an electric spark, an ignition source, in that starboard fuel tank. Or are you one of those guys who believe in spontaneous combustion? Or maybe you're going to tell the jury it was a lightning bolt that did them in? Come on, Bill, are you going to try this case on empirical evidence or science fiction?"

Abrams laughed out loud. "You should probably call the bomb fairy or even George Lucas as your first witness."

Canning fired back with a limp shot. "Those reports prove that fuel-vapor pressure built up and ripped one of those tanks open. Speaking of fictitious characters, why didn't you also name Mother Nature as a defendant in your caption, Frank? It was probably she who conspired to build up all that heat and internal pressure in that fuel tank."

Abrams smiled to himself as Canning stood up and paced back and forth, gathering his thoughts.

"Look, I'm sure you've read those reports, Abrams. The feds ruled out defective fuel pumps, static electricity, and any other logical cause. We know the missile theory wasn't a real possibility because there was no sign of explosive chemicals. And there was no structural damage or metal deformation from shrapnel or missile fragments. None of the bodies or the passenger seats showed any signs of a high-energy explosive. So, Frank, the sad truth is no one has any idea what the ignition source was. And more importantly, neither the hell do you!"

Realizing that his pacing back and forth was accomplishing little except to betray his frustration, Canning sat down abruptly in his seat at the head of the table. "Look, let's get it all out in the open now, shall we? If you think you're going to rely on that old hogwash that the FAA negligently refused to order the industry to use the same kind of nitrogen systems to vent the fuel-tank pressure the way the military used to do, you're dreaming, Frank. That dog won't hunt, and you know it. Everyone knows Boeing aircraft and military aircraft are totally different animals— like comparing apples and oranges."

Frank stood up and leaned to within a foot of Canning's now-reddened face.

"I think you're beginning to hear footsteps in the dark, Billy. I never said anything about the military vapor venting system. Once again, you're overthinking this one. Come on, Billy, have I ever disappointed you when it came down to admissible proof? How closely have you studied those FAA reports anyway? Or are you relying on a CliffsNotes-styled summary prepared by one of your esteemed young legal scholars here?"

Looking at the unnamed associates, who Canning hadn't yet had the courtesy to introduce, Frank said with a smile, "No offense, gentlemen. I'm sure your research skills are more than up to the standards of this illustrious firm." The two young men had no clue that they and their law firm had just been insulted big-time. *Pearls before swine*, Frank quietly thought to himself as he looked back at Canning.

"Look, Billy, let's get real here. Do you really think I would challenge you to a gunfight with a knife? Are you really going to sit back with your feet up on your opulent desk and tell me you're going to rely on the Warsaw Convention liability limitations argument? And do you really think I don't have something substantial to establish willful misconduct on the part of both TWA and the FAA to get me past that old canard? This will be like shooting fish in a barrel."

The confidence in Abrams's voice was thick and tangible, but not arrogant. Lee suddenly recalled, with glowing admiration, why her husband had relied so heavily on Frank Abrams for all their years as partners. No one seated at the long table, except Abrams, had noticed that while Frank spoke, Canning's shoulders slouched downward ever so slightly. Much has been written about the art of studying the psychologically driven body language of adversaries and prospective jurors. Frank Abrams was one of those instinctively gifted lawyers who needed no such training in reading the bodily movements of any living animal—human or otherwise. He could tell when a dog was about to growl and bare his teeth, lift his leg to take a piss, or submit to his master's stern voice. Canning had just put his tail between his legs and folded back his ears and wasn't even aware of it.

Canning's two young law associates were oblivious to what was going on in those few intense minutes of point and counterpoint between their mentor and Abrams. They would continue to dutifully exaggerate their billable hours to meet the mandatory minimum of sixty hours a week. They would do the monotonous trial research in the firm's musty-smelling, one-hundred-year-old library and fetch a lunch or two along the way. And maybe, if they were lucky enough to go the distance, they would have a ringside seat to a classic fight with a classy fighter—that was if they would be allowed to venture outside of these hallowed, blue-blood halls and enter the frightening caverns of the Federal Courthouse of the Southern District of New York. For the moment, however, they would have to be content, as part of their job description, to get up and bring some tea to the table for Canning's guests.

Canning realized that the meeting's momentum had shifted decisively in favor of his adversary and tried to change the subject quickly. "Would you like something to drink, Mrs. Mayfair? Some tea? Perhaps some spring water?" said Canning as he gave a quick nod to his young associates.

Frank Abrams smiled contentedly, knowing he could intimidate the hell out of guys like Bill Canning, almost at will. Yet at the same time, he worried privately how he was going to assemble enough expert proof to make out not just a prima facie case against TWA, but actually back up each of his bold allegations. Frank knew that it was time to end the bluff and bluster and put some evidentiary meat on those bare NTSB bones. Not today, perhaps, but very soon.

Just at that moment, Liam rushed through the door, slightly out of breath. "Sorry, Mom, Mr. Abrams. I took a wrong turn and got lost. I haven't stayed at the family condo for so long, I forgot my way around town."

How refreshing, the innocence of youth, mused Abrams. Colin and Alex, he was sure, would have been here on time, dressed and primped to the nines. He was suddenly glad for Lee's insistence.

Liam's pea coat and Red Sox hat suddenly put the meeting in a lighter mood and warmed the ice jam. Abrams got up and gave Liam a bear hug.

"Liam, my boy, I haven't seen you since the funeral. You look a little tired. How have you been? Oh, I'm sorry. Bill Canning, I'd like you to meet JW's youngest boy, Liam Mayfair."

Canning was surprisingly genuine in his greeting. "Liam, it's an honor and a pleasure. Please sit down. I didn't expect to see you or your mother this morning. But I'm glad you're both here. Maybe we can come to some equitable solution and put this case in the rearview mirror with very little fuss and fanfare. How does that sound?"

Liam shot a surprised look at Abrams. He thought, *Could this really be over so soon?*

Canning looked back at Abrams. "Frank, don't get me wrong, I know you'd give us a run for our money, but you just don't hold the right cards. Not this time. Not on this one. I'm sure you probably know that TWA—in fact, the whole industry—has been suffering from depressed airline revenues for over a year now. My client is interested in cutting litigation costs, even though they're confident they'll prevail in the end, maybe even as a result of an early summary judgment motion. But in spite of all that, my client is willing to accommodate the losses of the families and make what is more than a fair offer to put this tragedy behind us so we can all get on with our lives. But . . . and this is a firm, nonnegotiable 'but,' this offer is going to be made only once, Frank. I know you've heard that song before, but we're very serious. We've studied JW's case, his life, and his pecuniary losses and stacked that up against the remote chances of you winning a liability verdict."

Canning paused for a moment and skillfully shifted eye contact away from Abrams directly to Mrs. Mayfair and her son. "Mrs. Mayfair, I've been authorized to write you a corporate check this morning for $450,000, tax-free, no risks, no strings attached." When Canning spoke the number aloud, he slowly articulated every syllable of it. He let the words pour over them like a warm bath and echo in their heads. If Canning had been meeting alone with Abrams, he would have simply said, "We can go up to four-fifty and that's it!" But he was trying to grab a negotiating advantage by speaking directly to the client, in person.

"It's a very generous offer, wouldn't you say, Mrs. Mayfair? Liam?"

Abrams ignored the obvious impropriety of making the offer directly to his client instead of himself and just rolled his eyes. He gritted his teeth on the stub of his cigar, and before he could tell Canning to go to hell, Lee Mayfair spoke, slowly and deliberately.

"Mr. Canning, my husband was one of the most decent, loving, and exciting men you will ever meet. His death, because of your client's negligence, has created a financial and emotional black hole in the universe of my life and the lives of our four children. Your so-called offer can't even begin to fill it. I had hoped that you and your client would have taken this lawsuit much more seriously than you apparently have. Unfortunately, there's nothing more to discuss here. I think we'll go now. Thank you for the tea."

Her face was like flint, yet her voice was calm and almost sweet. Frank Abrams stifled a grin as he watched Bill Canning's jaw drop. Lee Mayfair had just told Canning to stick his "offer" where the sun don't shine, without any of the familiar vulgarities and bravado which that had already queued up in his head, ready to launch across the long table. *What class*, he thought. The unrehearsed words were so much more powerful and genuine coming directly from the client herself. He was glad he had broken with tradition and agreed to allow her and Liam to join him at this meeting.

"Alea jacta sunt," Abrams said aloud, with an exaggerated flair.

Canning looked up, his face twisted in confusion and annoyance.

"Come on, Bill. Don't tell me that a Jew from the Bronx has stumped a Boston Irish Catholic in his own native high school Latin? Don't you remember the famous words of Caesar as he crossed the Rubicon and began his fateful march on Rome? The bones have been rolled, Bill. Or as the phrase has been honed down for the rest of us over the centuries, 'The die has been cast.'"

Abrams enjoyed feigning loss of control over the meeting and his client as he threw his hands up over his head in mock surrender. "I'm afraid my hands are tied, Bill."

Liam had been observing all of this testosterone-laden swaggering from behind an opulent red leather chair. He looked like a deer caught in the headlights. *Geez, that's a lot of money to casually toss back across the table*, he thought quietly to himself. More impressive to Liam, however, was the sure display of strength by a mother who had always taken a backseat in every family conversation about money—except when it really counted. For someone who wanted no part of a protracted fight in court, Lee Mayfair had just taken off her black kid gloves. Lee slipped her right hand into Frank's as they excused themselves and walked out the room. Liam, still a bit shocked at what just happened, shrugged his shoulders and smiled at the stunned defense team. He leaned over the table and shoved his breakfast, a sugar-glazed apple turnover, into his right coat pocket as he trailed off behind Abrams and his mother toward the elevator.

Thirty minutes later, back in Abrams's Manhattan office, only three blocks away, Frank was beginning to outline his litigation strategy when Lee feigned the need to visit the ladies' room. Left alone with Liam, the attorney seized the opportunity given him by Lee.

"Liam, what do you know of your father's estate? Or more specifically, your mother's financial condition."

Liam looked puzzled at the question. "Not very much, why do you ask?"

Abrams got up from his desk, walked to the window, and looked down from his twenty-seventh-floor perch over the city.

Frank's mood grew somber. "Liam, your mother's in serious trouble. It seems your father's business dealings began to sour months before the plane crash. I won't bore you with the details, but it appears JW leveraged practically everything he owned—property, annuities, stock—into that Zurich/French merger, and now that deal appears to be stone-dead. He had lapsed all his life insurance . . . felt he didn't need it, what with such an impressive balance sheet, a few years ago. Do you understand what I'm saying, Liam?"

After a moment of silence and obvious confusion on Liam's part, Frank continued. "Liam, your mother needs to win this case against TWA if she is going to keep the properties in Manhattan and Shelter Island, not to mention the oceanfront house in Naples, Florida. The real estate, along with what's left of your father's assets, may have to be sold off to satisfy his debts and leveraging. Your mother has spent her entire adult life taking care of JW and you kids. She can't go out into the workplace now, not after all these years. She's not equipped to do that at this stage of her life. I—we—need to win this case. I don't like turning down $450,000 in any kind of litigation. But your mother is my boss. And if she wants to roll the dice, then those are my marching orders."

"Mr. Abrams, my father and I were not exactly the best of friends. He never discussed anything about his estate with me. I don't have the foggiest idea of what he's worth or what my mother's situation is. Why are you telling me all of this? Shouldn't you be talking to my brothers? They're both lawyers, you know."

"I know that very well, Liam. But your mother wants me to keep you not only at my elbow, but in the center of the loop. She hasn't said exactly what she has in mind, except that she apparently trusts your judgment, even over that of Colin and Alex. Your brothers, with all due respect, based on what I've heard from your mother, think they know everything there is to know about civil litigation. You know probably as much as they do just from just sitting around the dining room table with JW all those years you were growing up. She's adamant. She wants you to exercise that sixth sense of yours. That gift she's always talked about. She wants your opinion as to when and on what terms to pull the plug on this suit. Obviously, based on our little tête-à-tête with Canning today, she thinks $450K is not going to cut it. On the other hand, I saw your surprised reaction. Now let me hear from you. What do you think?"

"I don't want to have to think . . . not now. I've got too much on my plate. I'm here because my mother says she needs me to be here. I have no idea why."

Liam's voice was tightening. "Look, Mr. Abrams, I don't want any part of this. I just don't get it. What the hell does she expect from me? What exactly am I supposed to do? This makes no sense!"

The words were no sooner out of his mouth when he saw Lee Mayfair standing, watching from the doorway.

"Mom . . . I'm sorry . . . I didn't know . . ."

"Liam, don't worry about what you are supposed to do. Just stay close to Mr. Abrams while he prosecutes this case. I don't expect you to play the lawyer. I just want you to listen, observe, and tell me what your instincts tell you, especially when we get down to the trial—or as your dad used to call it, 'crunch time.'" What Lee didn't say aloud was that she had other, more important reasons on her mind to keep Liam involved in the case. She had long been acutely aware, for many painful years, of the depth of the estrangement between her husband and his youngest boy. She intuitively believed it important for his soul and peace of mind for her to seize every opportunity to bring the two back together, even from beyond the grave. Abrams instinctively began to better understand his client's unspoken agenda, without having it spelled out. He approved of it with conviction.

Liam grew visibly frustrated and upset by the conversation. He lowered his head and mumbled words that sounded like "Sure, Mom, whatever you want . . ."

Lee spoke with the compassion only a mother could have for a troubled son. "Liam, I won't force you to do anything you don't want to do. I have my reasons for asking you to do this. Reasons I can't, and quite frankly, don't want to discuss with you at this moment. Please go back to Shelter Island. Think about what you need to do to get on with your life and your future with Maggie. Think about what Mr. Abrams and I are doing here and the importance of this lawsuit.

"What Frank told you about Dad's estate is true. If I don't win this suit, I and all of us are in serious financial trouble. We may have to sell off our homes and all the other assets. I'm going to spend some more time here with Mr. Abrams discussing the case. You go home and sleep on it, OK?"

"Mom, you know I'll do whatever you want me to do. But I have to say this to you both. I seriously don't believe I'll be of any value to you, Mr. Abrams, or this lawsuit. My being involved in this is just a waste of time for everyone."

"Liam, I only want that you think about it. I'm sure you'll find a way to come to the right decision."

Liam turned and walked out of the room without saying another word.

"Lee, do you want me to talk to him?"

Lee lowered her eyes. "No thanks, Frank. He just needs some more time. He'll be fine."

After some prolonged silence, Lee got up from the chair and purposefully changed the subject. She walked over to her favorite object in the room, something that had become so familiar to her over the years. She traced her finger along the bottom of a bronze picture frame and smiled.

"You know, Frank, I've seen this for years, but you never did tell me how you managed to get it." Lee pointed to a framed letter hanging on the wall near the door. "And more importantly, why do you show it off for the entire world to see? Isn't it supposed to be embarrassing?"

Frank Abrams smiled. "Lee, the truth is, I would never have met you and John if I had not gotten this letter of censure. I would have been very happy to make a lifetime career as an FBI agent, but fate had other plans for me, thank God. You'll notice it's signed by J. Edgar himself."

Lee grinned and said, "I noticed the signature the first time I ever looked at it. Somehow the aquamarine-blue ink doesn't fit in with the tough-guy image I have of the infamous Mr. Hoover."

"Yeah, well, the old man had a method to his madness. He was the only person in the bureau who was permitted to use that color ink. It seems he likened it to the ring used by Henry VIII as his seal of office when embossing the wax on all his official orders. The English kings intended it as a symbol of unquestioned authority and authenticity. And so did John Edgar Hoover. If it wasn't signed in aquamarine blue, then you knew it was a fraud, plain and simple. Quirky, but very effective."

Frank looked at the letter and was flooded with memories. What he didn't tell Lee was that he had left the bureau under less than favorable conditions. That one letter changed the path of his life dramatically. It was well-known among the agents that Hoover would never push along an agent's career whose personnel folder was "topped off" by a letter of censure, no matter how petty the offense. It was unofficial bureau policy at the time that regardless of how many prior letters of personal com-mendation a young agent had accumulated, no matter how ingenious his investigations or brave his actions, no matter how skilled an agent was in the use of firearms, a letter of censure was always kept at the top of his personnel folder, like the eight-hundred-pound gorilla sitting on your chest. It could never be returned to its proper chronological place in the personnel file until a letter of commendation, regardless of the subject matter, postdated and physically covered it.

"Lee, this letter of censure, ironically, was given to me at the same time as a letter of commendation from Hoover. Both just happened to involve the same criminal investigation."

"You know, Frank, JW used to repeat all your FBI war stories to me. I feel like I've lived them myself. What was so important about this letter, anyway?"

"Well, I had tracked down this armed-robbery convict who had escaped from a prison-road gang in a rural farming area just south of Opa-locka, Florida. I did something then that I am not too proud of today."

Lee frowned and gave Frank a look bursting with curiosity.

"I bullied and threatened the man's father. I knew he was dying of cancer. But I wanted to make this arrest in the worst way. I said to him, 'Look, you'd better get to that reprobate son of yours before I catch up to him. I know he's in touch with you. If there's a showdown involving firearms, someone, and it won't be me, is really going to get hurt . . . if you catch my drift!'"

Lee said disapprovingly, "So Hoover was angry that you tried to intimidate a dying man? I can't say that I blame him, Frank."

"I wasn't censured for that, although I should have been. I was criticized for using 'poor judgment' in agreeing to the surrender of the guy in the newsroom of the *Miami Herald*, a paper known for its hostility toward Hoover and the bureau. Somewhere in that huge newsroom, a reporter was using fast film, on a flash-less camera, and recorded the entire event, every last detail of it. He wasn't just interested in a good story, he was trying to embarrass the bureau. What pissed off the director, as it turns out, was the fact that his brash, hotshot rookie special agent had allowed himself to be snookered by a cub reporter who dictated and orchestrated the terms and venue of the surrender and arrest. It wasn't that the arrest had become publicized in a major news story. What set the old man off was the fact that it had involved the publication of my photograph for all the world to see. It seems I had violated the bureau's eleventh commandment. 'Thou shalt keep a low profile at all times, in both thy public and private life.' The director was not pleased when he received a copy of the full-face photograph of one of his fledging agents filling up the front page of a major left-wing newspaper. But as it turns out, that was only half the story. I might have gotten away with just a slap on the wrist and only a reprimand if it hadn't been for one more embarrassing screwup."

Lee suppressed a smile. "You mean you screwed up even more than that?"

"Yep, 'fraid so. Hoover's official write-up pointed out that I had cuffed the convict with his hands in front of him, instead of behind his back, per strict protocol. Even worse, as I was leading my prisoner to the elevator, I made a lame joke about the handcuffs, which I had borrowed from one of my two backup agents, who had removed them from storage. I was quoted in the featured story: 'Sorry, they're an old, rusty pair.' When I slapped the cuffs on this guy, they actually broke the skin. This guy's wrists bled like a sieve. And it was all caught on film."

"But, Frank, that's actually a pretty funny story. Was Hoover that much of a cold fish?"

"The truth is, Hoover wasn't known particularly for his sense of humor. On the contrary, he was known for his immense pride in his men and the 'state–of-the-art' equipment at the bureau's disposal. There was no room in the bureau's iconic image for old, rusty handcuffs.

"As a matter of fact, Lee, I don't know how Hoover developed a reputation for being so humorless, especially since he had a long-standing drinking-buddy relationship with the notorious comic actor W. C. Fields. And how about the transvestite story that suddenly and conveniently first surfaced soon after Hoover's death? Both were just myths promoted by a media that had grown politically antagonistic and impatient with the old man. Hoover had plenty of flaws, Lee, but kinkiness in matters of sex and the inability to laugh, except sometimes at himself, were not among them."

"But how can you say that, Frank? Didn't everyone agree that he and his second in command were . . . well . . . you know . . . lovers?"

"Tell that to his personal drivers who used to set up rendezvous with his 'lady friends' while he was out of town. Those rumors aren't true."

"As for his sense of humor, I remember this fellow agent, another rookie, who brought a poster of Hoover into the office. It showed the old man sitting up in bed with a frightened look on his face, wearing a night stocking cap. The caption read 'J. Edgar Hoover sleeps with a night-light.' The guy decided it would be a hilarious to use it as his personal desk blotter, in full view of the entire office staff. His unit supervisor, who was a career good old boy from West Virginia, didn't see the humor. Instead of taking him aside and warning him to control his naïveté, he reported the incident by bureau teletype directly to Washington. Within two weeks, the agent was transferred to Butte, Montana, by a sternly worded letter personally signed by Hoover in his classic aquamarine ink. Turns out Hoover thought Butte was the worst assignment in the world. But it was the garden of Eden compared to places like Newark and Baltimore. Anyway, what made his message so unique was that it was probably the only time in the history of the bureau where the old man embellished his typed directive with a bold handwritten postscript. All it said about the nightlight poster was 'PS: I do not!'"

Lee's laughter finally broke the reverie and brought Frank back into the moment. "Frank, I, for one, am very grateful that Mr. Hoover cut short your career with this letter of censure. Without it, JW would never have met you. He would never have enjoyed your loyalty and friendship for all these years."

"I'm sorry I got so distracted there, Lee. It's just that this letter triggers so many memories. It reminds me, though, that I still have a lot of friends in the bureau. I'm going to contact a couple of them very soon to help us win our lawsuit."

Lee grasped Franks' hands. "Thanks, Frank . . . for everything. You're a good friend." Lee looked at her watch. "I'd better be going now. And again, don't worry about Liam."

"Give my regards to the rest of the kids, Lee."

As Lee walked out of the office, Frank stared at the framed letter and was transported once again back to a sullen, overcast Monday morning in Chicago. Frank stood, like a shaved-head recruit, in front of his unit supervisor, a longtime veteran agent from Marietta, Georgia, who explained, in a slow southern drawl, that no agent in his thirty years on the job had ever displayed such "unmitigated and ungrateful gall and audacity" to turn down Hoover's incredibly generous offer to report to language school. What he failed to mention however was that the "offer" directed him to report "forthwith," not to the beautiful Monterey, California, peninsula to study Russian at the famous Defense Language Institute, as had been promised by Frank's supervisor in Quantico, but to pack up and move to Washington, DC, to study Spanish. It had become painfully clear by then that, despite Frank's superior language skills, the bureau had decided to underutilize them and bury him in some small Texas border town to cozy up to Mexican informants while assigned to border drug-smuggling cases.

It dawned on Frank in that moment that his boyhood dream of engaging the "evil empire" in his personal Cold War of real, honest-to-God espionage and counterintelligence was dead. That morning, in a brief, bizarre, informal ceremony, Frank handed over his .38-caliber MP Special, his handcuffs, and the keys to his beloved black-walled-tire, navy blue, 400cc Ford Intruder.

His supervisor looked up and said, "Isn't there something else you need to give me, Agent Abrams?"

"Oh, right!" Frank immediately went into his suit breast pocket and slowly turned over his prized, leather-bound FBI credentials and badge. In the final step of this strange ritual, the dumbfounded supervisor leaned over the desk and silently and ceremoniously handed Frank a single sheet of paper. It was Hoover's personally signed one-line letter accepting Frank's resignation. Even upside down, he could make out the aquamarine ink signature and the words typed in caps at the bottom of the page: "WITH PREJUDICE." In Bureau-speak, the words meant simply "I'll let you go, you ingrate. But don't ever ask me for anything ever again."

"Fair enough, Edgar. You reneged on your promise, so I'm reneging on mine," Frank said to himself under his breath as he folded the letter and put it in his coat pocket.

As he slowly walked out of the field-office lobby, glancing at the photos of Hoover and Attorney General John Mitchell on the wall, Frank knew that he would miss the excitement and camaraderie of the bureau. Although not counted among the many Christians and Mormons with whom Mr. Hoover mostly filled his ranks, this Jewish special agent from the Bronx solemnly and slowly made the infamous FBI sign of the cross for the last time. "Spectacles, testicles, wallet, and creds," he said out loud as he walked off into the parking lot.

While not happy over the way he left the bureau, Frank had no regrets to speak of. Rather, he was immensely proud of having experienced the honor of serving his country in a tumultuous time in its history, alongside the many loyal and trusted agent friends he had made. He would maintain close friendships with many of them in the years that followed, contacts he knew he would soon be calling upon for help in his case on behalf of his lifelong friends John and Lee Mayfair.

Abrams would often joke with his former law partner that despite his transparent attempt to avoid infantry combat in Vietnam as a "low number" draftee, Frank saw almost as much action and had dodged almost as many bullets as JW had eluded North Vietnamese-fired, Russian-made, SAM missiles. Frank thought of the agonizing death JW must have suffered and knew in his heart that there was no fair comparison of the relative dangers each of them had faced as younger men. How ironic, and grossly unfair, he thought, that his good friend would die so violently so many years later, exactly where he had skillfully avoided death and fought so bravely for so long—in the sky.

THE DILEMMA

Back on Shelter Island later that evening, Liam saw Maggie's Volvo in the driveway and rushed into the house. He found her in the kitchen, making dinner.

"Maggie, what are you still doing here? I thought you had to get back to Boston?"

"I got as far as the ferry and turned around."

"Why? Didn't you have to meet a client in Boston last night?"

"Liam, I called my boss and told him I'll be out another couple of days with a family emergency."

"What emergency?"

"You, my love, are my emergency. You have all the lights and sirens and whistles blaring at the same time. I'm here to put out the fire. Do you have a problem with that?"

Liam walked over to her at the sink, put his arms around her, and sighed aloud.

She looked sympathetically at her troubled lover and said nothing at first. After a minute, she decided not to ask him any questions about the meeting with the attorneys and said, with an almost imperceptible quiver in her voice, "Liam, I have something to tell you. It's really important."

Liam immediately shot her that furrowed-brow, worried look men have been giving their lovers from time immemorial.

She sensed his thought immediately. "No, it's nothing like that! It's something much more important."

"You're not sick, are you?" he said. "Come on, tell me, what is it?"

Maggie slowly picked up an audio cassette tape from the kitchen table.

"Do you remember when you got the news about your father and Flight 800? You were in such a big hurry to get on the road to your family that when you loaded up your Jeep that night, and when you moved out the rest of your stuff a few weeks later, you left a few things behind. One of them was your old answering machine, the one you were taking your own calls on."

"Yeah, I remember that, but how is that important?"

"Well, I had thrown it in the trunk of my car, planning to bring it over to your place when you got home to Boston from the funeral. Truth is, I just forgot all about it. It's been hiding in the corner of my trunk under a bunch of papers and blankets for over a year and a half. All this time I never noticed it, even the one time I had the car washed last year. I just happened to find it last weekend when I finally cleaned out the car. I put in on the front seat a few days ago and finally remembered to bring it to you here on Shelter Island."

"Maggie, what is this all about anyway?"

"Liam, just be patient for a second and listen to me. I don't know what possessed me to bring it into the house and see if there were any messages on the tape, but I did. No more than a few minutes ago, just before you got back." Her look became strained and almost frightened.

Liam sensed the fear: "What is it? What's the matter?" He suddenly grew cold.

"Liam, it's your father. There's a message from him on this tape. It's really eerie. When I first heard his voice, it scared me a little. But when I heard him say he was calling you from the plane, I panicked and turned it off immediately."

Liam remained quiet and just stared ahead.

"Liam, did you hear me? He called you on the night of the crash!"

Liam grew pale, afraid to think or act. He looked at the tape in Maggie's hand but made no move to take it. Suddenly the nightmare images flashed back through his brain—the charred face, the fire and smoke, the screams. He froze and closed his eyes.

Maggie looked at him in disbelief. "Liam, you've got to listen to it! It's a message from your own father, for God's sake. These are probably the last words he ever spoke to you or anyone else. How could you not want to listen to them?"

"I can't . . . I . . ." Liam knew immediately that the message, if indeed there really was a message from his father on the tape, could only have been left within a few minutes before the plane crashed into the sea. Liam had routinely checked the answering machine every day and never let messages get stale. This one had clearly fallen between the cracks.

"But, Maggie, how could I have missed this message?"

"Because when you grabbed your stuff and threw it into the back of the Jeep, you weren't exactly thinking straight. And when you came back to Boston after the funeral, you moved right back into your old apartment. You never did take that machine with you. That's when you cut yourself off from everyone, including me, and refused to take phone calls. Don't you remember?"

Suddenly the time line of the missing tape made sense to Liam. "But what could my father possibly have wanted? We hadn't spoken for almost a year before the crash."

Liam suddenly envisioned the terrible shouting match with his father when he pompously announced that he was thinking of dropping out of school to "find himself and write a little music." Liam had visited the family condo on only two occasions to see his mother in New York during that year of JW's disfavor. He had spent both times overnight while his father was away on business. Lee Mayfair had never told her husband about the visits, one of which consisted of several predawn hours of deep soul-searching and tears shed by both mother and son. Liam had admitted to his mother that his plan to drop out of school was as a result of a deep depression, induced, as he had finally admitted, by alcohol abuse. It had nothing to do with writing music. He never had the guts or opportunity to tell his father that painful detail. Somehow, however, JW could smell every bit of it from all those many miles away. Yet he could never bring himself to face the truth about his youngest son. Lee had convinced Liam to persevere and finish his last year of college and graduate. Which he did. Albeit with very lackluster grades. Ironically, since his father's death, Liam had remained completely sober and was very much surprised by how easy it was for him to stay that way.

Maggie decided not to force the issue and simply placed the tape into Liam's right hand.

"It's up to you, Liam. I think you should listen to it alone. But for God's sake . . . just do it. I hate to sound like a broken record, but it's time for you to face this head-on and get on with your life."

Maggie turned and walked out of the room.

Liam looked out of the east window facing the bay. A full moon was rising behind fast-moving clouds, driven by warmer winds out of the southwest, unusual weather for March on Shelter Island. He remembered, as he loaded the cassette player, that the NTSB report said there was no moon that night. It reported light winds, scattered clouds, and good visibility for miles.

His hand began to tremble as he turned on the machine. He hit the rewind button and realized that the message was already cued up at the beginning of the tape. There was only one lengthy message. The voice that poured through the speaker was clear and familiar. It covered him like a blanket—warm yet, in a strange way, plaintive and melancholy.

At first, his father's voice sounded almost alien with a deep echo chamber quality to it. Yet there was no doubt; it was unmistakably JW's.

"Hello, son. I don't know when I'll get a chance to speak with you again. I'm calling from an air phone on my flight out of JFK to Paris. I'm in the middle of this European merger deal and things have been hectic and unsettled for months. My gut has been telling me for weeks to cancel this trip and call off the deal. I just found out that if we go through with this, hundreds of people, including some personal friends of mine, are going to lose their jobs. I think I may have let the almighty dollar get the better of me this time. I'm not feeling too proud of myself at the moment. I'm also not proud of the way I've handled our relationship.

"Listen, Liam, there isn't a day that goes by without my thinking of you and how I have fouled things up, coming down so hard on you. Although you have to admit you haven't exactly been easy on me either.

"Liam, I was sitting here on the plane waiting for takeoff and daydreaming about certain events in my life. I was thinking about that time we took one of our walks through the woods near the summer house, down that long sandy path to the beach. I remember it like it was yesterday. It was your fifth birthday. You bounced down the stairs early that morning and asked me to take you to that old pine tree with that nest of young red-tailed hawks near the beach. You wanted to see if the chicks had learned to fly yet. I remember telling you that on that very beach hundreds of years ago, the local Indians believed that when you spotted a young red-tailed hawk soaring in the sky, that was a sign that you would be blessed with a deep understanding of the big picture of life, especially if you were confused or worried about something. While we sat there on the beach, watching the waves come ashore, you spotted a young buck swimming toward us in the water. I made a joke about him not being allowed on the ferry because he couldn't afford the fare. Do you remember what you asked me? You wanted permission to do what only an innocent five-year-old boy would consider to be the right thing in that situation. You wanted to take money out of your own piggy bank and pay for that deer's next ferry ride to the island. I remember asking you in a spur-of-the-moment kind of thing, right then and there, to make me a promise. You wanted to know exactly how someone keeps a promise. I told you that the most important thing about a promise was not speaking the words, but making sure that the words became real. No matter what kind of trouble or pain got in the way, no matter how much the truth may someday cost you or hurt the ones you loved. What I said was half-intended to be rhetorical and symbolic, but you took it literally. You sat facing me on the sand, looking up at me, and you said something that knocked my socks off. With that serious frown on your little face, you just said, 'You can count on me, Dad.' My heart melted then and still does to this day, every time I think of it."

There was a long pause on the tape. Liam thought he could hear a break and some quivering in his father's voice as the message continued. "Well, Liam, I'm making this promise to you. I will mend this broken fence between us. At the very least, I'm going to try really hard. Listen, you know I'm lousy at expressing my feelings. But I've decided to slow down and take the time to somehow learn how to do that. Liam, I love you. I always have. From that wonderful day your mother and I first held you in our arms. I've always felt you were blessed with almost unlimited, untapped talent, which is probably why I have been so tough on you.

"Anyway, that needed to be said, and probably a lot sooner than now. Liam, I'd like to see you when I get home. Bring Maggie home for the weekend . . . separate bedrooms of course. I want to show her your poetry prize from the third grade, the one I keep in the den, next to the mounted bass. We'll have a good, long talk when I get back, man-to-man. What do you say? And when I do see you again, I want you to repeat the promise I asked you to make to me on that beach. Do you think you still remember it?"

Then just before the end of the message, there was a another brief pause, followed by an intensity in JW's voice that Liam had never experienced before.

His words began in slow motion then grew frenetic and loud. "What . . . the . . . fuck? Oh, my God! That's a SAM! Liam, I don't know what the hell's going on here. I'm looking out a starboard window, and I'm staring at a goddamn rocket with a white plume coming right up toward us from the bow of a freighter. I gotta go, son . . . Pray for me."

Liam finally realized that the message had ended abruptly. His father's voice was followed immediately by some muffled screams and then a loud, irritating blast of static. He found himself screaming into the machine. "Dad, Dad! Are you still there?" He could feel the adrenaline that must have been pouring through his father's body in those last few seconds of exquisite fear, as his own heart pounded wildly in his chest. Liam stared at the tape player, not believing or fully comprehending what he had just heard.

"Is this someone's idea of a sick joke?" he screamed.

Maggie ran into the room. "What going on, Liam? Who are you talking to?"

In his agitation, he sputtered, "Are you sure no one else has heard this tape for all these months?" Maggie nodded and said, "Yes, I'm sure. Why?"

Liam rewound the tape and listened to it again. This time, he strained to digest every word, every syllable. Maggie was dumbstruck and just looked at Liam, her mouth agape.

"Maggie, it's definitely my father's voice. I can't believe this!"

His head slowly began to clear. "Wait a minute. They never said anything about a missile. Their report only mentions a possible electrical wiring spark in a fuel tank, right?"

The implications of what he had just heard suddenly began to pour over him like a bucket of iced water.

Liam's eyes were wide. His voice sounded almost like that of a frightened child. "Do you realize what this all means? The feds have it all wrong! Their preliminary report is wrong! There was no wiring defect or fuel-vapor problem. This was a goddamned terrorist attack! But how could they not know that? How could they not have seen evidence of a missile hitting the plane? It makes no sense!"

Maggie looked up from the answering machine. "Liam, I remember the papers saying there were some eyewitnesses near the beach and on the water who claim they saw a missile rising from the surface."

Liam instantly recalled the NTSB representative who had recently contacted his mother. He looked at Maggie. "The man who returned my mother's phone calls at the NTSB told us that those eyewitnesses were confused because what they were really seeing was an optical illusion. This guy said that the fuselage, which was already on fire, continued to rise three thousand feet upward from the momentum of the jet engines, after the nose broke away, before it started to fall. He said that to someone at ground level, the burning fuselage would have looked just like a rising missile with a fire plume. But the bottom line, according to this guy, is that all of their experts say they found absolutely no traces of explosives or signs of contact with the pieces of the wreckage. And they managed to recover and examine almost 95 percent of that plane."

Maggie looked confused. "But I don't get it. How could your dad have seen a missile when all those experts insist there was no missile?"

"I don't know. But what the hell am I going to do now—with this?" he said, looking down at the cassette tape.

"Are you kidding? You're going to bring it to the FBI! That's what you're going to do!" Maggie said incredulously.

Suddenly, the thought hit him between the eyes like a lightning bolt. Liam felt as if the weight of the world had just crashed down on his shoulders. "Maggie, if I make this public, my mother's multimillion dollar lawsuit goes down the toilet."

Maggie didn't understand. "But why is that? What do you mean?"

"Mr. Abrams explained everything to me. A terrorist attack is defined as an act of war, not an act of negligence. You can't accuse the airline with careless maintenance or faulty electrical wiring if it's blown up by a missile! You can't hold someone responsible under the law for an act of war. My mother's case will be thrown out. Period. End of discussion. There's nothing Abrams can do to win the case if this turns out to be terrorism. I can't just run straight to the government with this!"

Maggie suddenly remembered something she had once heard in a sociology class. She learned that there are experts in human behavior who say that when someone first recognizes the clear profile of a profound and life-changing moral dilemma, the natural first instinct is to stand back from the breach, to retreat momentarily, rather than rush forward into the danger of the unknown. "Liam, I understand your hesitancy to do anything about it right now. But at some point, and soon, you'll have to act on this. You'll have to turn this tape over to someone in authority."

Liam ignored Maggie's comment and became mired in his racing thoughts. "My father was a huge fan of one of the most famous lawyers in history. I'm going to take a page from his playbook and study this from every angle before I rush into anything stupid or rash."

"Liam, what are you talking about?"

"I'm talking about Sir Thomas More, the patron saint of lawyers. You studied English history, right? King Henry VIII gave his trusted friend an ultimatum. He wanted to force Thomas to accept his faux marriage to Anne Boleyn and acknowledge him as self-appointed head of the church in England. It didn't take a genius to see the firestorm the king was setting him up for. But Thomas didn't take the bait at first. He refused to rush into Henry's trap. He took his sweet time and parsed and nuanced every word of the king's edict, looking for some legalistic escape hatch. It turns out though, in the end, he only had two choices. It was either go along or stand trial for treason."

"Liam, what are you trying to say? I'm not following you."

"Look, Maggie, the point is, he backed away from that cliff and tried to come up with an intellectual and scholarly way to avoid going over the edge. Some plan he could live with . . . some compromise that would satisfy both his king and his conscience."

What Liam didn't bother to tell Maggie was that, as JW had once explained to his young son, for a man with the character and intellect of Sir Thomas, there was no possible way out of his dilemma—not on this side of life. The Catholic chancellor of England was destined to forfeit his head, his family, and all the wealth, titles, and lands he had accumulated as Henry's loyal adviser. In the end, he chose honor over the friendship of the king. Or as JW had once piously described it, Thomas eschewed the king's crown and title "in exchange for his own crown of glory."

Maggie suddenly grabbed Liam's hands and looked into his eyes.

"Thomas More didn't betray his conscience, Liam. And neither will you. I'm sure of it."

"Yeah, well, I'm not really interested in sainthood or martyrdom anyway. Besides, I don't have what it takes."

Liam picked up the tape and quickly tucked it into his shirt pocket, as though concealing it from the world. He had made an immediate decision to throw aside all thoughts of honor and glory. Instead, his survival instinct kicked into high gear as he made a mental note to invent some plausible nonconfrontational means to skirt the dilemma suddenly staring him in the face. *I'll deal with all this later*, he thought. *Not now.* And with a little luck, perhaps he would never have to address it at all.

"Maggie, I've got a lot to think about here. I need some time to sort all this out carefully. I'm going to figure a logical way out of this mess without losing my head in the process."

Maggie, still unnerved by the voice of JW's ghost, held her tongue, hoping to find another and better opportunity to talk about it again soon.

GO EAST, YOUNG MAN

The next day before dawn, Liam slipped out of back door of the house while Maggie was still sleeping. He tiptoed across the creaky wooden porch, got into his car, and left the driver's car door slightly open as the tires slowly crunched their way down the long oystershell driveway to the macadam road. He caught the 6:00 a.m. ferry and rode it across the south race through the early-morning fog blanketing Shelter Island. He got on the Long Island Expressway and then drove on toward Manhattan in unusually light traffic. All the way in, as the sun rose in a fiery red sky in his rearview mirror, he could think of nothing else except the sound and the words of his father's ghostly message. How different JW's voice seemed on the tape compared to the last time he heard it about a year before his father's death. Then, the voice was angry and filled with shouting and cursing. It had been sparked by Liam's disingenuous announcement that he was planning to drop out of college to try his hand at writing some music. Liam remembered painfully the exact words he had used to slam the door shut on the conversation. He had told his father that he was an "asshole" and added, "The days of your trying to manipulate my life are over, old man!"

JW quickly rose to the bait and immediately drew the proverbial line in the sand. "Unless you apologize for that, you little ingrate, there will be no contact between the two of us ever again. Don't call me until you're ready to act like a man and apologize."

Liam remembered screaming into the phone. "It'll be a cold day in hell when that happens. I'm warning you. Stay the hell out of my life!" With that, he slammed down the phone, ending the call and starting their long war of silence.

Why did it all have to end like that? Why didn't I just swallow my pride and apologize right then and there? he thought. He would have given anything to have that explosive moment back. What a waste it all was. Liam wanted to crawl into a dark hole and disappear forever.

His thoughts drifted to the message and the childhood incident on the beach. Liam was surprised as to how easily and vividly he remembered the details: His birthday. The young deer swimming in the mist. The hawks in the pine tree nest. But what he recalled most easily was the promise he had made to his father. He would have given his life for another chance to have fulfilled that promise. But that was never meant to be. The finality and the irreversible pathos of it all drew a loud, primeval moan from deep within his wounded soul. The urge to cry suddenly reappeared and rushed over him like a tsunami.

As soon as he got to his mother's condo in New York, he asked for her copy of the bound preliminary NTSB report. She found it, brought it in to the kitchen, and handed it to her son.

"Why do you want this now, Liam? Didn't you already read this?"

Liam said nothing and thumbed through the first few pages of the voluminous document. He quickly found what he was looking for.

"Mom, can I have this for a couple of weeks? I'd like to go over it again."

"Why? What's going on? What are you up to?"

"It's not important, Mom. I was just thinking that if I'm going to help Mr. Abrams during pretrial discovery, I'd like to know as much as possible about the technical side of the case. That would make sense, right?"

Lee frowned at her son's poor attempt at candor. "Don't give me that. You drove all the way in to Manhattan from out East at the crack of dawn for something I could easily have mailed to you overnight. You know, Frank also has this in his office. I'm sure he would have made a copy for you."

"Mom, I can't talk about it now. I just need a little time to think some things out, that's all."

Lee knew firsthand about the impulsiveness of the Mayfair men and grew concerned.

"Liam, I don't know what you're up to, but promise me you won't say or do anything without clearing it first with Frank, OK?"

"Sure, Mom," he blurted out, as he hurried out the door.

Liam sat in the car with the engine running in the underground garage for almost a half hour, reading the summaries of the eyewitness accounts of the Long Island fishermen and others who were interviewed by the FBI within the first few days after the explosion. There was a specific reference to several fishermen who ran charter fishing boats out of Montauk. Their eyewitness stories were discounted almost immediately in a perfunctory way. They had each claimed to have seen, from two different boats no more than a mile apart, a bright explosion in the darkening sky. One of them, however, added a detail that was played up dramatically in the press in the months that followed. Harley Mathers, in two separate interviews with FBI special agents assigned to the New York and the Long Island Resident Agency offices, had insisted that he saw the bright white-gray plume of what looked like a rocket rising from the ocean surface, just to the south of his position, as he was returning from an all-day tuna fishing trip offshore. Although the report didn't initially explain why, it concluded that Mathers's account was "not credible," especially when compared with that of two commercial pilots who were over the area at the time and reported seeing nothing except the fractured plane descending in slow motion in a blaze of fire. One of the pilots was a former navy navigator. He boasted that on such a clear night, if there had been a missile, he would have noticed it streaking from the ocean surface. "No way," he told the young agents. "That fireball was the only light in the sky that night." Of course, what he had failed to mention was that he had no combat experience and, as a second seater, he had never personally fired any of the navy's arsenal of air-to-air missiles.

Liam noted the name of the boat owned by Mathers, put the car in gear, pointed it east on the LIE, and began to pry open what he feared might become the ultimate can of worms. He had no idea of what he would do or say when he got to Montauk, except to locate one Harley Mathers. Whoever the hell he was.

IT HARDLY MATTERS

The last few days of March were going out like the proverbial lamb. The wind out of the south was unusually warm, and the sea surface was as smooth as green glass. Liam stood at the end of the dock and enjoyed feeling the sun on his face. All around him, the smell of dockside creosote filled his nostrils. He watched as the fishing boats returned from the morning charters with catches of cod and a smattering of spring bass. He followed the familiar aroma of chowder into a bar and grill at the end of a small parking lot. As his eyes adjusted to the dim lighting inside the bar, he could see two older men hunched over the worn, green, cigarette-scarred felt of a pool table in the back of the long room. He immediately noticed on his right that the door to the men's room was open, with a mop and bucket blocking the entry. The stench of urine and Clorox overpowered the inviting aroma of clam chowder drifting out of the kitchen. Liam looked around the large barroom and determined that the kid behind the bar looked no older than sixteen. Moving quickly, he opted instead for the old-timers. As he approached, he focused on one of the men with a filter-less cigarette hanging from his lips, leaning into the arc of the light suspended over the table. The skin on the old man's face and neck looked like a leatherback turtle. His eyes were a light blue, clouded with cataracts. The man looked up and slowly surveyed the preppy intruder.

Liam met his eyes. "Excuse me, sir, but—"

"Sir? Did you hear that, Mike? I think the kid's gonna salute me!" They both laughed so hard that old Leatherface started to cough, with a hack so deep that it sounded like it was recorded in a tuberculosis ward.

"Whadya want, kid? If you're lookin' for fish, you've come to the right place." The old man's smile showed off a row of missing teeth.

Liam, somewhat annoyed at the noisy reception, spoke hesitantly. "Excuse me, but I'm looking for a gentleman by the name of Mathers, Harley Mathers."

"Gentleman? Ha! He ain't no gentleman, sonny. When he ain't drunk over at that bar rail, you can find him aboard that tub he calls a fishin' boat at the other end of the lake. I seen him go out with a charter this morning, as a matter of fact. What do you want with old Buzz Mathers? You one of his pissed-off customers who got skunked and come home with no fish? Buzz has got plenty of them kind of customers! Don't he, Mike?" Another round of laughs roared through the room as several other men, hidden in the shadows at the far end of the bar, joined in the chorus.

Liam tried to cut off the noisy chatter from these old derelicts. After all, he was the one who came all the way out here with questions. Just then, Liam noticed that a couple of men and a woman who had just walked into the bar had started to show interest in the discussion. *This was not the way I intended to make a few discreet inquiries*, he thought to himself.

"Look, I just want to talk with him. It's nothing important."

The old man stopped smiling and stepped closer to Liam, leaning closer into his face. The iron breath almost knocked him back on his heels.

"Say, does this have anything to do with that plane crash couple of summers back? You another one of them reporters? You're a little late, kid. That story's been told. Not for nothin', but old Buzz really went downhill fast after the feds made him look like an old fool, you know . . . Hardly done any serious fishin' since then."

The old man squinted hard into Liam's eyes. "You ain't no reporter . . . no fed either. My guess is you lost someone on that plane, didn't ya?" He paused, looked over at his pool partner, turned back to face Liam, and said quietly, "The last boat at the end of the dock on the other side of the lake . . . big old black hull. The name is the *Northern Star*. Just follow the dirt road out here." He pointed out the bar's side window. "If he's back by now from his morning trip, he'll be below, probably drinkin'. Just climb aboard and knock on the cabin bulkhead. He won't mind."

"Thanks, mister," Liam said as he looked once more around the suddenly quiet room. The smiles and laughter were gone. All eyes followed him out the door as he beat a hasty retreat into the bright sunlight.

Liam drove down an old dirt and gravel road to the poorer, underbelly side of the harbor. He moved slowly past a boatyard filled with old iron and wooden derelicts sitting up on blocks, almost audibly rusting and rotting away slowly in the sunlight. The badly rutted road narrowed, and Liam got out of his car. As he walked past the rotted ghost vessels, he noticed the names painted on the hulls. Every one, it seemed, bore the name of some long-forgotten woman. Painted on almost every transom was a faded ancient reminder of long-dead wives and lovers. It wasn't likely that any of these women were ever assuaged or comforted by their namesakes—the "other women" in their husbands' hard-knock lives. This boat graveyard was filled with the mistresses who lured their men to sea for so long—for too many years.

Finally, he got to the old dock and followed the pilings and the smells of fresh creosote, diesel fuel, and dead fish, until he got to a black-hulled boat, its double flying bridge rising high over all the others. Tacked to a wooden beam above a set of pilings was a crudely painted sign. "The *Northern Star*. Available for charter. AM and PM trips; Cod, Tuna, striped bass, blues; Capt. Buzz Mathers." *An odd way to drum up business*, he thought, *to advertise without listing a phone number.* There, hanging from a hook under the sign, was a huge striped bass, probably in the forty-pound range. He was surprised to see a bass this early in the season and thought maybe the warm weather had driven the fish north ahead of schedule. Liam remembered his own father holding up a similar fish for photographs on these same docks years ago, when JW would take all the boys out here a couple of times a summer to troll for these beautiful giants. He smiled when he thought of JW using the old fisherman's trick of holding the fish forward toward the camera at full arm's length, to make them seem bigger than they really were.

Liam stood near the stern of the *Northern Star* and was even more surprised that the fish had not yet been gutted and filleted. He wondered if Mathers, assuming he was even aboard, was aware that he had left it hanging out in the warm sun. He looked up and down the boat from bow to stern. The decks had been washed, and all the lines and bumpers were clean and in neat order. Or as his father used to say, everything looked "shippy."

Liam saw no sign of life aboard. Gingerly, he stepped over the transom onto the deck, feeling immediately like an interloper, as though he had just walked uninvited into someone's living room. The cabin door was shut tight. But through a bulkhead window, he could see below the profile of a man hunched over a chart table, with some kind of bottle in his hand. Steeling his courage, he rapped his right hand on the cabin door, suddenly realizing he had no idea what he would say or do if Harley Mathers answered the knock.

The cabin door creaked opened slowly. A man in his midsixties with a close-cropped white beard, disheveled white hair, and steel blue–gray eyes stepped into the sunlight, offering his hand. In his other hand, he held a bottle of Coke. "What can I do for you, son?" His voice was confident and clear. *No drunken fool aboard this boat*, thought Liam.

"Harley Mathers?" was the best he could come up with.

The captain surveyed the young man up and down in one sweep. "And who might you be?" He was curious but reticent.

"Mr. Mathers, my name is Liam Mayfair. You don't know me, but—"

"Mayfair." His eyes widened. "Right! You're John Mayfair's son, aren't you?"

"Yes, but how—"

"I know every name on that plane's manifest, son. I can still see it in my sleep. What brings you out here to the end of the island? You're not out here to fish, I'm guessing."

"I don't know why I came out here, Mr. Mathers. I felt this need to ask you about the NTSB report. Something about it doesn't make any sense to me."

The captain looked about the dock nervously, his aura of confidence suddenly gone.

"Does anyone know you came out looking for me? How did you find me? My number's unpublished." He quickly grabbed Liam by the arm and pulled him into the cabin, closing the door behind.

"Look, son, I can't talk to you about it. Especially not here. Please, just go home. Where did you say you were from?"

"My family's from the city."

"Just go home, will ya?" he pleaded nervously. "You shouldn't be seen on this boat. Did anyone see you come aboard?"

"Please, Mr. Mathers, listen to me! It's important! I have a tape of a phone call my father made that night from the plane, seconds before it blew up and crashed. He saw something. He said he saw a—"

"Missile." Their words overlapped at the same precise moment. Liam's eyes confirmed it all.

"Mr. Mathers, I have to know something. Why didn't they believe your story?"

Mathers slid down lower into the bulkhead seat at the table and buried his head into his large, calloused hands. "Son, I saw the same horrible thing your father must have seen. It looked like a giant Fourth of July rocket. I saw it rise up from the ocean about half a mile away, just off my port bow. I was at the wheel on the bridge. Believe me, I got a good look at it. Visibility was very good. Not quite dark yet. My charter . . . three Wall Street guys from Manhattan . . . they were all below, laughing and drinking up a storm. The FBI contacted them first, in the city. They didn't see anything. Even if they were topside like me, they were too shit faced to see or remember anything. It seems they told the feds I was drinking with them. That's a lie. They were just pissed. Thought I overcharged them for the trip. Cheap bastards. We were coming in from a full-day tuna trip offshore. Sure, I had a few beers that afternoon. It was really hot . . . a real scorcher that day, as I recall."

Mathers lifted his eyes toward the port side window and seemed to gaze at something far off in the distance. "I remember it like it was yesterday. I was alone at the helm—and stone-cold sober—when I saw that thing light up the horizon. I saw it climb from the deck of some kind of freighter toward that plane. Half a minute later, there was a big explosion that lit up the sky. The worst part of it was watching that huge fireball breaking up and falling in big pieces. It all seemed like it was happening in slow motion. I tried to change course and get to the wreckage to see if there were survivors, but my customers threatened to stiff me for the charter if I didn't get them back to the dock as soon as possible."

Mathers's eyes began to well up. "I should have done something to help instead of worrying about the damn money."

Liam tried to get back on topic. "Mr. Mathers, why did the FBI say that your story was unreliable? Weren't there plenty of other eyewitnesses who also said they saw something that looked like a rocket that night?"

Mathers looked up from the table with a look of exasperation on his face "Did you read the report? It also said that I had a reputation as a drunk for a lot of years. Sure, I might have had a drinking problem around that time . . . an occupational hazard for guys like us. But goddammit, I was sober as a clam that night. Matter of fact, I haven't had a drink since then. At first I talked to whoever was willing to listen. I made a big stink . . . even went to the papers. But the more I spoke out, the more I got knocked down. I told them nothing but the God's honest truth. That plane was attacked. Those people . . . your father . . . were all murdered. I know what the government is saying about the cause of the explosion. But that was no accident, son. No way on God's green earth.

Mathers grew suddenly quiet and sounded a little melancholy. "After a while, I began to doubt what I saw. Almost everyone started calling me crazy, even some of the locals. One Sunday afternoon, a man came out to see me . . . says he was some kind of federal agent from Washington. He said I was making too much . . . 'trouble' was the word he used. He said it was time for me to shut up and just accept the fact that this was a simple mechanical accident, nothing more. He said that it was important, for the sake of national security, that the preliminary findings of the NTSB be 'left alone.' When I told him to go stick the report up his ass, he put his finger in my face and threatened me. He deliberately opened his suit coat, put his hand on the gun on his belt, and said he would see to it that I would never work again . . . that something really bad could happen to me and my boat. He scared the shit out of me."

"Did you get the name of this guy? Did he show you his credentials?"

"Well, he showed me something in a leather case that had his picture and the letters FBI in bold print across it. And yes, I wrote his name and shield number down. I got the note somewhere here below with my charts. But there was something not right about this guy. I mean, he wore a fancy suit and tie and all, but the way he spoke was a little funny . . . very foreign sounding . . . definitely not American. Everything about him reminded me of this Arab guy who used to be my landlord when I lived in Queens many years ago. He was clean-shaven but a little too heavy in the gut and very swarthy looking. Didn't exactly fit the G-man image, if you know what I mean."

"Mr. Mathers, did you tell the FBI about this guy and his threat?"

"I tried to. I left two or three phone messages for one of the young agents who originally interviewed me. They said he had just been reassigned to another office on the West Coast and that someone else would get back to me. But that never happened. So I just gave up and shut my mouth."

"Would you mind digging out that note for me?"

"Not now. I can't spend the time looking for it right now. Besides, I don't want any of the boys to see you talking to me. So please get off my boat. I'll meet you tonight on the town beach, just after dark, about a mile and a half up the road toward the lighthouse. The moon is full, so you won't have any trouble finding me. I'll be at the near end of the breakwater. I don't want anyone seeing you with me here. Sorry for the secrecy, son. But like I said, this guy scared the living piss out of me. I don't need any more trouble than I already got. Please don't mess things up things for me now. It's tough enough trying to scratch a living out here on the water."

By the time Liam awoke in his car about two miles from the harbor, a few hours later, it was already dark. He had been to Montauk before with Maggie, during the peak summer season a few years prior, and was surprised to see it so deserted and quiet now. He found the town beach easily, following the old dirt road from the lake. A quick southwest wind was blowing low cloud cover past the moon just now rising in the east over the ocean. He could hear the sound but not quite make out the waves slapping up on the beach. Off to the left, in the dark distance, the unmistakable, erratic clanging of a bell buoy at the mouth of the harbor carried across the water and the humid night air. For the first time since starting this adventure, Liam was gripped by an overpowering sense of impending doom. A dull ache and tightness formed a knot in his stomach.

Liam slowly climbed out of the driver's seat and walked a few paces toward the beach. He almost jumped out of his skin at the sharp complaining calls of a few sandpipers he had disturbed as he watched them scampering away across the dunes. "What the hell am I getting into?" he mumbled to himself as he walked farther toward the beach and the jetty. Nothing but questions and doubt piled up in his head. *Why am I going through all this spy stuff over something seemingly as simple as the truth? Who is this man Mathers anyway? Who had threatened him so badly that he has to skulk along a deserted beach at night to stay out of sight? What would I do with the name of this "agent" who threatened him, even if I could find and identify him?* Liam was just about to give up his stupid adventure, jump back into the car, and hurry back to Shelter Island when he saw the profile of a man walking quickly toward him in the sand.

Mathers was slightly out of breath when he reached Liam. "Son, I found the name. I don't know what good it will do you. No one is going to believe that audiotape of your father is the real deal. The feds are too invested in their own story to listen to you or anyone else."

Mathers handed a piece of folded paper to Liam. His voice had tightened and now betrayed a heightened sense of fear. "Good luck, Liam. I don't know why you're getting into the middle of this, but I hope you can sort it all out. And remember, what your old man saw was a deliberate act of terrorism . . . so keep your head down and your eyes open. There's no telling what these guys are capable of."

Without waiting for a reply, the captain turned and started walking back toward the dunes as quickly as he had approached. Just as he was about out of sight, Liam saw, in the corner of his right eye, tiny flashes of light followed by several small popping sounds. He saw Mathers slump to his knees and then collapse forward, facedown in the sand. His mind immediately kicked into overdrive. Liam wheeled, started to move toward Mathers, but froze when he saw two men suddenly emerge from behind the dunes to his right. They walked briskly at first but then started to run toward him. One of the men, the taller of the two, wore a hooded sweatshirt, the other, a suit jacket. The moonlight reflected off a metal object in the taller man's right hand—looking like silver. Liam ran through the sand like a gazelle, never looking back toward the dunes. He reached his car and fumbled for the keys. As he pulled them out of his pocket, they slipped out of his fingers and fell to the sand. He bent down, groping in the darkness till he found them. Starting the car engine seemed to take an eternity. As soon as he put the car in drive, Liam turned off the automatic running lights, hoping that would remove any lighting from the rear of the car. A surge of adrenaline pumped through his body as he finally reached the dirt road. He gunned the engine, leaving a cloud of dust and sand over one hundred yards long. As he drove down the road back toward the harbor, doing sixty mph in the dark, he looked once in his rearview mirror. There was nothing there. The road behind him was dark and empty.

Suddenly, he heard a loud explosion. Off in the distance, directly ahead of him, Liam saw something that made his hair stand on edge. There, on the other side of the harbor, he saw a large fireball silhouetting dozens of boats tied up in a row at the end of a long dock. It was the *Northern Star*, engulfed in flames that shot a hundred feet into the air. As he continued to race the car toward the paved road, he felt sickened at the thought of what he had just seen. He was nauseous and wanted to stop and vomit but was too terrified to slow down. Once on the main highway, he looked in the rearview mirror again and, realizing he was not being pursued, loosened his grip on the wheel. In his right hand was a small piece of paper. He threw it on the seat next to him and kept driving.

Liam barely caught the last ferry of the evening to Shelter Island. Finally feeling safe in familiar surroundings, his nerves began to settle as he sat up till just before dawn on the front porch, trying to make sense of what had happened just a few hours before. Maggie was still sound asleep upstairs, and he didn't want to disturb her. How would he explain any of this to her? A man he had sought out for some simple answers was probably dead on the beach. His body may be lying there for days, assuming it was not taken away and disposed of. He thought back on his father's lessons of law and thought to himself, *Am I committing a crime by not reporting a murder to the police? What if those men got my license plate number? Jesus, what if they got a good look at me?*

Liam walked over to his car and, in the darkness, turned on his running lights. The license plate was illuminated by a small bulb, and the rear running lights cast even more light on it. He turned the light switch off—nothing. There was no illumination at all on the rear of the car. His instincts were correct, and he breathed a sigh of relief. As he stepped back toward the front of the car, he noticed something in the fading light of the moon. It almost took his breath away. In horror, he realized that there was a small hole in the door just under the driver's window. He knew immediately what it was. He traced the hole through the steel door and into the plastic interior molding. Probing with his finger, he found it. A twisted slug—the remains of a small-caliber bullet just protruding beneath the interior door handle. He grabbed it, pulled it out, and rolled it in his hand. It was a bent piece of soft lead, a hollow-point bullet, designed to break up and cause maximum damage to human flesh and bone instead of passing smoothly and cleanly through it. Liam looked around and put it quickly into his coat pocket. *Maybe,* he thought, *Frank Abrams could ask one of his FBI lab friends to do a forensic study of it. I've got to see Abrams fast.*

He started to walk away from the car when he suddenly remembered the object that may have gotten Mathers killed. He leaned over into the front passenger seat, picked up the piece of paper, and turned on the overhead light. Mathers's handwriting was surprisingly clear and legible. The name in block letters read "ALFRED P. LYONS." Beneath the name was a phone number: 202-555 6030. Under the number, in bold, were the letters FBI, followed by a large hand-printed question mark. Just above the name of the "agent," Mathers had printed the words "SHIELD NUMBER" and the number 465. Liam recognized the phone area code of Washington, DC. The rest meant nothing to him.

Over the next three days, Liam stayed alone on Shelter Island and spoke to no one. Maggie had left the morning Liam returned from Montauk. He had not said a word to her of his bizarre exploits the night before. Every hour, on the hour, he tuned in to a local East End Long Island radio station, hoping to pick up some news of the murder and boat explosion. Finally, on the second evening, when the radio reception was optimal, he heard it.

"A dramatic explosion rocked a popular tourist fishing dock at Montauk Lake early Sunday night, destroying two charter boats in a fire that could be seen for miles out to sea. Police confirmed that one man is dead and presumed killed in the blaze. According to the preliminary report of the Suffolk County Fire Marshall, one of the boats, the *Northern Star*, was totally destroyed when an electric soldering iron may have ignited a propane tank. The body of a man found aboard the boat was burnt beyond recognition but is presumed to be that of the boat's captain, Buzz Mathers, a local favorite among Montauk fishermen. While arson is not suspected, police theorize that Mathers may have been drinking and had fallen asleep while working with the soldering iron."

"Man, they think of everything, don't they?" Liam thought aloud, not knowing who "they" were. He imagined Mathers's body lying at the bottom of one hundred feet of water with an anchor tied to his waist. He continued to ponder what had happened. He thought of the body on the boat and suspected that it probably belonged to one of the old-timers who may have been grabbed coming home drunk from one of the bars. He pictured in his mind's eye the old toothless man at the pool table and could only wonder.

Unanswered questions nagged and pulled at Liam. *What*, if anything, *do I do with this note from Mathers? Should I tell the police about his murder? Do I have to wait for the killers to find me, or do I get help trying to find out who they are?* As his head ached and swam in confusion, he suddenly understood that only one thing was certain. Liam knew he was way out of his league. He picked up the phone and called Frank Abrams.

THE RETAINER

Later that afternoon, sitting nervously in Abrams's spacious New York office waiting room, Liam felt the sudden urge to walk out and just try to forget the events of the past few days. *Let sleeping dogs lie,* he thought. *No one will ever be the wiser.*

Just as Liam stood up and started for the door, Frank stuck his head through the doorway. "What's up, Liam? You sounded a little spooked on the phone. Is everything all right?"

Liam tried to curb his anxiety and decided to crawl out on the end of a long and narrow limb. There would be no turning back now. He got up and walked into Abrams's office, approached the desk, and put a dollar bill facedown on it.

"Mr. Abrams, my dad once told me that the attorney-client privilege doesn't kick in until your lawyer is actually hired under retainer, and even then, it's not official until he's paid. Is that true?"

"Well, yes, that's technically right, but that depends on a few things. But what is this really all about?"

"I need to hire you to be my attorney."

"I've already been hired by your mother in the TWA lawsuit. As a matter of fact, as JW's son, you automatically became one of my clients when your mother retained me to represent your father's estate. We already have a privileged relationship. Why do you need another?"

"Forget my mother's suit. I'm officially hiring you to represent me in another completely different matter. I need all the advice I can get, and I need it right now. Can I pay you the rest of your fee when I get some money together?"

Abrams cocked his head and stared at his young client, curiosity brimming from his eyes. He leaned forward and picked up the dollar bill. "OK, Liam, considered me hired. As of now, I'm your private attorney. Now, what the hell's going on here?"

Liam bent down and took out an audiotape player from his backpack, put it on the big oak desk, and hit the play button. His father's voice instantly filled the room. Abrams sat upright, startled for a moment, then leaned closer to the machine with a look of amazement on his face. "My God, that's JW! When was this recorded? How long have you had it?"

Liam interrupted him. "Wait, wait . . . listen all the way to the end of the message! Listen to all of it!"

The taped played out, and the room fell totally silent. Only the sound of city traffic twenty-seven stories below could be heard. Abrams' face was frozen in amazement.

Liam broke the silence. "There's more . . . a lot more than this. Do you remember the report of one of the fishermen who claims he saw a missile rising into the air? His name is Mathers. I got his eyewitness version from the official NTSB report."

"Sure, I remember reading that. What about him?"

"Well, I drove out to see him a few days ago in Montauk. A couple of guys in a local bar pointed out the boat to me. We had a conversation about what he saw. It's totally consistent with what you just heard my father say on that tape."

Abrams grew agitated. "Liam, this changes everything. I need to talk to your friend Mathers right away."

"That's not possible."

"Why the hell not?"

"Because I watched him get shot by two men on the town beach. I'm pretty sure he's dead. Two minutes later, I saw his boat blow up at the dock."

Abrams was stunned. He took out a yellow legal pad and began to take notes. "Give me the whole story and don't leave anything out."

Liam slowly and methodically filled in the gaps with all the frightening details. Abrams sat in silence, trying to take it all in and mentally digest everything in one serving.

Finally, Abrams put down his pen and spoke. "But why? To what end? None of this makes any sense! Have you gone to the police or the FBI?"

"No. I panicked and ran. You're the only person who knows what happened. I haven't told my mother or Maggie—no one. According to the local news reports, the Suffolk police think the explosion was an accident. There was a body aboard the boat. They're assuming it was Mathers. I heard it all on the radio last night."

"Liam, you're required by law to report this. You're a material witness to a murder, for God's sake!"

"But they don't even think it was a murder," Liam protested. "As far as they're concerned, there was no foul play. What's the point in my reporting it?"

"Because it's the law, Liam, that's why! They can't do their job if you don't tell them what you saw and heard."

"Look, Mr. Abrams, I've done nothing but stew over this for the last three days. I don't see the point in getting myself killed over something I don't even understand. I have no clue what's going on here . . . except maybe . . . "

Liam paused and finally allowed himself to say aloud what he had been shoving into the darkest and most remote corner of his mind.

"Unless, of course, whoever killed Mathers is part of a plot to discredit him . . . and—"

Abrams finished Liam's thought aloud. "And you think this plot to discredit him is part of a bigger conspiracy to cover up a terrorist attack on Flight 800? Do you realize how ludicrous that sounds? There are too many good and honorable people working for the bureau and NTSB for there to be a cover-up. That's crazy. Why would the government want to conceal an attack on an American airline company by a bunch of crazy terrorists? There must be something else at play here. Mathers must have been involved in some kind of mob thing, maybe gambling or drug running. Who knows?

"Liam, since I'm now your personal attorney, I have to insist you answer some questions. Let's start with this. Did you tell Mathers about the tape of your father's phone message and that it confirmed his sighting of a missile?"

"Yes."

"Was anyone aboard that boat besides the two of you?"

"No."

"Did these men on the beach get a good look at you? Do you think they saw your license number?"

"They saw me, all right." Liam reached in to his coat pocket and handed Abrams the lead bullet.

"They shot at you?"

"I pulled it out of my driver's side door. The closest they got to me was about seventy-five yards, I think. I doubt they saw the plate, though. I turned off the running lights as soon as I started the engine."

"Liam, have you considered the possibility that they might have known Mathers was going to meet someone on the beach and that it was you they wanted to confront, not him? And that maybe they saw you on the boat or in the bar earlier that afternoon and already had a gotten a good look at both you and your car?"

Liam surprised himself with the logic of his immediate response. "No, I don't think so. That would mean Mathers was being watched round the clock. That doesn't make any sense. Besides, I never told anyone I was going out there to see him. It was a totally spontaneous trip out east. Someone in the bar must have tipped them off that I was heading to the boat to talk to Mathers."

Again, the images of the toothless old man and his buddy Mike ran through Liam's head.

Abrams continued to deal from the what-if deck.

"Maybe they didn't actually see you at all. Maybe they heard you."

"But no one was with us. We were the only ones on the boat . . . "

"Except perhaps a little bug?" Abrams pointed a finger to his ear.

"Maybe the boat was wired, Liam. Maybe they didn't get a close look at you after all . . . I hope. Did you give your full name to Mathers while you were aboard the boat?"

Liam lowered his head and nodded in the affirmative. Abrams's shoulders slumped. He rolled his head back, looked up at the ceiling, and said, "Shit!"

After a minute of silence, Liam asked, "Now what?"

"Well, if you refuse to take your attorney's advice and won't go to the police, what I'd like to do is clear my head and then go talk to an old friend of mine. He was my first partner in the FBI. He retired just last year from the bureau. Conveniently enough, he lives very close by, in Westchester. His name is Bob Anderson."

Liam pointed to the dollar bill in Frank's hand. "Don't forget about my retainer. We have a confidential relationship now. Just so we're clear, you can't divulge what happened to me in Montauk to anyone, including retired agents, unless I give the OK, right?"

"Liam, I'll make a deal with you. If you let me fill in Bob Anderson, whom, you should know, I would trust with my life, I won't tell anyone else about your Montauk incident. If I'm going to get his help on the lawsuit, he needs to know what's going on behind the scenes. "Don't worry, I'll only give him the basics. I had intended to talk to Bob anyway about the suit to get some background information about the FBI interviews and the investigation . . . and to see if maybe he could fill in some gaps and point me in the right direction for some more evidence as to how deep they got into this missile possibility. And besides, who knows, maybe he can shed some light on this little ballistic souvenir you picked up."

"Oh, I almost forgot, while you're at it, would you ask him if he knows an agent by the name of Alfred P. Lyons, shield number 465? And this phone number." Liam handed him the crumpled piece of paper. "This is what brought Mathers out to the beach that night. I asked him to bring it to me. If he hadn't found it, he might still be alive."

As Liam got up to leave, Frank held up his hand as if to stop him and raised his voice. "Liam, I'm not done with you. I'm not kidding. We need to have a serious talk about your duty to report this."

"Not now, Mr. Abrams. I'm not ready to deal with this."

Liam started for the door, stopped, and turned. "Oh, and there's one more thing. I especially don't want my mother knowing anything about any of this. OK?"

"Wait a minute, son, I have to at least tell her about the tape. That's important evidence. I have an ethical duty to disclose it to her. As a matter of fact, because of this tape, the suit against TWA is now in serious jeopardy. I might even have to disclose the tape to the defense counsel and the court. If some wacko terrorist really fired a missile that night and destroyed that plane, that's the end of the official federal government's defective wiring theory. You understand that, don't you? I would be ethically bound to discontinue the case on behalf of your mother. We would all have to walk away from this adventure with nothing to show for it."

"With all respect, Mr. Adams, as of thirty minutes ago, your first ethical duty at the moment is to me and the confidentiality of everything

I've just told you and given you." He put his finger to his lips. "Remember, not a word to my mother or anyone except Anderson. At least not until I can think things through and figure out what has to be done next." Liam walked out of the room, leaving Frank Abrams as befuddled as a first-year law student.

Frank Abrams, seasoned trial attorney, had just repeated the rookie mistake he had made as a young agent. He had just allowed himself to be snookered by another twenty-three-year-old kid. Even if he felt morally bound, as an officer of the court, to disclose everything he had just learned, he may have just precluded himself from discussing any of this—the tape, the imminent danger to Liam Mayfair, the fact that the boy was a material witness to a murder—with his "other client," Lee Mayfair. Worse, he might have to go through the motions of prosecuting a civil action against an airline company that he now had good reason to believe may be entirely blameless and innocent of any negligence or wrongdoing. He could already hear the screams of charges of suborning perjury that would be thrown at him from all quarters.

What a classic conflict of interest, he thought. This was the kind of mess that could get him disbarred, or worse, send him to jail, if he didn't get on top of it fast. Abrams sat up straight in his leather chair, staring at the dollar bill in front of him. All he could manage to say to himself was, "Good God almighty! What have I just gotten myself into?"

A RUNAWAY TRAIN

Bob Anderson lay dozing in the warm golden glow of the late-afternoon sun on his backyard patio. A lit cigar dangled precariously from his right hand. As Frank was escorted out to the back of the comfortable Westchester home by Bob's wife, Kay, he recognized the same white-haired crew cut and black horn-rimmed glasses Bob had worn in the years leading up to his retirement from the bureau.

Kay, realizing her husband was asleep, spoke softly. "Well, here's the old man in all his glory. He's all yours, Frank. I'll go in and get you both some iced tea. Decaf, no sugar, right?"

"Thanks, Kay."

Frank stared down at his old friend and immediately thought of his first day on the job in the Miami field office. Bob had broken him in for about a few months, tutoring him in the art of prosecuting the Selective Service cases Hoover often reserved for the fresh graduates of the FBI Academy at Quantico. The unofficial consensus among the new agents was that Hoover was testing their loyalty to flag and country. Frank remembered the moment at Quantico when he and fifty other men stood with their newly issued badges held high in their left hands, poised to take the agent's oath of office. The shaved-head firearms instructor administering the oath squinted, scowled, and said to the young recruits, "Look to your right and left, ladies. Everyone in this room knows that some of you are here to avoid getting your balls shot off by the Viet Cong. But know this as well. As God is my judge, I will personally find and root out each and every one of you hippie pussies. I will drum you out of this program and ship your sorry asses off to Saigon before you can learn to spell Dillinger. Is that clear? Now, raise your right hand and repeat the oath after me."

There was no doubt that Hoover wanted to send a clear message to his young agents. The last thing he wanted was to be infiltrated by antiwar hippie sympathizers. As it turns out, Bob Anderson was assigned to personally administer this informal test of loyalty to Frank Abrams by making sure he vigorously hunted down and prosecuted every draft dodger whose case came across his desk to the fullest extent of the law. Bob taught Frank how to find and capture many of those thousands of young men who had either planned a hasty exit to Canada or buried themselves in the underground drug culture of the sixties. Frank actually enjoyed the thrill of the hunt even though most of his prey were not particularly dangerous. What did bother him a great deal, however, was a new phenomenon that started occurring with greater frequency at the local draft boards. Frank reported to these boards in Miami one morning each week to monitor dozens of newly drafted young men who were scheduled to be inducted and sworn into the US armed forces. Invariably, there would always be the one or two clean-shaven, tie-and-jacket types who refused to step forward and take the oath. Frank's distasteful job was to approach these young men and warn them with onerous language read from a preprinted card that if they refused to be sworn in, they would be arrested immediately. He remembered his embarrassment and his fumbled attempt to handcuff several young Jehovah's Witnesses as they clutched copies of St. James Bibles in their hands. *How incongruous yet poignant*, he thought.

After a month of rounding up these conscientious war objectors, Frank started referring them, in the privacy of his bureau car while driving them downtown for booking, to a local Selective Service attorney who specialized in defending these cases. Frank was relieved the day Bob Anderson finally announced that he had "passed the test" and would now move on into the arena of real fugitives—not those who carried Bibles, but those with loaded guns, the kinds used to rob banks.

As Frank debated whether to wake up his old friend, still sleeping peacefully on the chaise, he smiled as he thought of the time they got a radio call from the FBI dispatcher in Miami to respond to a "91 in progress," a bank robbery, going on only three blocks away. Frank, the young buck ready for the excitement of confronting a live bank robber, was stunned when Bob leaned over and turned off the radio. "What the hell are you doing, Bob? That bank is right around the corner. We can be on top of this in seconds!"

Bob just looked ahead and smiled as he continued to drive. "There are plenty of other bureau cars in the area, rookie. Let someone else cover it." After a short debate and some shameless groveling by Frank, Bob capitulated and sped off toward the bank. Frank dove under the seat, pulled out the red car dome light, and shoved it outside the passenger window, attaching it onto the roof of the Bucar with its magnetic base. As they pulled up in front of the bank, siren on and dome light flashing, Frank unholstered his newly issued .38-caliber MP Special. He flung the door open to jump out and, to his horror, watched as the red flashing light, still attached by the power cord to the cigarette lighter, was whipped off the roof and onto the sidewalk, where it crashed and fractured into a hundred pieces of red plastic. By now, a crowd of civilians had gathered to watch the exciting real-life drama. The startled bystanders stared in silence as Frank rushed into the bank, gun still drawn, only to find three other agents assigned to the same UFAP squad, calmly interviewing a couple of beautiful young tellers and the hyperventilating, overweight bank manager. The robbery was over—and had been for quite a while. The felons had already fled in a beat-up Ford pickup with about $1,300 in cash.

But Frank's embarrassment had only just begun. At the weekly FBI party that Friday night, all of the office's seasoned agents—a tough, cigar-smoking, two-fisted bunch of serious drinkers—mercilessly mocked Frank and roared over his Keystone Cop moment at the bank. This was their ritual immersion of the young rookie in a baptism of fire. When they were done skewering Frank, they moved on to the other veterans in the bar, one by one, regaling dozens of stories describing their own amateur screwups. No man was spared. This was an equal-opportunity bunch of critics, venting the stress and emotional steam that accumulated each and every week of their lives, all of which were lived out every day on the front lines of federal fugitive investigations. All of these men had shared the horrible fear of the sudden unexpected confrontation with a young, rogue, gun-happy fugitive with nothing to lose. On the other end of the emotional spectrum, they all had suffered the boredom of countless hours of sleepless, mindless surveillance, the frustration of covering up a superior's hubris and incompetence, and the anger that was born of the unrequited injustice and arbitrariness of bureau politics.

And yet, in spite of all their whining about the things over which they had little control, the one thing that every one of these men shared most intimately and happily was a deep sense of satisfaction in their work and the uncompromising loyalty of their fellow agents. Frank was learning from these men what this elite force for good was all about and was being schooled faster than he had ever expected. He was humbled by their acceptance of him and, at the same time, immensely proud to be counted among them.

Frank would often later recall, as he slid his tail between his legs and tried to pick up the broken pieces of red plastic on the sidewalk outside the bank, that he realized then and there that Bob was not carrying his service revolver that day.

After the excitement had settled down, Frank asked, "Where's your gun, Bob? What were you going to do? Sit in the car and let me shoot it out alone?"

Bob was nonplussed. "If you must know, rookie, it's in the trunk. Don't you know by now that those things are dangerous?" Frank couldn't say for sure whether Bob's calm response was serious or just his idea of a really bad joke.

Rather than challenge his older mentor openly, in front of the other agents, Frank said nothing at the time. But he was deeply troubled and stored the affair deep into his memory. Indeed, as Frank would often recall the event to his friends years later, he would say that the only dangerous thing about the incident was the fact that Bob knowingly chose to be unarmed. Frank simply chalked it up to a careless and naive habit developed by a good agent who, after many years of arresting young draft dodgers without incident, assumed that his luck would never run out. He had committed the first and most serious sin of fugitive apprehension. He had foolishly discounted the potential for danger and ignored the first line of defense against an unexpected disaster. Ironically, while these young draftees were almost never designated as "armed and dangerous" and were rarely considered a personal, physical danger to the agents who collared them, they nevertheless posed a different, more insidious, and ephemeral kind of danger in Frank's view. Their unique threat was to the already shaken morale of the tens of thousands of young men who, unlike those who scampered like roaches in the middle of the night to Canada, answered their country's call to pick up a gun and fight for its defense. And therein, during the tumult of the '60s, lay the rub and the sad irony that consumed a patriotic yet badly divided and war-weary nation.

Sensing Frank's hovering presence, Bob suddenly opened his eyes, looked up from his chaise, and smiled. "Hey, rookie, how the hell are you?" The affection in his voice was palpable.

"Hi, partner. Looks like I caught you napping again. Just curious, where's your service revolver—under the bed?"

The dig was a direct hit. Bob laughed out loud. "You know, if I was called on the carpet for every goddamned bureau infraction, I would have been fired and become a schoolteacher years ago. Sit down, rookie. Take a load off, and tell me what brings you out here to the hinterlands."

Frank turned to face Kay, who had just come back with the drinks. He politely told her how well they both looked and then gave her that knowing glance that all FBI wives have come to recognize from firsthand experience. Without another word, she retired to the den, leaving the two old friends alone under a giant maple, its lengthening shadows slipping across the back lawn.

"I can tell this is no social call, Frank. You sounded on the phone like something heavy was weighing on your mind. So tell me, what's up?"

Bob always did get to the point fast, thought Frank. Over the next thirty minutes, he condensed everything he knew about Lee Mayfair's lawsuit against TWA. When he got to the part about JW's audiotape and the likely murder of a key witness to the Flight 800 crash, Bob, who had not yet uttered a word, got up from the chaise lounge and moved to a nearby chair. He pulled the chair up closer to Frank and sat down. With a deeply furrowed forehead, Bob hunched in closer to his old friend, like a priest to a penitent, as though signaling to the world that he did not want Frank's words to be carried outside their immediate zone of intimacy.

When Frank had finished his story, Bob just stared at him in disbelief. "Judas H. Priest! That's the most incredible story I think I've ever heard, Frank. If any part of it is true, methinks you're sitting on a powder keg. I almost don't know where to begin."

"Let's begin with that little so-called 'official' FBI visit to our fisherman friend in Montauk during the crash investigation," said Frank.

"Who? Mathers? You mean the dead guy whose body was never really identified? Now there's a real solid starting point!" Bob said sarcastically.

"Come on, Bob, let's work with what we've got. OK?"

"OK, Frank, you're right. The whole thing stinks to high heaven, but you'll never get anywhere presuming that the bureau and the NTSB are involved in some grand conspiracy to cover up a possible terrorist attack. Do you really believe that is even remotely possible?"

"Not for a minute. But neither do I believe that Mathers was visited by one of our guys. And presuming it wasn't the bureau, then who the hell tried to quiet him up and then kill him? But the real million-dollar question is, assuming he was in fact murdered, why would anyone feel the need or even want to kill him? Why silence someone whose story was totally debunked by the forensic experts to begin with . . . especially when that someone was considered a loser and was written off by the FBI and the press as an unreliable witness?

"Here's the bottom line as I see it, Bob. Without any credible, forensic proof to support a missile attack, Mathers and the other missile eyewitnesses are almost irrelevant. They pose no threat to anyone. And if that's the case, then why the hell would anyone need to kill anyone, much less some flaky local drunk, right?"

Bob sat up straighter in his chair. "Let me guess, Frank. You'd like for me to do some digging and check out that name. What is it, Lyons? And that badge number, you want me to run it past the bureau and our friends at Langley . . . and while I'm at it . . . the military intelligence boys, to see if there any matches, right?"

Frank nodded and then continued. "Look, it seems pretty simple to me. If this guy Lyons was not 'officially' one of ours, assuming we get the truth out of the spy boys at the agency, then there is a pretty good chance he was some kind of foreign operative. Agreed?"

"Yes, that thought did cross my mind."

"Look, Bob, you finished up your last few years working counter-intelligence in Washington. I know you still have some great hooks with the boys in WFO, and I would love to have your help and advice. But I don't want to get you involved in this mess if you have any hesitancy or concerns about your credibility or reputation being hurt. Or worse, any worry about how this could affect your retirement and your overly generous pension."

"My reputation? Ha! I don't even know what the hell that might be. That's not even on my radar screen, Frank."

Anderson spoke slowly and smiled. "Look, to tell you the truth, I've been going a little stir-crazy sitting out on this patio every day sipping iced tea and watching *Rumpole of the Bailey* with 'she who must be obeyed,'" he said as he held up his fingers in the universal sign for quotation marks. "I have to admit, this is one hell of a story. You really have piqued my interest, rookie. To answer your question, am I concerned about any blowback? Absolutely not. So yes, count me in all the way."

"I was hoping you would say that, partner. Oh, I almost forgot a not-so-small detail."

Frank reached into his jacket and pulled out the slug Liam removed from his car door. "Could you have your friends run this through the lab for me? We might learn something important from it. My guess is it's a hollow point from a 9 mm. I would ask you for your personal ballistic opinion, but then you wouldn't know anything about guns, would you?" Frank smiled, rising to his feet.

Bob leaned on the arm of the chair, got up a little slower than his younger friend, and rolled his eyes. "You just can't help yourself rookie, can you? You know, you never did have any respect for your elders! You may be a fancy Manhattan lawyer now. But to me you'll always be that smart-ass Jewish kid from the Bronx."

Bob finally lumbered to his feet and gave his friend a long, warm hug. "Do you remember my telling you about my father and what he did for a living?"

"Yeah, he was a railroad man back in the day, wasn't he?"

"Yep, he was an old railroad engineer during the heyday of coal-fired locomotives. I remember him telling me once when I was a kid that for the longest time, he never could figure out why his company spent so much time teaching him the proper way to survive a jump and roll off a moving train. You know, down those steep cinder railroad banks? I mean, what's the point of that in the middle of a train wreck, right? Well, it seems my old man learned his lesson the hard way one cold night, when the engine controls and throttle locked up as he was doing forty-five mph through those steep hills of West Virginia. He couldn't slow her down as he came to a sharp curve and had to jump ship just in time to watch eight carloads of raw timber crash down the mountain into the Monongahela River. Pop wound up with only a separated shoulder and a few scratches.

"One thing he learned for sure, though. When someone offers to teach you how to roll away from serious trouble, just shut up, listen, and take notes. Pop was very grateful that the brass taught him how to pull off that tricky maneuver. I guess what I'm trying to say to you, Frank, is . . . please be very careful, my good friend. You might find yourself alone on a runaway train in very short order, if you're not alert."

"Don't worry about me, partner. I'll be fine."

Frank walked through the den and said "Good night" to Kay. As he reached the front door, Bob called out to him from the back of the house. "I'll be in touch when I have something for you. Meanwhile, learn how to jump and roll, rookie."

EYES IN THE BACK OF HER HEAD

Liam got out of the elevator and opened the door of his parents' East Side penthouse condo. Lee Mayfair was standing there, arms folded and with an angry look on her face.

Liam spotted the troubled frown immediately. "What's the matter, Mom?"

"Liam, is there something you should be telling me?"

He immediately thought of his confidentiality agreement with Abrams and swallowed hard. His mood grew defensive. Thinking that his newly retained attorney had already betrayed him, he braced himself for the next few difficult minutes of conversation. "Why do you ask me that? What exactly did Mr. Abrams tell you?"

"Who, Frank? I haven't spoken to him in days. What are you talking about?"

Realizing that he might still be holding on to some decent cards, Liam relaxed. "Nothing in particular, Mom. What are you referring to?"

"What am I referring to? I'm referring to that unmistakable bullet hole in your driver's door! That's what I am referring to!"

Liam laughed nervously. "Oh, that. That's not a bullet hole, Mom. That's a puncture hole from a forklift. The other day, while I was driving along one of the side streets in midtown, this delivery guy accidentally drove into the side of my car while I was stopped in traffic." As soon as the lie formed in his mind and flowed from his lips, he realized how ridiculous it sounded.

"Liam, I am the wife of a hunter and firearms expert who taught me how to shoot long before you were born. Don't give me that nonsense! I was walking past the car this morning in the garage and noticed it right away. The hole even extends into the inside door panel."

God, she has eyes like a hawk, he thought as he tried to compose himself. Liam just then remembered that he had left the car keys in the glass bowl by the front door and that he had parked in the family's reserved spot under the building. He could hear the echo of his father's voice as he often warned the Mayfair boys. "Don't try to pull a fast one on your mother. She's got eyes in the back of her head."

Liam stared at the floor and said nothing.

"Well, are you going to tell me what's going on, or do I have to stay up all night imagining the worst and getting angrier by the minute?"

Determined not to dig the hole any deeper, he tried the disengagement approach. "Mom, I can't discuss it with you right now. I promise you though. I'm not in any kind of danger. I'll explain it all later."

Yeah, much later, he thought to himself. Later, when he could come up with a much more plausible explanation—one that did not involve the use of firearms.

Liam put his arms around his worried mother. "Mom, you've always trusted me to do the right thing. There's no reason to stop now. Everything is fine, really!"

Lee Mayfair was totally dissatisfied with her son's answer. She decided to let this play out a little while longer, knowing she wouldn't let the subject rest until she knew everything she needed to know. She quietly resolved to discuss it with Abrams, hoping he would know how to pry the truth out of her evasive son.

After a long moment of silence, Lee Mayfair spoke in a very slow, measured manner, a familiar giveaway that her level of anger and disappointment was climbing off the charts. "This morning, I got a call from a reporter at the *New York Times*. He says he's doing a follow-up feature story on the families of the Flight 800 victims and wants to talk with us. I'm not interested. You can deal with him as you please." She handed Liam a piece of paper with the name and number of the reporter. "If you decide to talk with him, I would strongly suggest you clear it with Mr. Abrams first. The reporter's name is Mike Ketchum. Get cleaned up and I'll make you some lunch."

As Lee Mayfair spun and walked quickly toward the kitchen, she stopped, turned, and looked at her chastised son. "And by the way, did you find the slug?"

Liam pretended not to hear the question, went into the den, and dialed the number for the *Times*. After a dozen rings, Michael J. Ketchum, twelve-year veteran beat reporter, finally picked up the phone. Ketchum spent the next several minutes doling out pro forma niceties and delayed condolences.

Finally, Ketchum got to the stated purpose of his contact with the family. "Liam . . . may I call you Liam? My editor has asked me to do a follow-up piece on the Flight 800 story. Pretty standard stuff in these kinds of cases. You know, the deeper, human interest side of the equation. Pretty straightforward questions like how are your mother and siblings coping with and adjusting to your horrible loss two years after the fact? Are there any annual memorial services or scholarship funds in the works? What do you think of the FBI's conclusions on the cause of the crash? That sort of thing. You know . . . strictly routine, mundane stuff."

Liam surprised himself with the bluntness of his response. "OK, Mike, let's cut out the crap. What do you really want to write about?"

"Wow, you don't mess around, Liam. I heard from a few sources that you just got a degree in journalism. Sounds like you might have chosen the right career path. Listen, I'll be equally as blunt. I heard your family is being represented by your dad's former law partner, Frank Abrams, in a multimillion dollar lawsuit against TWA. I'm hearing reports that he and lead defense counsel, Bill Canning, are old courtroom rivals and that there is no love lost between the two of them. If this case goes to trial, I could probably sell ringside seats to one hell of a fight. Am I on the right track so far?"

"Go on," Liam said laconically.

"Well, I'm no lawyer. But I do know that in order to make out his case before a jury, Abrams has to prove that the electrical spark that ignited that wing fuel-tank explosion was the direct, foreseeable result of some kind of defective material, improper installation, or negligent maintenance of the hundreds of miles of wiring in that plane. Is that a fair summary of Abrams's theory of law in this case . . . from a layman's point of view, of course? Am I using the right formal legal terminology?"

Liam was getting annoyed and impatient with the direction this conversation was going. "Why are you asking me these questions? Shouldn't you be talking to my attorney, Mr. Abrams? He's the lawyer on the case, not me. As a matter of fact, shouldn't you have gotten his permission before contacting us about the lawsuit?"

Ketchum ignored the rebuke and moved forward. "Actually, it's the other way around, Liam. As I understand it, if I had tried to contact him directly, he would have just told me that he would first need your permission for him to talk with me. So you might say I'm going directly to the horse's mouth and avoiding the middleman altogether. This way, you and I can have a direct, unencumbered conversation. You know, man-to-man, with no mouthpiece filter to waste anyone's time. That way nothing gets lost in the translation. I'm sure you get the idea."

"Oh, I get the idea loud and clear. Nice try. Look, I'm not answering any questions about this case without Abrams present. But I'll tell you what, Mr. Ketchum. Why don't you tell me what you want and I'll do the listening for a while. Let's see how it goes. How's that sound?"

"That's fine with me. So allow me to get the point. Here's what I'm really calling about. In the first few weeks after the explosion, some folks in the media, based on eyewitness accounts, thought this plane was blown up by some kind of missile. But the feds and all the experts ruled out terrorism. They insisted that heated vapors and a spark from faulty wiring was the only logical explanation."

Liam remained evasive. "And just how am I supposed to respond to that?"

"I'm really curious. Don't you find it more than a little coincidental that one of the loudest, most vocal, pro-missile eyewitnesses—the one guy who refused to shut up about seeing a missile trail rising from the surface of the ocean that night—was also killed in an explosion? And according to what I hear from some of the locals out there in Montauk, under some very strange circumstances."

Liam was startled. He caught his breath and was suddenly grateful that Ketchum was not standing there in person to see him flinch. Pretending to play dumb, he said. "You mean that fisherman guy out east? What's his name? He was killed?"

"I'm really surprised you haven't heard about it. Although, with you living here in the city, I could understand that you wouldn't pick up on Long Island news stories. Yeah, well, anyway, his boat was blown up at the dock with him in it. Strange, isn't it? At first I thought it sounded like another story of an electrical-wiring defect. But this time, the cops think it was a combination of a spark from a soldering iron with a leaky propane tank that did him in."

"That's too bad. But what does that have to do with our lawsuit?"

"Not sure that it has anything to do with it, Liam . . . at least, not yet."

"Not yet? Where exactly are you going with all this, Mr. Ketchum?"

"You know what the really weird thing is about that boat explosion, Liam? It seems some young guy was seen poking around the local docks out there asking a lot of questions about this old codger just before he and his boat wound up being fried to a crisp."

"Is there a question in there somewhere?"

"Oh, sure. Sorry. Here's my question, Liam. You wouldn't happen to have any idea who that preppy-looking young man who was snooping around that afternoon might happen to be, do you?"

After a long awkward silence, Liam spoke deliberately. He feigned a quick laugh. "Preppy? Boy, that really narrows it down. That could describe almost half the population living out there on the East End. Is that the best description you got from the people in the bar?"

"Bar? Who said anything about a bar? I don't believe I ever mentioned that detail, Liam. And by the way, 'preppy' is only one of the many descriptive words I wrote down in my notes. Like the fact, for example, that this kid, about five feet eleven inches, 180 pounds, straight dark hair, was seen driving a black Jeep with an out-of-state tag . . . Massachusetts, I believe. Liam, I'm a reporter, remember? This is what I do for a living."

Liam froze and was afraid to speak.

"Listen, Liam, I think we should meet in person. From my vantage point, this is what I'm coming up with so far . . . strictly on a hypothetical level, of course. Just suppose that plane explosion wasn't due to faulty wiring after all but in fact was caused by a missile attack? What if Harley Mathers's death wasn't an accident? What if someone was trying to neutralize the noisiest proponent of a missile attack by shutting him up permanently? And by the way, did you know that Mathers was the poster boy for an equally noisy conspiracy cult out there? You've heard of those folks who are openly challenging the government's findings, haven't you?"

"What exactly is your point, Mr. Ketchum?"

"Seems to me, the multimillion dollar question that remains is whether your case against TWA would, excuse the pun, go down in flames if this missile theory suddenly grew legs and reappeared on the horizon with some renewed credibility. I'm just wondering out loud. Has any of this kind of conjecturing ever crossed your mind? Has it come up in conversation with Frank Abrams? Or are you and Abrams more comfortable resting on the convenient and friendly conclusions of the NTSB report? Surely you've noticed that their conclusions happen to give you the greatest chances of success at trial against TWA."

"Mr. Ketchum, you have a lot of questions there, not to mention some very nasty innuendo. I need to talk to my attorney and get back to you. I'm going to need a few days, OK?" Liam was really feeling the panic set in about now and worried that the sudden break in his voice, with its higher pitch, was betraying his fear. He needed to get off the phone.

"Great. Why don't you do that, Liam. I look forward to hearing from you soon. And just one more point. The last thing I want to do is cause any trouble for you or your family or do anything to derail your lawsuit. But in my business, facts are stubborn little critters, and they are very hard to ignore. Like the fact, for example, that you happen to drive a black Jeep with a Massachusetts registration and that you happen to fit the description of that kid sniffing around the docks. That would be quite a coincidence in the scheme of things, wouldn't you say?"

There was another long awkward pause. Ketchum moved in for the kill. "Please tell Mr. Abrams when you talk with him that my follow-up piece has to be put to bed in three to four days and I would love to hear your side of the whole story before we go to print. And please remember, Liam. I'm not out to hurt you. OK? But make no mistake. We are going to print with or without you. Do you understand?"

Liam kept his knee-jerk retort to himself. He bounced the words around in his head but didn't have the guts to speak them aloud. *Yeah, sure, but if someone or some little fact "critter" gets between you and a Pulitzer prize nomination, someone might get hurt, and it won't be you Ketchum, will it?*

Liam hung up the phone without saying another word. He felt his heart begin to race and began to feel light-headed.

"Shit!" he mumbled to himself through clenched teeth.

TIME'S UP! PUT YOUR PENCILS DOWN!

The sun was just beginning to settle behind the city's concrete canyon walls on Manhattan's West Side. Liam was glad that Abrams asked that they meet not in his stuffy office, but out here in the broad, airy expanse of Sheep Meadow in Central Park—a bucolic refuge from the noise and car exhausts of Midtown Manhattan. It had been a beautiful, unseasonably warm afternoon, and the meadow was being overrun with dogs, Frisbees, and winter-weary lovers. As Liam saw Frank approaching from the Sixty-Ninth Street entrance to the park, he noticed that the years had taken a bit of steam out of his gait. His shoulders were a little more stooped than he had ever remembered.

"You look like I feel," Liam said as Abrams got nearer. "Are you OK?"

"I'm fine. Just need a little fresh air. What a day, huh?"

"Yeah, a beautiful day. Until a few hours ago."

Frank stopped short, frowned, and stared into Liam's face.

"Mr. Abrams, I want to apologize for something I did today. It was really stupid."

Frank's voice betrayed his deep concern. "OK. Let's hear it."

"I think I just incriminated myself to a reporter from the *New York Times*."

Abrams, holding his hand over his eyes to shield them from the lowering sun, squinted at his young client. "What did you tell him?"

"Mr. Abrams, I'm so sorry I ignored your advice . . . I figured I could handle him . . . I didn't know . . . "

Visibly irritated, Abrams raised his voice and repeated the question. "What exactly did you tell him? Give it to me slowly, every damn word of it."

Liam relayed the entire conversation and the alleged purpose of the contact from the *Times*. His voice quivered as it trailed off into a whisper.

"First of all, take a deep breath and follow me closely. There's no question he threw some fresh bait in the water, and unfortunately, you bit. So he thinks he's about to land a big one. But if he really is as thorough a reporter as you seem to think he is, I doubt he seriously believes you were involved in Mathers's death. That would make no sense. He's trying to scare you into running at the mouth. However, what I am worried about, depending on the slant of Ketchum's story, is what the reaction of the objective observer and the average *Times* reader might be. They could easily be led to suspect something I want to avoid here. A lot of folks might think that your vested interests in the outcome of your mother's case, and the well-being of Harley Mathers, might not exactly be compatible, if you catch my drift."

Abrams continued to try to calm down his frightened client. "Let's talk this through logically, shall we? Because of either sloppy forensics or amateur police work, the body they found on the boat was never definitively identified. It was presumed to be Mathers, but it sounds like no one took the trouble to compare dental records, for example. That's assuming, of course, that this old-timer had ever stepped inside a dental office. So at least, for the moment, and based on what you actually saw, Mathers's real body was definitely not on that boat and is nowhere to be found. And without his body, there can be no autopsy and no ballistic study. Right? That is, at least for the moment."

Liam said, "You think they'll find the body?"

"Yes, I do. Make no mistake about it, Liam, I doubt these two men had the same level of expertise of the mob in disposing of bodies and incriminating evidence. I'm sure that once the body decomposes enough and the lines they used to tie it to some weighty object break down, your friend Mr. Mathers will bob to the surface and some fisherman will find him. And with all those rough bottom currents out there in Montauk, I wouldn't be surprised if it happens within a few weeks."

Liam merely gazed out across the meadow and remained silent.

Frank continued. "Oh, and speaking of ballistics, I spoke with Anderson a little while ago about the slug you dug out of your car door. The preliminary findings suggest a hollow-point .380-caliber bullet fired from probably a Walther PPK. A very compact and very reliable German semiautomatic. The FBI and CIA don't authorize their agents to carry this weapon. Maybe a Glock or Smith & Wesson 9 mm., yes, but not a PPK. The fact that the gun has historical Nazi connections might have something to do with that kind of bias.

"Anyway, based on your description of the appearance and accent of that so-called agent who bullied Mathers on the boat, my bet is that we're dealing with a foreign operative, maybe of southern European or Middle Eastern descent.

"But what really concerns me most is what Ketchum intends to do with the fact that his source out there saw you and your Jeep around the docks, asking for directions to Mathers's boat, within a few hours before it exploded. If he goes to the Suffolk County Police, the bigger question is, what, if anything, would they do with that information? How far would they go with it? It seems to me, at the very least, they would want to interview you about it. But that's not going to happen. Not while you're my client."

Liam suddenly grew very annoyed. "And why the hell not? I haven't done anything wrong, except maybe sit on this a little too long. I have nothing to hide!"

Abrams' eyes grew wide as he suddenly raised his voice. "Really? Nothing to hide? Are you kidding? When they start drilling you for information, are you going to tell them about how you met with the victim on his boat? That you were probably the last person to see him alive? Are you going to describe how these two thugs killed Mathers on the beach right in front of you? Are you going to tell them you were shot at too? And that you decided to do your own little crime scene investigation by digging that slug out of your car? That instead of calling the police immediately, you went into seclusion for a few days? That your delay in reporting all of these facts could very well have hampered their investigation of a murder?"

Liam's head and shoulders slumped as Abrams continued to pound Liam with the inconvenient reality of what he was about to face with the police. "Are you going to tell them that your inaction probably prevented a timely, thorough autopsy, not to mention a complete investigation of the crime scene before it could be fouled up by weather and beach traffic? How do you think they would react to all those little details, Liam? Do you think they would consider you the model citizen, say thank you, and let you walk away?"

Liam, by now, had become totally overwhelmed. "Mr. Abrams, all I know is I'm tired of all this skulking around like I was some kind of criminal. Look, I met you here today to tell you that I've made up my mind on what I should do about the tape . . . actually, about this whole Mathers affair."

Sensing what Liam was about to say, Abrams tried to divert his attention, at least momentarily. Looking him squarely in the face, he said, "Son, I want you to think very clearly about what you are about to do. And please understand that I am not advising against it. However, I want you to also understand very clearly that if any evidence comes to light suggesting that Flight 800 was blown up by a missile, your mother's case will have to be discontinued with prejudice. Any possibility of a financial recovery for her and your family will be lost forever. Do you understand that?"

"Yes, I do. I'm going to let my mother listen to the tape tonight and ask her to decide whether to give up the lawsuit. This has to be her decision. But I'm going to do my best to try and convince her to walk away from the suit. Knowing her as I do, I'm positive she'll agree with me. I know this business with Mathers doesn't look good for me, but I'm going to go to the police and the FBI and tell them everything. I should've followed my instincts from the start. I should've cleared the air about all of this a lot sooner."

"And what do you want me to do?" asked Abrams.

"I want you to be ready, after I talk with my mother, to formally discontinue the lawsuit. I want you to call Canning directly to tell him we are dropping the case and that we don't want his $450,000 dollars either."

Suddenly, the rest of Liam's thoughts became crystal clear to him. "I'm going to see the *Times* reporter tomorrow, hopefully with my mother present, and tell him everything. If Ketchum goes to the police and the police think I was involved in Mathers' death, then so be it. Let them try and prove it. They're not going to get anywhere with that." The boldness of his statement surprised him and somehow ratcheted down his level of anxiety.

Frank's eyes widened and he grinned. "Liam, it just occurred to me, you're so much more like your old man then I ever gave you credit for. Stubborn as a mule, but as honorable as the day is long. Give me Ketchum's number. I'll call him and schedule an appointment for tomorrow morning in my office. I insist on setting up how and where this is done."

Remembering another meeting with a young reporter in the newsroom of the Miami Herald many years prior, Frank continued: "Our meeting with the *Times* will be on my terms, on my turf, not theirs.

I refuse to let this spin out of control any more than it already has. Agreed?"

"Agreed."

"In the meantime, please . . . Liam, talk to your mother and share every last bit of this information with her. And get back to me right away. As of this moment, we have officially run out of time and options."

A FAMILY AFFAIR

That night, the entire Mayfair clan gathered for dinner in Lee's Manhattan condo for the first time since JW's funeral. Liam was the last to arrive. He entered the door, carrying the tape and his old cassette player in an old, faded backpack. As he walked into the family room, Colin, Alex, and Darcy were seated talking quietly among themselves. He noticed right away that there was none of his brothers' usual laughing and banter. Instead, he was greeted by three very somber faces that now looked wide-eyed up at their brother.

"Hi, guys. Where's Mom?"

Darcy stood up, ran to him, and threw her arms around Liam, holding him close. "She's in the kitchen. Liam, I'm so sorry I haven't been in touch with you. I had no idea you were still having such a rough time. I'm so glad all of us are here together again." She glanced over at the family photograph of JW on the mantle. "Well, almost all of us." Her warmth and sincerity reminded him of his mother.

Must be a female thing, he thought. His brothers would never be caught dead in a display of any affection like that. Suddenly, he realized that he, too, inherited JW's cool, aloof style. Ironically, his father, especially as the boys grew older, showed more signs of open affection for friends and mere acquaintances than he did for his own family. He and his brothers were all alike in that same department. Thank God, Liam thought, for the rare feminine qualities supplied by his mother and little sister in this testosterone-driven family.

Lee Mayfair walked into the room and smiled warmly. "Liam, I thought I heard your voice. Come and sit down, we'll be eating in a few minutes."

"Mom, before we eat, I have something very important to tell you. Actually, I want all of you to hear this."

Colin interrupted. "What's this all about, little brother?"

Liam decided to set some parameters from the outset. "First of all, Colin, let's get this out in the open, I'm not your 'little' brother—I'm your youngest brother. Second, I don't want anyone interrupting me in what I'm about to say. I'll answer all of your questions when I'm through, not before. If anyone has a problem with that, let me know and I'll leave now!"

Colin, Alex, and Darcy all shot a look of surprise at each other and wondered where this forceful side of their quiet, demure brother had been hiding all these years.

"Mom, please sit down. To start with, I'm sorry for not being honest with you about that hole in my car door. You were right. That was a .380 slug fired from a Walther PPK, directed at me personally. I should have known you were way too smart when it comes to firearms to fall for the wool I tried to pull over your eyes, Mom. But let me start at the beginning."

Colin sat upright on the couch. "What? Someone shot at you? When? Where?"

"Are you going to shut up and listen or not?" Liam fired back. Colin quietly slumped back down into his seat.

"When I was evicted from my piss hole of an apartment in Boston and moved into the house on Shelter Island right after Christmas, I left almost all my personal stuff behind in Boston. I couldn't care less about that crappy furniture I left for the sheriff on the sidewalk. But there was one thing I wanted but forgot to take with me. That was my old cassette answering machine. I thought it was among the stuff grabbed by the eviction crew. But fortunately, I had left it at Maggie's, and believe it or not, she's had it in the trunk of her car for the past year and a half. A few days ago, she gave me the tape and player. It had one long phone message on it. It was from Dad." Liam took the tape out of his pocket.

They all looked over at the backpack Liam had laid down on the glass coffee table and watched Liam remove the machine, plug it in, and insert the tape.

"This is going to be tough and a little weird for you to hear. Dad left me this message from aboard the plane seconds before it blew up. No one's heard it for almost two years."

Liam hit play and studied the looks on the faces of his family, paying particular attention to his mother's reaction. The emotions ranged from horror to fear to sadness. Darcy sobbed quietly to herself. Colin clenched his fists and stared at the floor. Lee Mayfair grew teary eyed but remained stoic.

After the tape played out, Liam spoke up. "I'll explain about the bullet in my car door in a minute, Mom, but first I want to hear all your questions about the tape itself."

Lee spoke up first. "Liam, has Frank Abrams heard this tape?"

"Yes, I played it for him soon after I first heard it myself. And yes, what Dad describes is almost certainly a missile. He called it a SAM, a surface-to-air missile, the kind that Dad evaded on all those bombing runs in North Vietnam. I know what the FBI and the official NTSB reports say, but they haven't heard this tape yet."

"What do you mean 'yet'?" barked Colin. "Christ almighty, if they get their hands on that tape, Mom's lawsuit will have to be discontinued! We can't let that happen!"

Colin's voice grew frenetic. "Look, there was absolutely no physical evidence of a missile explosion. How do we know Dad didn't see something that only looked like a missile being fired? This was July. Maybe it was a fireworks kind of rocket. Every expert who has looked at the debris and the wreckage field says there was no missile. How can we be sure that you're right, Liam, and everyone else is wrong? Christ, can't you see there's too much at stake for us not to be 100 percent sure?"

Alex joined in next. "Colin is right, Liam. I say we sit tight on this tape until we have some corroborating evidence, until we have something more reliable. Who knows? Maybe some new evidence will pop up."

Liam shook his head and looked at Alex. "All the evidence that has been found to date has been documented and examined from a hundred different angles. There *is* no new evidence, except for this tape. There *is* no other corroborating evidence. This is it, Alex."

Colin was getting even more agitated. "The tape is not enough, standing alone, to back up a missile theory. If we try to prove something the government says can't be proven, we'll all look like fools. We will have given up on the only theory that can win the case against TWA. For what? Do you intentionally want to lose this case before we've had a chance to fight? What about the offer they've already made? Do you want us to give that up too? Why? As a matter of principle? Do you want to see Mom destitute, for God's sake?"

Liam looked down and took a deep breath. "Of course not. But it doesn't matter what I think. This has to be Mom's decision. If it were just up to me, I would release the tape and let the chips fall where they may. I personally won't be part of a lie." Liam looked directly at his mother. "Mom, before you give us your answer, you need to hear the rest of the story."

"I was wondering when you were going to get around to that, Liam. Don't leave out any detail. I want to hear all of it."

Liam looked directly at his brothers. "Well, now for the part that really gets messy. The day after I heard the tape, I drove into the city and saw Mom. I asked her for the preliminary government report and reread the narrative about one of the fishermen who claims he saw a missile plume rising up from the ocean surface . . . not just a fireball falling down toward the water. That same day, I drove out to Montauk. And I found him. It was a lot easier than I thought. I had a conversation with this guy, Harley Mathers, aboard his fishing boat. He told me about being dismissed and ridiculed as an unreliable drunk by the FBI. I think they might have bought his story if there had been some forensic evidence of an external explosion. But since they made up their minds early in the investigation, that a missile was out of the equation. To them, Mathers was just a crazy old drunken coot who wouldn't shut up."

"So why do you insist on giving him credence now when no one else has?" asked Colin.

"I believe Mathers's story because I saw him murdered on a beach where he and I met later that night. I had asked him to give me a piece of paper with the name of someone who contacted him, claiming he was a federal agent. This guy basically threatened to kill him if he kept going to the press and insisting that he saw a missile."

"Liam, is that the person who shot at you?" said Lee.

"I think so, Mom. And probably the same person who blew up the *Northern Star*, Mathers's fishing boat, that night."

"Jesus, you saw that happen too?" said Alex.

Colin fired another question. "What about the body? Did you see what happened to this guy Mathers?"

"I saw him collapse after the shots were fired and didn't stick around when these two guys started coming at me. I just jumped in the car and tore the hell out of there. I was able to get away, but not before one of them fired a bullet into the driver's side door. Mr. Abrams believes that I should not discount the possibility that the killers may have already identified me."

Darcy finally composed herself enough to ask a question. "Liam, did you tell the police what you saw? Can't you get in trouble if you don't tell them you witnessed a murder? Isn't there a law that says you have to do that?"

Liam immediately noticed that this thorny legal problem hadn't popped up yet in the scholarly minds of his two lawyer brothers. Of all his siblings, Darcy was the sweetest and most pure minded. *From the mouths of babes*, he thought.

"Yes, I should have reported it the night it happened, but it's not too late. I've made up my mind to go to both the Suffolk County Police and the FBI and give them the tape, along with everything else, every detail of the story . . . that is, if Mom approves.

"I discussed this today with Mr. Abrams. Colin is right. If and when I disclose the tape, the lawsuit is effectively over and done with. And with no suit, there will be no money coming to Mom. Not even the $450,000 already offered by TWA.

"But there is a bigger problem we all need to talk about. Mr. Abrams is setting up an interview tomorrow morning with me and that reporter with the *Times*, Mom. Do you remember him? He's the guy who called you about a follow-up story on the flight victims. I want you to be there with me tomorrow. Abrams wants to try to control what he calls the 'spin' of the story before it breaks in the papers, TV news, et cetera. This reporter, his name is Ketchum, dug up some witnesses who will confirm that I was the guy out in Montauk poking around the local bars and docks and asking questions about Mathers only hours before he was killed and his boat was blown up. He has strongly implied that he is going to print the whole story, including my involvement in the Mathers incident. The point is, I'm tired of not doing the right thing. Darcy is right. I'm going to get out in front of this, now. I should have reported the murder right away. But I'm going to make up for that tomorrow morning and come clean with everyone: the police, the FBI, Ketchum, everyone." He paused and looked at his mother. "But only if Mom gives me the green light."

Colin stood up and tried to say something.

Liam held up his hand. "Sit down for a second and let Mom speak."

Lee Mayfair, the family matriarch, got up and stood in the middle of the room. "Liam, this is a lot for me to absorb at once. I have to tell you that I'm already leaning in one direction, but I want to hear from each of my children first before I say anything else". She looked directly at Colin, seated to her left. "OK, Colin, let's hear what you have to say now."

Colin Mayfair got to his feet and walked over to Liam. "A few minutes ago, I thought you were out of your mind for suggesting that we publish this tape. But now that you've explained about the murder and the legal mess you could be in . . . and especially the danger of being hurt by the people who killed that fisherman, that changes everything. I say, screw it all. Let everyone hear the voice of J. W. Mayfair. You're right, Dad wouldn't want us going after all that money if it meant one of us was at risk of going to jail for obstructing justice or for committing perjury. Besides, it's beginning to look pretty clear that Mathers's death is no coincidence. I want to know who killed him and how it all ties into Dad's death and Flight 800. If Dad says it was an unmistakable missile attack, then I suppose we shouldn't be afraid to let the world hear him say it. We'll survive. We always have."

Lee next turned to Alex. "Alex, before you give me your opinion, I want to tell you all that your father had every bit of his portfolio and assets tied up in that merger deal. However, I just found out yesterday, when I went through his papers again, much to my pleasant surprise, that he had quietly transferred the deed to the condo from our names jointly to my name, almost three years before the crash. He never told me he was going to do that, although I vaguely remember Dad asking me to sign some document around that time. Anyway, the good news is our condo won't go on the auction block after all. So to answer Colin's question. No, I won't be destitute. I won't have to move out. I'll manage just fine. Besides, I have a few marketable talents left in the arsenal, not to mention those I've perfected in raising four wonderful kids. I'm sure I'll be able to find some kind of part-time job if I had to."

Alex spoke up. "Liam, you would have made one hell of a trial attorney. Your arguments have completely turned me around on this. Mom, I have to agree with Liam and Colin. I say we should release the tape and see where it takes us. Maybe Mr. Abrams can figure a way to salvage some kind of case. But if he can't, I'm OK with that, if you are."

"Count me in too, Mom. I know it sounds trite, but there are things much more important than money. Like us sticking together as a family," added Darcy. "I agree with Colin, we'll all be fine. I'm not concerned about losing the case. I'm concerned about this family and us not doing what Dad would have expected us to do."

Lee Mayfair smiled. "Well then, that makes it unanimous. Do what you have to do, Liam. I'll be with you when you meet with the reporter tomorrow. I'll be alongside you every step of the way."

OLD FRIENDS

Bob Anderson was escorted into a large, stately, walnut-paneled office by a young, tall, blond secretary. "Mr. Jones will be right in. He asked that you make yourself right at home. May I get you some coffee?"

"No thanks, I'm fine, Miss."

The young woman smiled and extended her hand. "My name is Carolyn. I've been Mr. Jones's secretary for almost eight years. I understand you and he served together in the bureau and actually graduated from Quantico in the same class."

"That's right." Looking around the office at all the career photos on the wall, he added, "I understand that, Merle—excuse me, Mr. Jones—is getting ready to retire himself." Bob walked over to the picture of his graduating class from the FBI Academy. He laughed as he noticed that every one of the new fresh-faced agents in the picture had struck the same official and customary "crotch pose." All of their hands were held low in front of their bodies like a row of soccer players in front of the goal, trying to protect the family jewels from an impending penalty kick from one of the strongest scorers in the league. "This is Merle right here in the third row. That's me standing directly in front of him."

"I know. He pointed you out to me when he asked me to confirm your appointment for this morning. What distinguished-looking young men you all are," she added politely.

"But of course, Mr. Anderson was a lot better looking and in a lot better shape in those days." The rough voice behind them came from the special agent in charge of the New York office, Merle Jones. Bob turned and saw Jones's huge frame step through the doorway. Jones smiled and put his arm around his old friend.

Merle Isaiah Jones, former Arkansas Razorback football legend, was a massive, tough-minded man, well suited to both the regimen and politics of the bureau. He had risen to the top of the heap in the country's largest and most prestigious FBI office. Part of his longevity had much to do with the fact that he knew where all the bureaucratic bodies were buried and had paid homage at the feet of all those who needed to be recognized and stroked along the way. In short, Merle Jones was, above all else, a survivor, a prehistoric throwback to the last years of Hoover's reign of power.

"Come, Bob, and sit down. It's so great to see you again. Tell me, how are you and Kay adapting to retirement?"

"Well, fine, I guess. On some days, I love rolling over and going back to sleep. On others, I miss the thrill of the chase, if you know what I mean."

Jones laughed out loud. "I miss the thrill of the chase myself! I haven't personally tracked down a fugitive in years. I spend way too much of my time now, chasing away the mayor and all the bullshit politicians who all want a piece of my time. I didn't sign up to be a CEO administrator type, but I must say, I'm pretty damn good at it. Did you hear, by the way, I'm pulling the plug myself by the end of the year?"

"Yeah, I heard." Bob paused and tried to shift gears. "I also heard you've officially closed your investigation on the Flight 800 explosion and have adopted the same conclusion as the NTSB."

Jones smiled. "I was wondering when you were going to get to the real purpose of your visit, Bob. I knew it wasn't to squeeze an invite to my retirement party. Tell me, what might your interest be in that file?"

Bob returned the smile. "First of all, I don't need no stinking invite to your party. I know where you live and I'll be there, no matter what. But seriously, Merle, let me tell you why I wanted to see you. It seems someone impersonating one of our agents paid a little visit to your fisherman friend Harley Mathers and threatened to kill him if he didn't shut up about the missile theory."

"Really? Is that a fact? Well, it seems Mathers never bothered to report that piece of information to us. Why do you suppose he didn't want to come in and tell us about that little detail?"

"Actually, Merle, I'm told that Mathers did, in fact, try to report that incident twice but never got a return phone call from one of the RA agents on the island. He was told the agent was transferred to the West Coast."

Jones immediately got defensive. "That's bullshit. Sure we had some personnel changes around that time, but that's not the way we operate. You know that."

"Regardless of the reason, Merle, it looks like that impersonation incident was never followed up on. In any event, as it turns out, the threat on his life was actually carried out a few days ago. Mathers was killed out in Montauk."

"Yeah, I know. I heard. But he wasn't killed, Bob. The idiot blew himself up in a propane fire aboard his boat. He was a drunk, you know."

Anderson ignored the comment and moved forward. "Merle, I'm here on behalf of a fellow former agent, a good friend of mine, Frank Abrams. He's a trial attorney who happens to represent the Mayfair family in a wrongful death suit against TWA. He has evidence that Mathers didn't die in a fire on his boat. He has a witness who says Mathers was shot to death by someone who claimed to be an FBI agent . . . someone by the name of Alfred P. Lyons, badge number 454. The man even displayed what appeared to be valid FBI credentials."

"Whoa there, Bobby! We were told by the Suffolk County Police that Mathers was a victim of an explosion and fire, not a homicide. What exactly do you have that proves otherwise?"

Anderson pulled the lead slug out of his pocket and handed it to Jones. "This .380 slug was fired, we believe, from the same gun that was used by foreign operatives to kill Mathers, not on his boat, but on a beach in Montauk. This particular bullet entered the car door of an extremely reliable eyewitness as it sped away from the scene of the murder. Merle, I can't tell you yet who witnessed this shooting or whose car was involved. I ask that you please give me some room on this."

Jones studied Bob's expression carefully. "I can't imagine what your connection is to this witness, but you do understand, don't you, that this individual is a material witness to a capital crime?"

"Of course. Believe me, Merle, everything will fall into place very soon. It won't be long. More importantly, I think if you follow up with the Suffolk County Police, you'll find that the body aboard the boat was never forensically identified. It was so badly burned, I doubt whether anyone took the trouble to look for another possible cause of death—like maybe a few more of these, fired at close range," he said pointing to the slug in Jones's hand.

"Look, Bob, I'm not saying that if we had handled that crime scene and ordered that autopsy, we wouldn't have done a more thorough job, including dental and medical record comparisons. But let's talk some common sense here. You're telling me that a body fitting Mathers's general description in size and height was found alone aboard his fishing boat but that the facial features were burned beyond recognition. I'm not going to second-guess the police for coming to their conclusion, even if the way they got to that conclusion was a little sloppy and not up to our own standards."

"Merle, my point is that no one, least of all the medical examiner, knows for sure to this day whose body that was. Our eyewitness says he saw Mathers killed on the beach only minutes before the boat explosion. There's no way his body could have ended up on the boat in that time frame. Do you think that he was beamed aboard by Captain Kirk? The bottom line is that the so-called official identification of the body would never hold up in court under those circumstances, and I think you know that."

Jones just rolled his eyes, ignored the sarcasm, and changed the subject. "Bob, let me check on that name and badge number real quick for you. Hold on a second."

Jones picked up the phone. "Carolyn, would you ask Agent Lynch to come in here now, please."

There was a crisp knock at the door as Jones looked up. "Enter."

A tall, middle-aged man with a crew cut stepped up to the desk. "Yes, sir."

"Jay, I want you personally, not one of your team, to do me a favor. I want you to run this name, as well as this possible badge number, against all active and archived records of bureau personnel. Don't tell anyone else what you're doing or why. When you've done that, do the same with CIA and military intelligence. By the way . . . Agent Jay Lynch, I'd like you to meet retired agent Bob Anderson." The men shook hands briefly as Jones handed Lynch a piece of paper.

"Where do you think this is this going, Bob? Do you have any theory as to how Mathers's death could possibly have anything to do with our Flight 800 investigation?"

Bob measured his words carefully. "Merle, isn't it true that Mathers was the most vocal and insistent eyewitness that this was a missile attack? As I recall, every time you guys sneezed, Mathers went running to the press. He was like a modern-day John the Baptist crying in the desert. In fact, he even had a kind of cult following out east. He was sort of a combination of crazy and annoying kind of guy. Am I right?"

"Yeah, that's him. Bottom line, though, we determined that he just wasn't reliable. And every bit of the forensic evidence ruled out a missile. Look, I'm not telling you something you didn't already have access to in the preliminary report. It's been well publicized."

"Merle, all I keep hearing about Mathers is that he was 'unreliable.' Tell me, did you conclude that he was unreliable before or after NTSB decided that there was no sign of an external explosion?"

Jones was obviously annoyed by the question. "And what the hell does that mean?"

"Look, if you had some corroborative evidence that he was really drunk that night, or even certifiably crazy, that's one thing. That would make his testimony, by definition, unreliable. But if he wasn't drunk or nuts and you decided not to give him any credibility because what he swore he witnessed that night makes no sense to you personally, well, that's something entirely different. If you dismissed him, not because he was affirmatively contradicted by someone else, but because what he said made no sense to you in light of the absence of physical evidence of a missile, then that changes the whole dynamic of the investigation. Wouldn't you agree?"

Jones was reddening a little under the collar. "Are you saying my investigation lacked integrity?"

"No, not at all. What I'm saying is that just because one set of eyes happens to notice something that goes unnoticed by another ten witnesses, doesn't mean that the lone witness is unreliable or wrong in his description."

"Bob, I'm a damn good agent. There are times, when the evidence locker is dry, that you have to rely on gut instinct and follow the proverbial hunch. You've been there. How many cases have you broken wide open because you followed your nose and not a rote set of facts? Plenty of times, I would guess.

"In fact, do you remember the last case we worked together in Miami? That guy Milton Niport? He was the infamous FedEx serial killer, that cold-blooded dick who lined up those seven employees on their knees and put a bullet into the back of each of their heads. The only partial description we got on him was from that one woman who somehow survived her head wound. The point is, we had nothing . . . absolutely nothing, except an anonymous tip that he might be coming in on a flight from LA within a twenty-four-hour window. I remember you had this nagging hunch that he would try to slip into town when the airport was really quieted down for the night. You forced me to stay at the damned airport till after midnight. Sure enough, there he was, large as life, strolling out of that gangway tunnel on the last flight. We took him down to the ground and cuffed him. Do you remember what this 'armed and dangerous' killer did when you identified yourself as an FBI agent, Bob?"

"Yeah, he bawled like a baby."

"Right you are. Now, some would call that bust pure luck. But the funny thing about luck though, Bob, is that the more years you spend in hunting down fugitives and studying human nature, or for that matter, working in any other line of work, the luckier you seem to get. Do you get my point?"

"I do, and I agree with you, Merle. But one of the things I've learned over the years in studying human behavior is that the more people who come forward as witnesses, the harder it is to get a useful consensus about what they really saw and heard. I know for a fact that you interviewed hundreds of people in this case."

"And what's your point?" said Jones.

"Merle, do you remember what happened in one of our first law classes at the academy, when most of us were bored out of our skulls and half of us were nodding off? I remember it like it was yesterday. It was a sweltering day in August, and there was no air-conditioning. Suddenly, someone burst into the room and attacked the instructor. This guy was in and out of the classroom in less than five seconds. Do you remember the point of the exercise? There were thirty new recruits writing down thirty different physical descriptions of the attacker, who, by the way, turned out to be an FBI firearms instructor. Ford, I think, was his name. Anyway, you were the only agent in the class who described this guy with short, curly, red hair. Turns out he had no hair at all. He was a shaved head. Do you remember that?"

Jones was getting visibly annoyed at his old friend and a bit embarrassed over Bob's trip down memory lane. "Tie this up for me, will you, Bob?"

"Merle, I'm not saying I would not have come to the same conclusion as you under the same circumstances. But, and you know this full well, some people, including well-trained engineers, tend to see what they want to see. Or sometimes, even what they think other people expect them to see under the circumstances. Are you following me?"

Anderson saw the frown on Jones's face and moved the discussion along a little faster. "But I digress. This is what has been really nagging at me. In the case of Mathers, what in the hell would be the motivation in anyone both threatening and then killing one of the few purported eyewitnesses who insists this was a missile attack, other than to shut him up?"

"Come on, Bob, there could be a dozen unrelated reasons someone wanted to do the old man harm. Could have been a gambling loss or a drug deal turned ugly. Besides, technically speaking, I still have no evidence that Mathers was even murdered, despite what you're now telling me. Look, as far as the Suffolk County Police Department is concerned, this was an accidental propane-tank explosion. Nothing more. What the hell would you have me do? Ask the court for an order of exhumation, dig up his body, and try to pull some slugs out of him? What would I put in my sworn supporting affidavit to the court? A little bird told me he heard from an unnamed witness that Mathers was shot by unnamed, unidentifiable assailants? Are you kidding me?"

"Fair enough. But what if I were to get you a real eyewitness to not only the murder, but also the launching of the missile? Someone far more credible and reliable than all those inconsistent people you interviewed."

"We combed every bloody backwater on Long Island from Manhattan to Montauk, Bob. There's no one out there we haven't taken a statement from."

"Really? How about a witness with a heavy military-combat background, a pilot who knows from his own personal experience, in avoiding hundreds of them over North Vietnam, what a SAM missile really looks like in flight?"

"We interviewed every pilot and navigator who was in the air that night, within a three-hundred-mile radius of Flight 800. Not one of them saw a missile profile or plume trail rising from the ocean. Period."

"Well, unfortunately, there was one pilot in particular that you never had a chance to interview. What if I were to bring this witness to you? Would you follow up and reopen the investigation?"

Jones stared at Bob across the large oak desk and rubbed his big hands together. "I don't know exactly what you're up to, Bob Anderson, but I know you well enough to be sure that you wouldn't come to me and go out on a limb like this if you didn't think you had something substantial. Bring me that witness, Bob. If he's as credible as you say he is, I'll reopen my investigation. I'll have to get approval from the director, but I doubt that will be a problem."

"I apologize for being so secretive, Merle. But a lot of what I am able to do here will depend on some basic rules of attorney-client privilege. I have to speak to several people and get permission to pursue this. You'll have to cut me a little slack on this."

At that moment, Agent Lynch reappeared at the door. He looked quietly at Anderson and then at Jones, waiting for some direction.

"It's OK, Jay, Agent Anderson here has sufficient clearance. Give us what you have."

"I searched all the relevant databases, FBI, CIA, all the armed services intelligence agencies, NTSB, even the White House National Security folks, and there is no such person on any federal payroll. The badge number doesn't match up with anything real or active either.

"But there is one interesting thing I did find however, sir."

"Really? What's that?"

"That phone number you gave me matches up with a retired listing in DC. It used to ring at the Syrian embassy years ago."

"Thanks, Jay. Keep all this to yourself OK?"

"I knew it!" Bob mumbled under his breath to himself.

Jones missed Bob's comment. "Look, Bob I know the best the NTSB could come up with was a 'probable cause' theory, involving heated fuel vapor and a rogue spark in the center-wing tank, but I had hundreds of experts a lot smarter than me telling me there was no evidence of an external source of ignition. So let's keep this real simple. No external ignition source, no missile. No missile, no crime. My job is to determine if a crime was committed. I found none, so I closed out my investigation. End of story. If you have something or someone credible—and I emphasize the word 'credible'—to counter all these engineers and forensic experts, bring it to me and I will run with it. Agreed?"

Anderson rose to his feet. "Thank you, Merle. I knew I could count on your help."

"I haven't helped you with anything yet, Bob. The ball is your court, big-time. I'm not going to lift a finger to reopen this thing unless and until you deliver. Please don't forget that."

"Understood." Anderson started toward the door and turned around.

"Oh, there is one more thing I need to ask you, and you can tell me to go to hell if you want."

Jones smiled. "I know. You want an engraved invitation to my retirement party. Is that it?"

"Seriously, Merle, here's my final question. We have reason to believe, since we now know this so-called agent's name and badge number are fictitious, that the person who threatened and killed Mathers—"

"Allegedly, Bob. Allegedly threatened and killed Mathers. Let's not get ahead of ourselves."

Anderson plodded ahead. "We believe that this person, whether it turns out he is a murderer or not, is some kind of foreign operative, maybe Middle Eastern. My question is this. Did your investigation develop any leads or information from any of the usual foreign informant sources?"

"Information? About what? The fuel-tank configuration and the hundreds of miles of complex electrical wiring in a Boeing 747?"

"No, come on, Merle. I'm serious,. I'm talking about information contained in our 137 folders. You know . . . informant files. The kind of information that would suggest that this may have been a missile attack put together by a foreign terrorist cell, regardless of how remote you may have considered the possibility at the time. I'm also talking about the kind of information that would suggest that it was a specific individual on that flight, and not the plane itself, who may have been targeted."

For the first time since the two old friends sat down together, Bob thought he saw Jones's face and body flinch ever so slightly. The warm facial features were now gone, replaced with tightening brows and pursed lips.

Jones folded his arms and leaned back in his chair. "Even if there were any foreign informant sources in our investigation, you know I can't discuss any of that with you, Bob. If there were any such sources, and I'm not saying there were, we would have investigated every last one of them thoroughly. What I can tell you is that my counterintelligence agents are constantly developing foreign informants. As you can imagine, a lot of them these days happen to be Middle Eastern, for reasons I don't need to point out to you. That's no secret. But as you well know, having served in COINTEL yourself, 90 percent of these mutts turn out to be lying sacks of shit. They're either looking to throw us off our game by disseminating and planting faulty, unreliable information or trying to take advantage of the Bureau's generous cash giveaway program. I can't decide which group I hate more.

"But here's the bottom line, Bob. Once our experts were satisfied, forensically speaking, that there could not have been any missile involved, any related informant information we may have developed, no matter how enticing, would have become academic. It would have been of very little value in pursuing."

"Yes, I know that, but—"

Jones cut Bob off quickly. "That's all I'm going to say on the subject, Bob. Please respect my position."

Anderson held up his hands apologetically in front of him. "Of course. I understand."

"So remember what I said, Bob. The ball is in your court."

"I'm aware of that, Merle. I'll get back to you as soon as I can. You have my word."

As he left the downtown FBI building, Bob Anderson was now 100 percent convinced that buried somewhere in the extensive Flight 800 investigation records in the database, there existed an official FBI 302 interview form with information that might very well not only identify Mathers's killers but possibly reveal who masterminded the missile attack. And if they got really lucky, it might even point to the names of those involved in what Anderson was beginning to suspect was a possible cover-up. If he weren't already retired, he was sure he would have found a way to access it himself. But that would have to wait for another day and another opportunity.

A POINT OF NO RETURN

The director of the FBI was ushered into the Oval Office as the president rose to greet him with a warm smile. "Good morning, Lou. My chief of staff tells me you needed to see me right away. What's going on?"

"Good morning, Mr. President. Let me get right to it if you don't mind. Late yesterday afternoon, I had a communication from the New York SAC, Merle Jones, about a subject in which I know you have a particular interest."

"It must be important for the director himself to come all the way up here to the White House, especially on a Saturday morning. What subject is that?"

"Well, sir, do you remember the PLO official who gave us copies of all his organization's records at his debriefing in the New York FBI Office, just before the Flight 800 disaster?"

"Yeah, I remember. He's dead, isn't he? Wasn't he aboard that flight?"

"He may be dead, but his files are very much alive."

"Meaning what?"

"We have reason to believe that those PLO records, including their extensive donor lists, could soon be subpoenaed into the US District Court in Manhattan in a high profile lawsuit against TWA by an attorney named Frank Abrams. Who, by the way, happens to be one of our former FBI agents."

The president's face reddened as he shifted uncomfortably in his seat. "I thought I ordered those documents classified as top secret. Has there been a leak somewhere in your organization?"

The director, taking serious umbrage at that remark, stared coldly at the president. "No, sir, I don't believe so."

"Listen, as I told you many months ago when we first discussed this situation, those records are to remain highly classified and are not to be released to anyone until we decide what to do about them. Am I clear on that?"

"Mr. President, we haven't yet even publicly acknowledged that these records exist. Abrams, I suspect, is fishing at this point. SAC Jones recently met with another retired agent, Bob Anderson, who is a close friend of Abrams. Agent Anderson used to work in counterintelligence and, like most experienced agents, has developed a heightened, intuitive sense of smell, if you follow me. He probably has a hunch that Abrams might be onto something and is obviously helping his old friend. He just doesn't know exactly what that something looks like . . . yet."

"What makes you say that?"

"Well, according to Jones, Anderson's questions implied that he's looking for a particular file containing information obtained from foreign informants, having some direct connection with Flight 800 and our aircraft accident report. And as I have already reported to you, several such connections do, in fact, exist. Including that Iranian who called the New York office a week before the explosion. Then of course, there is the matter of the PLO informant who was killed aboard that flight, not to mention his records."

The president's voice grew tense. "It all sounds very vague at this point, Lou. I think it would be best if Abrams is allowed to continue to flounder in the dark. Let him serve his subpoena. Without anything much more specific, like the name of the PLO official who provided those records or the name of the file itself, you'll probably be able to fight the subpoena as overly broad and maybe even quash it. Correct?"

"Sir, you've said before that those documents are to be protected as a matter of national security. Now that the man is dead and his documents have been studied by our own counterintelligence team and the boys at

Langley, it's pretty clear, at least to us at the bureau, that they pose no real threat to national security. Do you still really believe that they should be considered highly classified?"

The president's voice betrayed sharp anger as he exploded. "Listen to me carefully, Lou. We've talked about all of this before. I do *not* want those records released to the public, under any circumstances. Have I made myself clear?"

"With all respect, Mr. President, that decision will not be made by me, but by a federal judge who will have to address the subpoena if and when it's filed. And unless you give me some tangible, logical basis for a credible national security argument, something that will stand up in court, I'm not inclined to fight a subpoena if I should be served with one."

The president raised his voice, held up his index finger, and pointed it menacingly at the director. "This is not a matter for debate, sir. Do you understand me?"

"Mr. President, I understand, but—"

"There are no buts on this one, Lou. You have your directive. Now carry it out, damn it."

The two men stared at each other in silence. The president shifted his gaze out into the Rose Garden. "I would imagine by now that all of the PLO documents on that floppy disc have been scanned and are in your computer database, correct?"

"That's correct, sir."

"And the duplicate original documents that were handed over by the PLO informant in New York? Where are they being kept now?"

"They're being physically stored in the basement of the New York office as part of the official investigation of the Flight 800 explosion."

"I want you to remove the PLO records from the overall Flight 800 investigation file and reassign them to another filing classification . . . maybe some other nonrelated informant folder. That way, you won't have to lie when you tell Abrams that there's no such document that is officially part of the aircraft accident report file."

44The director decided to toss in all his chips. "Sir, I don't believe you've ever really practiced law, so let me share some legal realities with you. In my considered opinion, as a former federal prosecutor myself, there is no judge in the world who is going to conclude that those records pose any risk to national security—certainly not great enough to override the plaintiff's right to fair discovery in the TWA trial. The simple truth, Mr. President, is that the only thing at risk here are those idiot friends of yours whose names appear on that money donor list to the PLO, and you know it!"

The president, by now, was red faced, as he sputtered his words. "The only thing I know is that you serve at my specific discretion, or do you need a civics lesson in the powers of the office of the president?"

With that, the director stood up and tightened the knot of his tie. "Apparently, the only one in this room who needs a refresher course in the

American Constitution is you. This meeting is finished, sir. Thank you for giving me the opportunity to clear the air. I'll let myself out."

"I'll tell you what's finished! You are, you goddamn insubordinate ingrate!"

As the director stood and started to walk out of the room, he stopped momentarily, turned away from the door slowly, and faced the president. He walked back, leaned against the edge of the Resolute desk, and spoke with surprising restraint and calm. "If you want my resignation, just call my secretary and ask for it. But understand this, sir. If you force me out of office over this political bullshit, to protect some of your cronies on the Hill, I will not fade away quietly into the night. The constitutional and political firestorm you will have set off will make the Flight 800 explosion look like a fucking Chinese firecracker."

He moved even closer to the president's startled face. "Now, is that clear?"

THE OLD GRAY LADY AIN'T WHAT SHE USED TO BE

Michael Ketchum was led into the conference room where Liam, Frank Abrams, and Lee Mayfair were seated at the huge glass-topped table. Abrams got up to greet the *Times* reporter. "Come in, Mr. Ketchum. Please sit down and relax. I have a pot of fresh coffee over here at the end of the table if you're so inclined. Please help yourself."

"Mr. Abrams, thank you for agreeing to this meeting. Liam, Mrs. Mayfair, it's an honor to finally meet you both." Ketchum sat down, opened his backpack, and wasted no time as he took out a small tape recorder and put it down on the table.

"Put that thing back in your bag, Mike," said Liam. "This will all be off the record until I say otherwise. If you don't agree to that, this meeting ends right now."

Ketchum was taken aback and was visibly annoyed. "Liam, this is pretty standard practice. We can all save a lot of time if I don't have to write down every word. With a recorder, there is no misunderstanding as to who said what to whom. It protects all of us, actually. Besides, I can't write my notes that fast while focusing on my questions."

"Well then, maybe you should have taken shorthand in college, Mike, because nothing will be tape-recorded here this morning."

Abrams was surprised at Liam's forcefulness. "I'm afraid I have to agree with Liam, Mr. Ketchum. We asked you to come in today to clear up some of the issues you raised with Liam the other day about Harley Mathers. I understand you have some information you would like to share with us. Apparently, you believe that Liam was the person seen asking questions about Mathers the day he died out in Montauk."

Ketchum laughed out loud. "I thought I was the one who's supposed to ask the questions here and not the other way around?"

Liam spoke up. "Why don't we both lay our cards out on the table and see what we can come up with, OK? Let me start the ball rolling."

"Be my guest," Ketchum said with a forced smile.

"But first, Mr. Ketchum, I need to lay down some ground rules, if you don't mind. I need to know that you and I are on the same page."

"What do you have in mind, Liam?"

"I am giving you an exclusive interview here. You're the only media outlet I am talking to. In return, I want your promise that you won't discuss anything I'm about to tell you with anyone and that you won't print anything about this until I give you the OK. In the meanwhile, I will not speak with any other reporter or news service. You will not be scooped. Those are my terms. Will you accept them?"

Ketchum looked down at this notes and picked up his pen. "Agreed."

"You say you spoke to someone who described a young, preppy-looking guy driving a black Jeep and that this person was seen asking where he could find Mathers's boat. Before I answer your obvious first question, I want to know how, and from whom, you got that information."

Ketchum slowly put the recorder away in his bag. "It was the young bartender. He overheard the entire conversation between you—excuse me, the preppy dude—and that old guy at the pool table. He described both the kid and the car to a tee."

"Well then, as you correctly surmised, that person was, in fact, me. I asked an old toothless guy playing pool where I could find the *Northern Star*, Mathers's boat. That was the extent of my so-called 'snooping.' The boat was all the way down at the other end of the lake. I found him aboard and spoke to him briefly."

Ketchum was scribbling on a paper pad. "Do you mind telling me why you came all the way out to the East End to see this guy?"

"Mathers was one of the few outspoken eyewitnesses to what some have described as a missile that struck Flight 800. But excuse me, you already knew that. I contacted him in person on the spur of the moment."

"OK. But why? For what purpose?"

"I recently found an audio cassette tape of a phone message my father left me. It was a call he made to me from his seat aboard that plane, on an aircraft phone, within minutes before it blew up. The tape had been essentially lost since the day of the crash twenty months ago, until recently."

"What does that tape have to do with Mathers?"

"Mr. Ketchum, before I tell you what's on that tape, may I remind you of our agreement? The reason I don't want you to divulge anything I'm about to tell you is that the FBI has to examine the tape and verify its authenticity."

Ketchum's curiosity was about to explode as he spoke quickly. "OK. Understood. Now, what about the tape?"

"On this cassette tape, my father confirms seeing the same missile Mathers saw that night, except he saw it at twelve thousand feet in the air out the plane's window, rising up from the water, from the deck of an oil freighter. Mathers saw the same attack, except only from the other perspective, from below."

Ketchum appeared stunned. "Jesus Christ! Are you serious? You know I have to ask you to play that tape for me, right?"

"One step at a time, Mike. I wanted to see and talk with Mathers in person. I wanted to check for myself if the reports about him being an unreliable drunk were true."

"Were they?"

"Not in my judgment. He was sober, logical, intelligent . . . and, more to the point, very frightened."

"Frightened? About what?"

"He told me he had been threatened. He was told that if he didn't stop making so much noise in the press about a missile, the same missile, by the way, which the government had already insisted did not even exist, he would be hurt."

"So are you saying the explosion on his boat that night was no accident?"

"Mr. Ketchum, Mathers was not killed on his boat. He didn't die in that fire."

"What? And exactly how do you know that?"

"Because I saw him shot to death on the beach not far from the docks, only minutes before I saw his boat go up in flames. That couldn't have been Mathers's body on that boat. It was physically impossible."

"Holy shit! When did you report all this to the police?"

Liam sheepishly lowered his eyes. "I haven't done that yet. But I intend to do so very soon."

Ketchum shot a quick glance over at Abrams.

Abrams's response was quick. "The law requires notification within a reasonable period, Mr. Ketchum. By my calculation, that clock is winding down but is still technically running. The only crime committed here, as I see it, was the murder of Harley Mathers."

"You realize that this is one unbelievable story, don't you? How does all this tie into the FBI and NTSB investigation? And who exactly threatened him?"

Abrams glanced over at Liam and then back at Ketchum. "We're still working on that. I hope to have some more information for you in the next few days. I can't prove anything yet, but we think that the shooters were foreign operatives of some kind. We think they were trying to prevent the feds from resurrecting the missile theory, for reasons we don't yet fully understand."

By this time, Ketchum had developed a serious case of writer's cramp. He shook his right hand and tried to regain some circulation in his fingers.

Liam took advantage of the hiatus. "Now, I have a question for you, Mr. Ketchum."

Ketchum unintentionally added to the palpable tension in the room by misspeaking. "Shoot. Excuse me, I mean, go ahead."

"What do you intend to do with the information you learned about my visit to Mathers?"

Ketchum put his pen down and looked pensively at his notes. "It seems to me, Liam, that's an issue you're going to have to work out with your attorney. Mr. Abrams appears to have a plan to fix that problem, at least for the moment. That is, provided that you don't let any grass grow under your feet, if you know what I mean. If you are asking me if I'm going to run to the Suffolk County Police to report this conversation, I figure that would be a wasted and duplicative effort. Wouldn't you agree, Mr. Abrams?"

Abrams nodded. "I couldn't agree more."

Ketchum redirected his attention. "Mrs. Mayfair, now I need to ask you a question, if you don't mind. That is, if your attorney will permit me."

Abrams fired a surprised look at Ketchum. "About what?"

"Every major investigation always seems to have not just one, but several conspiracy theories spinning around them at the same time. Don't be surprised if someone suggests out loud that the Mayfair family's interest in a sizable verdict against TWA would have been helped along considerably by the death of Mathers. In other words, those two events are not exactly mutually compatible."

Abrams shot Ketchum a nasty look. "What the hell do you mean by that?"

"Think about it. The less said publicly by this so-called screwball about a terrorist missile theory and the less attention drawn to this audiotape, the easier and the more likely it is to focus a jury's attention on the other 'official' cause of the crash of Flight 800. I have to admit, when I first learned that Liam was the one last seen with Mathers before he was killed, this thought occurred to me too. Do I have to draw it out on a blackboard?"

Lee Mayfair finally spoke. "Mr. Ketchum, that's absurd. My son had absolutely no reason to cause harm to Mr. Mathers. I can say that with certainty because he had already made up his mind, even before he went out to Montauk to talk with Mr. Mathers, that he would have to face the decision to discontinue our lawsuit against TWA. I've listened to the audiotape of my murdered husband. It is compelling beyond words. I'm now convinced, as is Liam, that it was a missile, not a wiring defect that brought that plane down. As to how, why, and who was involved, I have no idea. Those questions don't affect our decision to discontinue the lawsuit."

Ketchum sat silently with his mouth hanging open. "This is unreal! Do you realize what you're saying? Are you seriously considering walking away from millions of dollars by exposing this tape?" He turned and looked directly at Liam. "You could have destroyed it in seconds and no one would have been any the wiser! I'm dumbfounded!"

Liam remained silent.

"I've got to hear this tape, Liam."

"Not now, Mr. Ketchum. It has to be analyzed by the FBI lab people first, to be 100 percent sure it's authentic and hasn't been tampered with. When you do finally hear it, please understand you will be one of many other reporters and news outlets being given simultaneous access to it. I'm not going to give you an exclusive on the tape. You already have your exclusive in this interview. No one else will be allowed to interview anyone in the Mayfair family except you. Provided, of course, that you stick to our agreement. If you don't do that, I can't and won't give you anything more."

Ketchum packed up his notes. "I have no problem with that, Liam."

As the meeting broke up and Ketchum walked out of the office, Lee Mayfair turned to Abrams. "I don't trust that man. His eyes were shifting all over the place when he spoke."

Abrams took Lee's hand. "Don't worry, Lee, we'll get out in front of him."

MOVING UP THE CHAIN OF COMMAND

Early the next morning, Frank Abrams, Bob Anderson, and Liam sat together in the outer waiting room of the New York SAC's office. As they sat in silence, Frank smiled and looked over at Liam. "You know, Liam, I would have thought your father raised you better than that," pointing to his Red Sox hat.

Liam was taken off guard. "What do you mean?"

Frank laughed aloud. "Liam, I was born and raised in the Bronx. What do you *think* I mean? Even Mr. Anderson here is a true-blue Yankees fan. Right, Bob? I can picture old JW spinning in his grave. Isn't it a little treasonous for his son to have defected to the Red Sox? Didn't your dad bring up his boys as proper and loyal Yankee fans?"

Bob chuckled and quickly piled on. "You're deep in pinstripe country, Liam. You may get away with the hat for a while here in Manhattan, but don't go up to the Bronx for a night game if you know what I mean. I'm with Frank. Yankee loyalty is a father-son thing. Sort of like an inheritance." No sooner had Bob spoken the words that Frank began to regret their chiding. Suddenly, he had a clearer insight into the tense father-son dynamic that must have festered between them in the years before JW's death. *The strained relationship that so concerned Lee Mayfair must have even spilled over into sports,* Frank thought to himself. How sad it all was. Frank thought of changing the subject, but it was too late.

Liam suddenly grew very defensive. "Yeah, well, this is the year Boston will have its revenge. You heard we picked up the Cy Young winner Pedro Martinez from the Expos during the off-season, didn't you? He's the hottest pitcher in baseball, you know. Boston will demolish your Yankees and the AL East this year. You wait and see what happens."

"Tell you what, Liam. Let's make a friendly wager. If the Yankees win the World Series this year, which they will, you'll give me that silly cap so I can dispose of it properly. On the other hand, if Boston wins the pennant this year, you can have all my Yankee gear, including my Mickey Mantle autographed bat." He leaned over and shook Liam's hand. "Agreed?"

"Hell, yes! You've got a deal."

Just at that moment, Merle Jones's secretary entered the room. "Mr. Jones will see you gentlemen now. Please follow me."

As they were ushered into Jones's stately and spacious office, Anderson spoke first. "Thank you, Merle, for seeing us on such short notice, especially so soon after our last meeting."

SAC Jones rose to his feet to greet his guests. "It's my pleasure, Bob. Well, who do we have here?" he said looking at Liam and Abrams and then down over the edge of his glasses at the guest log on his desk.

"Merle Jones, I would like to introduce you to Frank Abrams and his client, Liam Mayfair, the son of J. W. Mayfair, who, as you know, was one of the passengers who died aboard Flight 800. They have something they would like for you to hear."

Jones responded quickly and with a bit of annoyance. "Bob, before we get into any of this, is it all right to speak freely in front of your friends? About our first meeting?"

"Of course."

"First of all, I believe the last time we spoke, Bob, you said you had a live eyewitness . . . a navy pilot, who saw a missile blow up Flight 800. Is this your combat-tested pilot? The son of one of the victims? What exactly are you trying to do here?"

Anderson suppressed a smile. "Merle, I never said my eyewitness was a *live* witness." He walked over to Abrams, who handed him a cassette tape.

"Bob, I'm not following any of this. What are you up to? Speak plainly, for God's sake."

Holding up the tape in front of him, Anderson said, "This is the voice of John Mayfair, recorded on Liam's answering machine minutes before JW was killed in the explosion of Flight 800. I've brought you the original and only copy of this recording. I'd like to play this for you right now. It hasn't been edited or enhanced in any way."

"Wait a minute, Bob. Before I listen to it, I'd like to know who else has had access to it, if you don't mind," said Jones.

Liam answered. "The only people who have heard this tape are my immediate family, my fiancée, Mr. Abrams here, and Agent Anderson, who just heard it for the first time an hour ago. I met with a *New York Times* reporter yesterday and told him basically what's on the tape, but I refused to let him listen to it. You're the first law enforcement official I've given it to."

"And why is the *Times* involved in this?" asked Jones, with some measure of contempt in his voice.

Abrams interjected. "We'll explain that to you in a minute, but first I'd like for you to listen to the tape."

Jones sat back down in his chair and folded his arms. "I'm all ears."

Liam inserted the tape and hit the play button. He turned the volume up to its highest level. As the tape played through the very personal message from JW to his estranged son, Frank noticed that Jones looked very uncomfortable as he squirmed and fidgeted in his seat. His body language shouted impatience. Finally, as the voice of J. W. Mayfair grew loud and frightened and the screams of the other passengers poured through the speakers, Jones squinted and leaned forward.

At the end of the tape, Jones looked over at Anderson, raised his eyebrows, and said, "Well, this certainly could cast a slightly different light on the situation, couldn't it, Bob?"

"Yeah, you might say that, Merle. That's probably the understatement of the year."

Jones looked over at Abrams. "Please explain the delay in bringing me this tape, counselor. This would have been nice for me to have in the first few weeks of the investigation, don't you think?"

Abrams ignored the sarcasm. "The simple truth is that this tape sat in the trunk of Liam's fiancée's car for nearly twenty months, totally forgotten and ignored. Why and how that happened is not important. There was nothing sinister involved."

"Fair enough, we'll get back to that later. Do you mind if I jump ahead a little and ask you exactly what was discussed with the *Times* reporter?"

"No, not at all. Right after Liam listened to the tape out at the family home on Shelter Island, he reread the preliminary NTSB report, got the name of the fisherman witness Harley Mathers, and spontaneously drove out to Montauk to find him and talk with him. Do you recall who he is?"

"Sure I do. But what does he have to do with the *Times* reporter?"

Abrams said, "Well, as I'm sure you may already know, Mathers was reported killed in an explosion and fire aboard his boat recently."

Jones nodded. "I'm aware of that."

"Our young Liam here was the one who got the name and shield number of the so-called agent who visited Mathers. That information, on the scrap of paper I showed you, turned out to be bogus, as you'll recall . . . thanks to your help."

"Go on, please."

Abrams turned to Liam. "Liam, why don't you finish the story?"

"Mr. Jones, Mathers told me he had been threatened that if he continued to talk publicly about a missile attack on Flight 800, he would be hurt. I met him out there on the beach after dark to retrieve that piece of paper. That's when I saw two men kill him with what I think were semi-automatic weapons. I believe Mr. Anderson gave you a bullet fired from of one those guns. I dug it out of my driver's side car door."

Jones held up his hand. "I'm sorry to interrupt you, Liam." Looking over at Anderson, he said, "I don't mean to put a damper on things here, Bob, but what you seem to have brought me today is a witness to the possible murder of a discredited witness with a history of alcoholism . . . at least according to our investigation. On top of that, you've given us a voice-recorded statement, albeit from a now-deceased witness, of what appeared to him to be a missile plume rising vertically from the surface of the ocean off eastern Long Island. I have to admit, this recording is very dramatic stuff, especially coming from a former navy Intruder pilot who ought to know about such things on a firsthand basis. But how do you, or anyone else for that matter, explain the glaring absence of any physical evidence of a missile detonation?"

"Who says there has to be detonation, Merle?"

Jones realized the trap he had just set for himself and tried to squirm out of it. "Look, I realize that NTSB has already looked at that issue in depth. But here's what you haven't seemed to consider yet. Even without detonation, there still has to be some significant impact by the missile with some part of the plane that has some fuel-ignition potential. There wasn't any obvious metal deformation anywhere on that plane. Nowhere. Nothing consistent with a projectile striking it. And more importantly, there were absolutely none of the missile fragments you would expect to find in the wreckage field, even without detonation."

Bob grinned and said, "Well then, Merle, it seems to me that at the very least, your experts are just as stumped as the rest of us."

"What the hell does that mean?"

"It means that their overheated fuel vapor and wiring defect explanation is just another theory . . . a theory no more credible than any other involving a missile at this point. In fact, from what I hear, NTSB couldn't even replicate their theory in a controlled mock-up experiment. So I'd say the score in the battle of the forensic experts is pretty well dead even.

However, after this tape is exposed and the truth about Mathers' murder comes out, it will no longer be tied."

"And what exactly is your point?"

"As I see it, Merle, this Mathers piece of the puzzle and all of the devious, far-ranging implications it holds, could very well be the tie breaker . . . at least in the court of public opinion."

Jones sat pensively for a few more seconds. "I don't prosecute my cases in the court of public opinion, Bob. The press manages to screw that up pretty well on its own." After a long pause, he asked, "So what exactly is your next move, Mr. Abrams? Do you really plan to expose that tape publicly?"

"Whether I make it public or not, the information on it changes everything, Merle."

Bob interrupted and said, "Do you mind if I ask you a question, Merle?"

"Of course not."

"I seem to remember reading some interesting intel about some American Stinger shoulder-fired missiles falling into the hands of the bad guys in Afghanistan after the war with Soviets."

"Yeah, that's true. What about them?"

"Well, assuming some wacko terrorist managed to come up with one, were they still capable of detonating after all those years of sitting in some damp cave?"

Jones rolled his eyes. "How the hell would I know, Bob? I'm no ordnance expert."

"Are you saying that you and your team never considered that possibility, Merle?"

Hoping to get Bob off the topic, Jones said, "But aren't we getting a little far afield here?"

Abrams took the cue and tried to move the discussion beyond the academic and into something a little more pragmatic. "Look, I think it's only fair to give you a heads up about something coming your way in a matter of days. As the attorney for the Mayfair family in their suit against TWA, we will be issuing subpoenas for not just the entire FBI aircraft accident report file and all the supporting interviews and exhibits, but specifically any information that may have been obtained from foreign sources concerning that flight. And when I say foreign sources, I'm referring not only to your customary contacts, but also to anyone who could be considered a non-American informant. I understand Mr. Anderson may have mentioned something about that to you."

Jones bristled for a brief moment. "Mr. Abrams, you're free to subpoena anything you think is relevant to your case. I don't know specifically what you may be looking for, but I can tell you the bureau will not look kindly on what may appear to be a fishing expedition. May I ask what the basis is for a request for foreign informant information?"

"Well, for starters, there is certainly enough circumstantial evidence, based on conversation between Liam and Mathers, to suggest that the men who threatened and then killed Mathers were likely foreign operatives of some kind. After all, as you've already determined, even though they claimed to be FBI agents, we now know they certainly did not work for our government."

"Is there anything else?" Jones asked curtly, not wishing to do anything to further this discussion.

"Yes, there is. Getting back to the tape, we also know the odds are excellent that the kind of freighter described by John Mayfair in his message was most likely of foreign, not American, registry. That's just a simple reality in today's ocean commerce. And foreign registry usually means a foreign crew. That alone should be enough to convince a federal judge to sign a duces tecum subpoena for foreign informant sources and all related 302 reports. That's assuming, of course, that the bureau followed up on any such leads. And that they did so with the bureau's customary level of thoroughness and meticulous professionalism."

Abrams paused, stared directly at Jones, and let his words pour over him slowly. "That's a given, right?" His contrived flattery was not lost on the New York SAC, whose face by now had turned a bright red.

After some more awkward silence, Jones looked at his watch and stood up. "Would you folks excuse me for a few minutes, please? I have a prescheduled phone conference at noon on another very important matter. I apologize. It shouldn't take that long. I'll be back as soon as possible."

Jones walked out of the room, closed the door behind him, and lowered his voice as he approached his secretary. "Carolyn, get me the director on a secure line ASAP and put the call into the conference room, please. Tell him it's urgent."

Back in Jones's office, Frank, Bob, and Liam all looked at each other with puzzled stares.

"Are you buying that 'I have another phone conference' thing?" said Frank. "He's acting like a horse who's been spooked by a snake. Whoever he's 'scheduled' to talk to, I think they're about to discuss us and this tape. I wouldn't be surprised if he is getting on the phone with his boss right now."

Bob spoke up. "With who? The director?"

"Look, as far as I'm concerned, the sooner he fills the director in on what's going on here, the better it is for all of us. And the sooner we can get this investigation reopened."

THE PLOT QUICKENS

Five minutes later, Carolyn buzzed into the conference room. "Mr. Jones, the director is on red line one."

The FBI director sounded annoyed. "Make this quick, Merle. I'm in the middle of an important meeting."

"Yes, sir. I have some very important new developments concerning the Flight 800 investigation that you need to know about, now."

"I'm listening, Merle."

"I have former agent Bob Anderson, attorney Frank Abrams, and Liam Mayfair, the son of one of the deceased passengers, John Mayfair, in my office right now. I just listened to a cassette tape of a phone message recording made from Flight 800 by John Mayfair seconds before the plane exploded. The tape was lost for the past twenty months and was just discovered. It sounds legitimate, but it will have to be lab analyzed to be sure. On the tape, Mayfair, who happens to be a former Vietnam War navy pilot, describes seeing a SAM missile with the usual plume profile rising from the surface of the water, within seconds prior to the crash."

The director was obviously not impressed. "So did some other so-called eyewitnesses on the ground. What makes this version so special, Merle?"

"Do you remember that Iranian informant who called one of my agents here in New York a few days before the explosion?"

"Yes. What about him?"

"Mayfair says on the tape that he clearly saw the missile being launched off the forward deck of a large freighter heading out to sea. An oil freighter, Lou! He was in a starboard window seat of the plane and saw the missile from an altitude of about twelve thousand feet."

There was no response, just dead air on the phone.

"Lou? Did you hear what I just said?"

The director's response was clearly agitated. "Holy shit! That Iranian described the same exact set of facts. Didn't your original report say that he claimed he was one of the deck hands on an oil freighter and knew of a plot to fire a missile from the deck of his ship by other crew members who were also Iranians?"

"You have a good memory, Lou."

"Do you realize what this means, Merle? This tape would be the first and only credible corroboration of what that Iranian told us. I thought he was nuts, remember?"

"Yes, I know. So did we."

"More importantly, I thought we had identified all of the ship traffic in the area at the time. At least I hope to God we did. Please tell me that you identified that ship and have the names of the entire crew."

"Yes, sir, we eventually got almost all of that information from that same informant. But it wasn't at the time of his first phone call."

"What does that mean? Summarize it for me quickly, Merle."

"Let me go back to the beginning. This whole thing started with a strange call from a guy who we eventually identified as one of fourteen Iranian crew members aboard an oil tanker headed up the east coast. The call came into the New York office about three days before the Flight 800 explosion and was routed immediately to one of my best agents. In that conversation, he told us that the PLO, with Iranian government backing, was behind a plot to fire a SAM missile from the deck of his ship, specifically targeting a TWA flight to Paris. You'll see in my report that even though we didn't give much credence to the information at the time, we passed along written and oral notification to the FAA and TWA, just to be safe. Apparently, neither the FAA nor TWA did anything to divert or cancel that flight.

"In that first phone call, this guy refused to identify himself. He sounded crazy, a little hyper, like he might have been on drugs. He said that he was a member of the crew aboard an oil tanker that was scheduled to unload refined product somewhere in Newark. When we tried to get the name of the ship and registry, he laughed like a crazy person and hung up. But not before he told us about the plot to fire a missile.

"We immediately checked the phone logs, tried to trace the call, and followed up with the local port authorities. It took us days to get a complete list of all of the hundreds of oil tankers coming in and out of New York Harbor for a one-week period on either side of the date of the explosion. We narrowed down the search by checking the ships we believe were in the immediate area around the time of the explosion. We finally identified the name of the ship this guy was aboard and tracked down the owner in Greece. But that wasn't until about six days after Flight 800 went down. When we finally confirmed the ship's itinerary, we learned that it had put into Caracas overnight, exactly one week after the explosion. By the time our agents in Venezuela boarded the freighter the next morning, fourteen of the original crew, all Iranian nationals, had disappeared. We interviewed everyone on board and searched every dark corner of that ship. No sign of any missile or launch equipment. We figured whatever may have been used to fire the missile may have been dumped over the side somewhere at sea en route to Caracas."

"What about the captain? Refresh my memory. What did he have to say?"

"The captain and chief engineer gave us the complete crew roster, including the names of all the Iranians who didn't return to the ship the next morning. The captain told us that he knew of no reason why his crew would just walk away from the ship. He said these maritime guys know that by deserting their ship, they automatically forfeit their pay. Our agents got the impression that he honestly didn't know anything about the missile or any conspiracy among his crew. He said he was below decks, having dinner at the exact time the plane blew up, and didn't hear anything unusual. The rest of the crew, four Brits and six Greeks, were also on their dinner shift. None of them saw or heard anything unusual that night. We interviewed all of them and concluded that they didn't know anything about any conspiracy to fire a missile from the deck."

"Merle, did this guy ever describe the missile?"

"Yes, he did. We're assuming that in using the phrase 'small, older-style missile,' he was referring to a shoulder-launched Stinger-type missile. Probably a leftover American FIM-92 Stinger or the Russian Strela used in the '80s. There were a lot of those that fell into the hands of the mujahideen after the Russian invasion of Afghanistan. The other older SAM missiles are much bigger, over ten feet long, and need heavier launch equipment that would need hydraulics to move them into place.

It would be almost impossible, even for a trained jihadist, to get the larger missile ready to launch on the deck of an oil freighter. With that kind of mechanical activity above deck, the captain would certainly have heard the noise. So we believe that whatever missile was fired that night was probably done by a shoulder launcher that could very easily be thrown over the side.

"And by the way, Abrams and Anderson are already asking questions about Stinger missiles. I'm playing dumb for the moment."

"What else did the captain say about the other Iranian crew members, Merle?"

"The only thing unusual he noticed that night was that none of them came into the mess for dinner. That, combined with the fact that only the Iranian members of the crew deserted in Caracas, really grabbed our attention at first. We thought we were onto something really big at that point.

"In any event, the captain ended up hiring local seamen from Caracas to replace the missing crew and went on his merry way. We have photographs of the entire ship, bow to stern, topside and below, and especially the layout of the forward deck. That's about all we were able to come up with at the time."

"But, Merle, how could they have brought the missile and launch equipment on board and kept it hidden from the captain and the rest of the crew for all that time?"

"Sir, have you ever been aboard one of these supertankers? They're three football fields long and almost four hundred feet wide at the beam, with dozens of dark corners below deck to stow this stuff. Hiding a five-foot rocket and a thirty-five-pound launcher on one of these giants is a piece of cake."

"I can understand that. But how are we going to corroborate what your informant said with any of his fellow Iranian crew members if we can't even find them to talk to them? Christ, we don't even know if any of the names on the ship's roster are real."

"We had no idea if the names were real at the time. And when those guys bolted into the Caracas underworld like rats in a dark alley, we had no way to pick up their trail. We even checked with the local airport and bus terminal but came up dry. We never got any more information from that guy. That is, until a few days ago."

"A few days ago? What the hell are you talking about?"

"As bad as all this might sound, Lou, there is some good news to report."

The director tried not to sound too hopeful. "What kind of good news?"

"Amazingly, that very same anonymous Iranian who called and warned us about the attack just showed up on our doorstep like a stray cat. Our guys in Baltimore just happened to pick him up on a routine stowaway bust on another Greek-registry tanker entering the port there three days ago. He had been locked up in a maintenance closet somewhere down in the bilge, sitting in his own waste without food or water for three days. He was never so happy to be freed and brought out into the sunlight by our agents. He even kissed their feet when he was taken topside and was arrested. He immediately told them who he was, that he was the one who called the New York office almost two years ago and that he was now, quote, 'willing to deal.'"

The director lowered his voice slightly. "The timing of all this is incredible, Merle. To tell you the truth, until you just told me about this tape, I couldn't care less why he would suddenly want to talk to us. Now I can't wait to interrogate the son of a bitch! What do you think he's up to?"

"Not sure. Maybe he's suffering from pangs of conscience, or maybe he had a falling-out with his former crewmates after not being able to extort money from them. My guess is that he wants us to pay him some kind of bounty fee to identify and roll over on his friends. The bottom line is, we found him and have him by the nuts. We're not going to let him get away from us this time. He's already given us some very good leads to help us positively identify and maybe even locate at least five or six of the missing Iranian crew, including the three men who actually fired the missile. But grabbing them won't be easy. They're probably hiding out somewhere in Tehran under the protection of the ayatollah. But remember, even if we can't find the others, this guy, standing alone, is a pivotal independent eyewitness. In just the last few hours, he's already given us a detailed description of not only how the conspiracy was carried out, but also the names of those in the Iranian government who gave the orders. He knows exactly how, where, and when they smuggled the missile aboard. He told us that these guys were worried at first that their rust-covered rocket might blow up in their faces. When they realized that the plane was actually hit and destroyed, they ran around the deck screaming 'Allahu Akbar.' In their excitement, they even almost forgot to throw the launcher equipment overboard.

"More importantly, he's given us the names of those who actually fired the missile and can tell us everything we need to know to get a conviction, assuming we can ever grab one or two of them. The US attorney here in New York has been briefed and, as of this morning, has authorized us to offer this guy immunity if he leads us to the others."

"Great work, Merle. Now tell me more about the notice we sent out to TWA and the FAA. How did it go out and when? How quickly did we act on the tip this guy gave us from that first phone call?"

"Our lead agent is Don Nelson. Not only did he fax an official written warning to both TWA and the FAA, but he also followed up with a personal phone call to upper management in their New York offices the same day. You can access the exact letter he sent out. It's an exhibit to my initial report."

After a few moments of awkward silence, Jones continued. "Look, Lou, I know what you're thinking. This is not meant as an excuse. But the reason we didn't follow up aggressively with that ship and its crew in the first few months after the crash is really very simple. Within a very short period of time after the explosion, we were all being told by NTSB's forensic experts that the missile theory was a physical impossibility and basically a waste of our investigative time and effort. Their opinion was pretty rock solid. Those guys were pretty damn convincing. So once the missile theory was ruled out, we didn't feel the need to assign any further manpower or effort to track down the ship or speak to any of the crew members beyond what we did in Caracas. That's what happened, Lou, plain and simple."

"Merle, I'm not faulting your decision not to follow up at the time. As a matter of fact, I also remember the NTSB was so cocksure of their opinion. But more importantly, you say you now have this guy under control. Where is he?"

"He's right here in New York. We had him flown up yesterday, as a matter of fact. Nelson has been working with him all night. I was literally just briefed a few hours ago. Don't worry. He's on a very short leash. He's not going anywhere."

"Merle, I don't want this guy walking around. I want him locked up in protective custody starting today. Don't let him talk to anyone. You got that?"

"Yes, sir. Consider it done."

"Good. Now I want you to put your best agents back on this immediately and try to salvage some decent interviews with however many
members of that missing crew you can come up with. I don't care what
part of the Middle East they may be hiding in or on which rust bucket
they may be sailing at the moment. Just get going on this right away. I
want every stone turned over twice."

"Do you want me to get some help from CIA?"

"No, not yet anyway. But in the meanwhile, I want you to formally
contact the NTSB and ask them to have their divers and SONAR team
go back out there and expand the radius of the wreckage field by at least
three miles. I've got a hunch I think we should pursue."

"What are we looking for?"

"We're looking for the rest of the story, Merle. We're looking for
that phantom missile and, if we're lucky, the launch equipment. Based on
the Mayfair tape and the direction of Mathers's boat, we might be able
to figure out the exact position and compass direction of the freighter
when that missile was fired. And from that, we might be able to plot the
missile trajectory and figure out where everything might be sitting on the
bottom."

After a brief pause, the director spoke haltingly. "Merle, does anyone
else, inside or outside the bureau, know about the Mayfair tape besides

the two of us? Did they tell anyone else in law enforcement or, I hope not, the press?"

"According to their attorney, Abrams, they're about to disclose everything to the Suffolk County Police Department. And yes, Liam Mayfair did talk to a *Times* reporter who was told the basics but wasn't allowed to listen to the tape itself. So far, the only other people who have actually heard the tape are Abrams, Agent Anderson, the Mayfair family, and Liam's fiancée. Unfortunately, the *Times* reporter knows enough to be dangerous, if you know what I mean."

"Damn it. I'll bet the White House already knows about the tape. Well, so be it. Let's try to keep it under wraps as best we can for just a little while longer."

The director quickly changed subjects. "Now, what about your hunch that this lawyer Abrams intends to subpoena all the foreign informant files related to Flight 800, including the file on the your Iranian snitch?"

"Based on what Abrams has said so far, I don't think there's any doubt about it. He's driving forward, full bore, like a man possessed. He's going after all our foreign informant leads in this case with subpoenas. How do you want me to handle him?"

"Just tell him we'll respond to his subpoena as best we can. A lot depends on what he is looking for and what he thinks we may have."

The director again shifted gears. "Look, I know we'll have much more intel from our Iranian informant in very short order. But what about that Palestinian bookkeeper, what's his name, Hassad? He's the guy who turned over all those PLO records to us around the time of the explosion. Is there a separate informant folder on him and his documents?"

"No. Both the Iranian informant file and our extensive debriefing of Hassad are all consolidated. They're still part of the overall airline investigative report. I thought it best to keep them all filed in one place. After all, Hassad, as his bad luck would have it, turned out to be one of the passengers killed on that flight."

Remembering his recent conversation with the president, the director said, "Good, Merle. I want you to keep both those files consolidated in one place."

After a brief pause, Jones spoke. "By the way, Lou, as long as we're on the subject, you know I've been waiting for almost a year now for some direction as to when I can open a full-fledged investigation on those PLO documents. There are a lot of prominent political names and organizations on those secret money-donor lists, including a past president, two senators, and a handful of congressmen. We not only know who their American and foreign money backers are, but now have a lot of details about past terrorists raids and attacks, including dates, times, places, names, methods, et cetera. This PLO informant was a virtual intelligence gold mine."

"I know, Merle, I haven't forgotten. I've been under a lot of pressure here to step gingerly around that issue. Meanwhile, I've been getting even stronger pressure from our friends in Mossad. They keep asking me to act on this information. They're putting a lot of it to good use on their end, but they want to coordinate strategy and counterintelligence with us directly instead of running off on their own. They're the ones who developed Hassad through a female operative in Tel Aviv, after years of hard work. I don't blame them for being frustrated. They must think our government has gone soft on terrorism and thrown them under the bus."

Jones pursued his request. "So when can I expect to get a green light and get started on this? I have a team of agents chomping at the bit to interview all those big money donors and throw the light of day on these scumbag jihadists and their supporters. I'm dying to see exactly how many of those PLO donor names are interrelated and which ones are laying in the weeds right there in DC throughout the halls of power.

"And while they're running around celebrating their sloppy victory in taking out one of our planes, Lou, we can start to expose them. Every last one of them. Wait until that PLO backer list hits the front pages of all the major national newspapers and the nightly news. All hell will break loose. They think they're all in the clear, hiding behind the skirt of an official American government report that insists this was not an act of terrorism but a simple wiring defect. I'm sure there was a collective sigh of relief from the West Bank to Washington when Hassad took his last breath. But what the idiots still don't realize is that Hassad had already turned over all those records to our New York office, the day before he was killed on that flight. The only thing they know for sure from their own sources is that we haven't yet interviewed any of the individuals and organizations on those lists. None of this has been made public. They're probably assuming that even though Hassad may have defected, maybe they got lucky and caught a break. Maybe they suspect that he disappeared without having taken any records with him. If that's what the PLO thinks, then so much the better for our counterintelligence guys."

"So what's the bottom line?"

"Look. With or without records, in the limited time we were able to debrief Hassad, he proved to be a tremendous source of intelligence on the PLO and their renewed connection with Iranian government terrorist operations. He would have been an even greater help to our country if he had lived."

After several long seconds of silence, Lou spoke with a sense of force and conviction: "Release the hounds, Merle. There's a long trail of blood here, and I suspect it leads all the way up to the White House and the Hill. The PLO and a few nervous higher-ups right here in DC had every reason to cheer when Hassad was killed. I know what the doubters and critics will say. 'His people could have killed him anywhere—in his car, walking his dog on the street in Jerusalem. Why did they need to blow up that plane to get at him?'

"Well, Merle, it seems to me the answer is pretty clear. They just couldn't find him. During the three months leading up to the crash, Hassad and his family had been kept in hiding in two different locations in Israel by the Mossad. They were protected by round-the-clock Israeli security. The PLO had no idea where he was or why he and his family had suddenly disappeared. But somehow they found out he was in New York and that he would be aboard that flight to Paris. By my calculation, they had more than an ample window of time and opportunity to get that shoulder-fired missile aboard the tanker and ready to go. All the moving parts must have come together for them in a hurry. An oil freighter with sympathetic Iranian crew members . . . readily available PLO funding . . . a missile supplied by the Iranian government . . . a ship's itinerary and schedule that matches up perfectly with that of Flight 800 . . . and most important of all, a perfect cover for the assassination of Hassad. They made this hit look like a garden-variety terrorist attack on an American jet airliner. On top of that, I'm sure the Iranians think that the PLO trail won't lead back to them because of strained relations with Arafat over the past few years. But we'll take care of that.

"Merle, I've given this a lot of thought over the last few days. As I've said, I've been operating under some intense political pressure for quite a while to sit on this. But that's all about to change. Look, I know you've been really busy with other hot issues lately, but I think it's about time we stir up that hornet's nest. What say you? Are your guys ready to go to work?"

"Lou, you know I'm getting my gold watch, or whatever piece of Waterford crystal they decide to give me, at the end of the year. But I think I can get a lot done on this investigation between now and then. I don't think it will take more than a few months to get some indictments. Personally, I think this could be very big."

"Yeah. Big enough to make or break a career."

"Meaning what, Lou? I don't follow."

"Oh, never mind. It's nothing."

Jones could sense the director's hesitancy to open up. "Lou, why do I get the feeling that you want to tell me something?"

The director paused for a few seconds, weighing the conflicting thoughts bouncing around his head. He decided to lay everything out on the table. "Well, I suppose now is as good a time as any to show my cards. Merle, I want you to take special note of what I'm about to tell you. This must remain strictly confidential between us. Can I rely on you to do that?"

"Of course."

"Something very controversial is brewing below the surface here in HQ. I can't give you too much detail about it right now. But this much I can share with you.. If and when the day comes that you hear that I've submitted my resignation or been asked by the president to quit, understand that it will be a forced and not a voluntary step-down. I want you to promise me that you won't be deterred or slow down in any way on this PLO investigation. I also want you to know that this file, despite what the bold red letters on the cover suggest, is not, and should never have been, treated as classified national security material. If it's subpoenaed by Frank Abrams or anyone else, I expect you to turn it over to whichever federal judge signs the order, without offering any resistance. If I'm no longer the director when that happens, don't worry about that. I doubt that my permanent successor will be appointed and approved in time to stop you from turning over the records to a judge. As a backup, I've already briefed my number two man here on everything, and he's prepared to follow my wishes to the letter, presuming he'll be named the interim director. I don't want any delays or any weasel excuses given to the court or the press. Those guys will be all over this issue like a wet blanket when it all hits the fan.

"And by the way, that goes double for that Iranian informant file. If there really was a missile fired from the deck of an oil freighter, there is no way in hell that information should be considered classified either. I don't care what anyone from the White House or the attorney general's office may tell you. If you're contacted directly by the attorney general, remember, you're answerable only to the director of the bureau, not anyone else.

Be respectful but firm. Tell him to deal directly with the interim director and say nothing else. Do you understand?"

"Yes, sir."

"Thanks, Merle. I have to get back to my meeting now. Let me know right away whatever more you learn about the Mayfair tape and the press. And see if you can learn what specific documents Abrams is looking for. "

"OK, Lou. I'll get back to you when I finish up with my own meeting with Abrams and Anderson.

"And, Lou?"

"Yeah, Merle?"

"Whatever the hell is going on down there, I hope everything turns out well for you. Keep your head down, boss."

"Thanks, Merle. I intend to. Keep me posted."

Jones hung up the phone and immediately headed back to his guests. His mind raced through the professional and political implications of what he had just been told. He decided to put those thoughts on hold for the moment. He also made a mental note to put together a team headed up by Agent Nelson to immediately launch an official bureau investigation into the Hassad records by interviewing the American names on the donor list.

SIMPLE POWERS OF OBSERVATION

While Jones was out of his office and on the phone with the director, Liam had become bored and restless. He had spent the time wandering about the spacious room, examining the private life of the man whose photographs, mementos, and awards covered the walls and desks. But what really intrigued him was a small glass aquarium tucked away in the far corner of the room. In it were two green turtles. Somehow they seemed out of place for one of the most powerful men in the FBI. Liam chalked it up to eccentricity and thought nothing of it.

Suddenly, he heard the door open. He turned and saw Jones walk briskly back into his office. "I'm very sorry for that interruption, gentlemen. It was a call I could not put off. Unfortunately, it ran a lot longer than I anticipated. I hope you understand."

Abrams looked at his watch. Almost forty minutes for a scheduled phone call? Abrams couldn't resist the opportunity and the temptation. "So, Mr. Jones, how is the director? I presume he's been brought up to speed on all of this, right?"

Jones grunted, bit his tongue, and pretended not to hear the comment. He immediately re-engaged Liam with the question that had been bugging him since the subject was raised.

"Liam, please explain something to me. What exactly is the *Times'* involvement in all of this? You said they haven't heard the tape. Do they intend to print a story on it?"

"I think so. I also think they may try to throw me under the bus on the Mathers incident. Their reporter, Mike Ketchum, spoke to a bartender in Montauk who places me and my car out on the docks shortly before Mathers was killed. I told him everything about what happened out there. To be honest with you, I wanted to talk to Ketchum in person because I was afraid he might run to the Suffolk County Police and blow the whistle on me for not reporting the murder. Fortunately, Mr. Abrams has begun to take care of that problem for me. He's already called the police to offer my complete cooperation and a detailed statement."

Jones turned to Frank: "Mr. Abrams, I would appreciate it, while you're setting up your meeting with the Suffolk County Police, that you schedule it to be held here with me in my office. I doubt they would mind coming into the city for that."

"Consider it done."

Jones looked back at Liam. "Liam, I can't order you not to talk to the press about any of this, but I would ask that you first give me a few days to have our forensic team go over your father's tape to authenticate it before you go public. Do you think you could do that for us?"

Liam looked over at Abrams. "I guess so. If it's OK with my attorney."

"Merle, I don't have a problem doing that for you. But I have a favor I would like in return. If you don't mind, I'd like to engage you in a little old-fashioned horse trading . . . for our mutual benefit, of course. And while we're doing that, maybe we can even do something to further the cause of justice. What do you say?"

"I'm listening. What exactly are you proposing?"

"Look, I've been a trial lawyer and an FBI agent myself long enough to know how the game is played when a trial lawyer wants access to certain official government records and when some law enforcement bureaucrat just doesn't want to turn them over. Sometimes that person cites national security reasons, sometimes he is concealing records for purely political reasons, and sometimes, to be blunt, he is simply being true to his bureaucratic nature as an officious dick.

"I think we all know, in light of the NTSB finding, that there was no missile, that there is very little likelihood that national security concerns play any role in their investigation of the explosion. I meant what I said before about foreign informant information."

"Your point, Mr. Abrams?"

"I want to see every informant file that relates directly to your Flight 800 investigation, properly redacted, of course. And I don't want to spend the rest of my life embroiled in a paper war with the Department of Justice. I don't need to waste time fighting over scope, specificity, and all of the rest of the knee-jerk excuses the government usually throws up as roadblocks to valid subpoenas. I'm sure you know exactly what I'm talking about."

"Yes, unfortunately, I'm familiar with what you're describing. But what is it exactly that you want, Mr. Abrams?"

"If I may be blunt, Mr. Jones, I have a very strong case here against TWA and possibly the FAA. They are my true targets, not the NTSB and certainly not the FBI. I want to be able to try my case without one arm tied behind my back. I don't want to be forced to grovel for every sheet of subpoenaed paper to be brought before a judge for an in-camera inspection, only to be told what we already know. And that is that these informant documents, which you and I both know exist, are not privileged or protected or deserve classified status in this case. I'd like to have your personal assurance, and I don't need it in writing, that you and the bureau will not deny me access to properly subpoenaed records for the reasons I just cited. No political nonsense. No bogus, make-believe national security crap. And no acting like a dog in the manger, if you catch my drift. In return, I will delay our press conference with all the national media until your lab guys have authenticated the tape and have given me the OK to proceed. Those are my terms."

"Mr. Abrams, if I can help you without violating any specific orders of the director to the contrary, I will. So yes, we have a deal."

Jones smiled knowingly at Abrams. "As a matter of fact, based on a very recent conversation with my boss, I suspect he will agree to them as well. That's the best I can do for you under the circumstances."

Abrams stood up and extended his hand to Jones. "That's good enough for me."

Jones walked his guests to the elevator and said good-bye.

Bob, Frank, and Liam remained silent as they rode the elevator down twenty-eight floors to the ground level. They walked across the lobby and turned in their visitor badges. As the two retired agents were retrieving their weapons from the locked box in the lobby, a short, heavy-set man with thick eyeglasses stepped quickly from the security desk and approached Anderson.

"Bob, is that you?"

Bob turned toward the familiar voice, smiled broadly, and said, "Clyde! What the hell are you doing in New York? The last time I saw you, you were managing the computers in WFO."

"It's really great to see you, Bob. What a coincidence running into you like this today."

"But what are you doing here?" said Bob.

"Well, right after you retired and came back to New York, I was transferred here as well to whip the active files and archives into shape and reorganize everything in the database from top to bottom."

There was an awkward pause before Bob introduced FBI Squad Supervisor in Charge of MIS, Clyde Watson, to Frank and Liam. Watson had risen high in the ranks of the bureau as a nonagent clerk. Bob had always considered him the smartest man in the bureau, and perhaps the most eccentric.

Clyde smiled knowingly and said, "To be perfectly honest with you, Bob, I knew you and your friends were meeting with the SAC this morning about this Flight 800 lawsuit, and I just wanted to catch you and say hi before you left."

Bob looked at Frank and Liam. "Clyde here used to work with me in Washington. In fact, we would have lunch together almost every day in the bureau dining room. We spent most of our time solving the day's *New York Times* crossword puzzle. Clyde is somewhat of a savant and a perfectionist when it comes to words, not to mention the thousands of bureau files he's in charge of safekeeping."

Suddenly, the smile on Clyde's face retreated as he stared intently at Bob. "Tell me, Bob. Do you remember the last day we had lunch together in Washington? It must have been three to four years ago. You were hopelessly stuck on the last word of the Sunday puzzle. You couldn't figure it out even after you pulled out your cheat dictionary."

"No. Can't say that I do. Why don't you jog my memory?"

"I'll only give you the clue and then I have to get back to my office." Clyde looked slowly around the lobby and lowered his voice. 'An ancient curved blade of Middle Eastern origin.' Do you remember the answer?"

"Wait, wait! It's right on the tip of my tongue."

Clyde leaned closer into Bob's face. "Keep it to yourself, Bob. And remember, it was the final and most important word of the puzzle."

Just then, Liam spoke the word aloud. "Scimitar!"

Clyde put his finger to his lips and said, "Right you are, Liam. But let Bob figure this one out on his own. He's very good at putting puzzles together."

Bob started to ask Clyde why he was taking this little trip down memory lane when Clyde suddenly turned to walk away. "Well, gotta run, boys. Keeping America safe for freedom and democracy and all that good stuff. Keep the faith, Bob, and don't forget to say hi to Kay for me." As he walked away, Clyde turned back momentarily and said, "Oh, I almost forgot. Regards from another old pal, Don Nelson. He's working here in New York . Why don't you give him a call, Bob? He's a good puzzle solver too."

The three men watched in silence as Clyde disappeared into the elevator. "Well that was a little bizarre," said Liam.

"Perhaps not as strange as you might think," said Bob as he squinted and stroked his chin.

Suddenly, the thought of the meeting with Merle Jones rushed into Liam's head. For some inexplicable reason, the crossword puzzle word he had just uttered triggered an image of a green folder he had noticed sitting open on the edge of Jones's desk. In his naïveté, Liam never considered the impropriety of looking at anything on the SAC's desk. But he had. And as a result, he remembered seeing a series of large numbers at the top of the page—137, in bold, black numerals. On the upper left edge of the page next to the word "Subject" was the name "el-Kabir." Immediately beneath that name was another, "SA Donald Nelson."

"Frank, I think we need to talk right away."

LAZARUS, COME FORTH

An old wooden Cape Islander lobster boat motored slowly out of Montauk Harbor, its bow pointed toward the sun, which was just starting to creep up over the ocean. The sky on the horizon was layered with low-hanging red and pink clouds. Barely visible on the boat's stern was a wooden name plaque, with the faded painted words "Lazarus, Montauk, NY." Bud Holmes, the grizzled, leather-skinned captain, was at the helm. He had gotten up, as he had for nearly thirty years, an hour before sunrise. Like his father before him, he needed no mechanical alarm clock to know the ebb and flow of the hard life of a Montauk lobsterman. He had fished these waters so long, he could move along the miles of his traplines in his sleep. He brewed himself a cup of fresh coffee, grabbed the lunch pail his wife had left in the fridge for him the night before, and drove his pickup down to the dock. By the time the first rays of sunlight poured over the boat's dew-covered bulkhead, he had already begun to warm up his engines.

Folks in town knew him only as Bud. They just assumed, based on the name of his boat, that his given birth name was Lazarus. What he never bothered to tell anyone was that he named the boat after the biblical story of Lazarus whom Jesus had raised from the dead after being in the tomb for three days. Charles "Bud" Holmes had been diagnosed with deadly pancreatic cancer many years prior and had had an extremely rare and, as his wife would say, miraculous cure. Since then, every day out on the water represented new life and new opportunity for Bud Holmes. He breathed in the cool morning sea air and was grateful to be alive.

As he cut back on the engine throttle and drifted up to his first trap position, he flicked his filter-less cigarette over the side, leaned over the starboard gunwale, and gaffed the trapline. He grabbed the red buoy, slid the line through the pulley, and started to haul the trap up from the bottom. Realizing that the trap was not coming up as easily as it should have from the deep, cold, green water, he hooked the line up to his power winch.

The winch creaked and whined under the load. "Somethin's not right here," the old man said aloud. As the trap finally appeared near the surface, he saw it was filled with a dozen or more large green-brown lobsters. He immediately noticed something out of the ordinary among the claws and shells. It was pale white in color. The old man squinted and nearly jumped out of his skin when he recognized the object as a human hand, wedged into the mesh of the trap netting. As the trap finally started to emerge out of the water, the hair on the back of his neck stood on edge. He let out a shout. "Sweet Jesus, what the hell do we have here?"

There, just below the clear, smooth surface, was the blanched, bloated body of what appeared to be an older-looking white-haired man who had apparently run into some bad luck. His right arm was tangled in the trap line. A few barnacles had attached to the dead man's face, and his eyes were still open—staring back up at the old lobsterman. As Bud jumped backward, the winch slipped and the trap and body began to sink back down into the water. He locked up the winch and ran to the radio.

Forty minutes later, a Coast Guard patrol vessel was tied up alongside the *Lazarus*, its crew carefully lifting the partially decomposed body out of the water. In searching for some kind of identification, one of the men leaned over the body and noticed three small puncture wounds in the upper torso. "This is not a drowning, sir. This looks like a murder. Those look like bullet entry wounds."

Chief Petty Officer Gross thought there was something very familiar looking in the dead man's face. He was sure he had seen him before. "Let's get him back to the dock and put him on ice until the medical examiner can have a look at this."

THE VISIT

Liam sat across from Frank Abrams, who was sitting silently behind his large mahogany desk. Frank stared past Liam over his shoulder. *This is odd*, Liam thought. Abrams had asked him to come in today to discuss the case yet had not said a word since he sat down. Suddenly, Abrams's face grew pale; his mouth fell open. Liam noticed that the light spilling into the room from the office window above the desk was otherworldly, almost surreal. Liam turned around. There, in the open doorway, as though standing in the flesh, was John W. Mayfair. Startled, Liam jumped up and backward, knocking over his chair. He was seized by a sense of both fear and excited anticipation.

JW's appearance was vibrant and surrounded by a bright, glowing aura. His face, broadly smiling, looked like a richly colored still life painting. Liam's heart raced as he blurted out, "Dad, what's going on? How . . . how can this be?"

Liam turned back to look at Abrams, who had vanished completely from the room. He stood alone staring in utter disbelief at his dead father.

JW spoke slowly as he continued to stand at the threshold of the large office. "Liam, your gut instincts, as usual, are terrific." His voice resonated with a stark clarity and an almost musical quality yet somehow seemed to defy the laws of sound and physics. It was almost as though JW was communicating telepathically. "You and Frank have teamed up extremely well on the case, but you both have some more work to do."

"I know, Dad. We need to subpoena the exact FBI files that will break the case wide open. The judge will come down on him like a ton of bricks if his subpoenas are too vague. He has to be as precise as possible."

"Liam, do you believe there is an FBI foreign informant file on the Flight 800 case?"

"Yes. Frank and Bob Anderson are convinced of it too."

"And if that informant file had a code name, what do you suppose that word might be?"

"I don't have a clue," said Liam.

"Really? But weren't you handed a clue the other day by Clyde Watson? And didn't you actually solve the crossword clue yourself?"

Liam was surprised as to how readily the recall came to him. "Oh, you mean the word 'scimitar'?"

"Yes, and correct me if I'm wrong, but didn't the sound of that word trigger a memory of something you inadvertently noticed on Merle Jones's desk?"

"Yes, I saw information in an open file, but I don't know what it all means."

"You don't? Have you asked Agent Anderson yet what the numbers 137 mean?"

"Yes, I did ask him that. They're the filing prefix numbers for an FBI informant folder."

"So then, you know the name of the foreign informant, right?"

"No, how would I know that?"

"Whatever you noticed on that page, Liam, is important in some way."

Suddenly, a lightbulb went off in Liam's brain as he visualized the rest of the page in the green folder. "El-Kabir! The informant's name is el-Kabir!"

"And that would mean that the FBI agent who is probably handling el-Kabir is Agent . . ."

Liam interrupted. "That's right! It was Nelson. Special Agent Donald Nelson. Is that what you're telling me, Dad?"

"No, Liam, that's what you're telling *me*. Thanks to your keen powers of observation, you've had the information all along, haven't you?"

"I suppose I have," said Liam, still somewhat confused.

"And if el-Kabir is as valuable a witness informant as you and the FBI apparently think he is, do you suppose it's reasonable to presume that he knows how and where the missile was stored aboard the ship and who may have actually fired it?"

"Yes, that makes perfect sense. And I guess the person who would have all those details is his handler, Agent Nelson?"

JW smiled. "One down and one more piece of the puzzle to go, Liam. Who or what do you think was the real target of this missile attack? What was their ultimate goal?"

"At first Frank thought it was a simple terrorist attack. But now I'm not so sure."

"Why do you say that?"

"I thought that it was more than just a coincidence that there was only one passenger on that plane whose name sounded Middle Eastern. I noticed his name right away. It was Ahmed Hassad."

"Very good. What's his nationality, Liam?"

"I think Frank said the name sounded Arab, possibly Palestinian."

"I presume you did a thorough background check on Hassad?"

"At first we thought he might be a Palestinian observer representative to the UN. Then we found a profile in which he listed his occupation as an accountant, not a diplomat. He actually identified his employer as the PLO. That's all we were able to come up with."

"And if he was not attached to a delegation at the United Nations, why would he have been in New York? Does he strike you as someone the FBI might be interested in talking with?"

Liam smiled knowingly. "I know, Dad, speak with Agent Nelson, right?"

"Liam, it sounds to me like you already have most of the information Frank needs to draft some very powerful subpoenas."

Liam began to understand what was happening in this strange discourse with his father. All he could think to say was "Thanks, Dad."

"For what? It was *your* intuition and *your* observations that led you to the answers, not mine."

"But what about the missile, Dad?"

"The government is claiming that a wiring defect ignited the center fuel tank. But let's not forget one simple fact. I was actually there, Liam. There was no way I could have mistaken that demon coming up toward the plane from that freighter for anything other than a missile. The description I left you on the tape is exactly what I saw out the starboard window that night. Liam, have you discussed with Frank and Anderson the type of missile that I must have seen?"

"Yes. Bob thought it might have been an old shoulder-launched American Stinger left over from the Russian-Afghan War. He thought it was probably one of the hundreds of missiles that later fell into the hands of the Iranians and/or the mujahideen. Bob found out from one of his military sources that these ordnance relics have a high failure rate."

"Did you do any research on why those old missiles are so unreliable?"

"Yes, I did. I was able to find out from some of Frank's contacts that many of them were stored in caves in the mountains of Afghanistan and that the fuses in those old Stingers were probably rusted and corroded. Frank said that it didn't take a rocket scientist to figure out that this might have been a dud."

JW wagged his head and said, "Frank was always fond of puns. But he's right. This was a one-in-a-million lucky shot. That missile barely penetrated the trailing edge of the starboard wing and provided just enough spark to ignite the center fuel tank. It brought down that plane without ever detonating. Can you imagine that?"

"But, Dad, the NTSB didn't come up with any missile fragments in the wreckage site."

"That's true. But why do you think they didn't search the bottom beyond the immediate wreckage field, Liam?"

"Because once the NTSB accounted for almost 95 percent of the plane and found no signs of a missile impact or detonation, they probably had no incentive to look for anything else beyond the limited area that they actually searched. You can't really argue with their logic, I suppose."

"Would you be prepared to argue against their logic once you make the tape public? What do you think NTSB will do then?"

"I don't know, Dad. But if I were in charge of the investigation, I would have doubled the size of the search field."

"And if you were in charge, Liam, they would have found the missile and launcher a long time ago."

There was a long period of silence as Liam made a mental checklist of things he needed to discuss with Frank. "Dad, who's going to believe any of this? Exactly how are we supposed to use any of this information at trial? And how do I explain how I got it? From a friendly ghost?"

JW spoke slowly, with the boundless patience and kindness of a father toward a confused and impatient son. "You still don't get it, Liam, do you? You won't have to explain anything. You and Frank and Bob have already uncovered all the information you need to know. You just didn't fully realize it till this moment. The only thing left for you to do is to finish connecting the dots, serve your subpoenas, and go win the case."

"Actually, there is one more thing I really need to do, Dad. I need to resolve the problems I inherited from Buzz Mathers. I'm in a lot of trouble because of his murder. The investigation of his death and the way I screwed it up is all weighing heavy on my mind."

"Liam, don't be concerned about Mathers. As you and Frank already know, that wasn't his body the police found aboard his boat. It was old Leatherneck from the bar . . . the old toothless guy who pointed you toward the *Northern Star*. Just as Frank predicted, Mathers's body wasn't disposed of properly. It was only a matter of time before he paid us all a little visit from the dead. You weren't able to recover my body, but the medical examiner will have his soon. Be sure to tell Frank to pay close attention to his autopsy report. I'm sure you and Frank must realize by now that it will clear you of any suspicion of involvement in his death.

"And finally, Liam, I know that you and your mother are worried that Mathers's killers are still lurking out there. Don't concern yourself with them. They're about to be taken out of the picture for good."

After a long silence, Liam finally asked the question that had been lingering in the back of his mind. "Dad, if you here handling this case, what would be your next move?"

"Liam, you've been working side by side with Frank for a while now. Knowing what you do, if you could take just two pretrial depositions, who would they be?"

"That's easy. Nelson and el-Kabir."

"Exactly. Tell Frank to serve those subpoenas as soon as possible. They're your keys to victory, Liam. Hassad and his records are just the icing on the cake."

Liam was beginning to sense the excitement and thrill of a dramatic win. He grew saddened by the thought that his father would not be in the courtroom to see it and savor the victory.

JW looked at Liam and grinned. "I wouldn't miss out on this for all the world, Liam. Don't worry, I'll be in the courtroom with you when Judge Schindler takes the verdict from the jury."

"But, Dad, we don't have a trial judge assigned to the case yet . . . How could you possibly know . . . ?"

JW held up his hand. "Don't ask me any more questions, Liam. Just continue to trust in your intuition and Frank's trial skills. That's all you need."

JW smiled and invoked a familiar phrase he used whenever Frank was about to start a long, tough trial. "I'd like for you to convey this exact message to Frank: 'Don't screw this up.' And when he stops laughing, tell him that I miss him."

During the entire out-of-body encounter and conversation between JW and his son, Liam had stood motionless, hanging on every word and sensation. A bizarre level of awareness suddenly overcame Liam as JW's calm, sonorous voice continued to pour over him like a warm, soothing bath. It reminded him of that precise moment when someone suddenly realizes that what had only been a steady yet barely perceived low-level background noise had come to an abrupt stop. On one hand, Liam reasoned that he was immersed in the most vivid dream he had ever experienced. And yet he was not convinced that any of this was a dream at all. Every one of his senses felt like it was pumped up on steroids. His depth and range of perception of every color and every sound of this mysterious encounter carried him far beyond anything that existed in the natural world. He felt his father's firm, warm grasp on his shoulder, more real than any sensation he had ever enjoyed this side of life. He knew intuitively that because his mind lay in a subconscious state of deep REM sleep, none of this could be real. How could it be? And yet it seemed that somehow, mystery and reality had merged into one. Liam felt confused yet clearheaded. Exhausted yet exhilarated. He desperately clung to every second of this strange event and wished that it would linger forever.

JW smiled knowingly. "I know, Liam, I know. It's truly amazing, isn't it?" He drew yet closer and hugged his youngest son. "I have never been more proud of you than I am at this moment, son."

There was a long pause before JW spoke. "Liam, do you remember the promise I asked you to make on the beach on Shelter Island on your fifth birthday?" Without JW uttering a sound, Liam suddenly heard his father's words softly echoing in the recesses of his brain where the memory had been stored for over eighteen years.

The words rang in his head as clear as a bell. "Promise me, son, that you will never let money stand between you and your conscience." Liam basked in the recall. "I remembered, Dad."

"Well done, son. Consider your promise fulfilled, Liam."

The smile faded from JW's mouth. "Give a big kiss and hug to your mother and siblings for me, will you? Tell them all that I love them very much. Tell them that there was no pain and that I'm in a wonderful place, waiting for them all. And by the way, Maggie is a keeper. Don't let her get away. Open your eyes now, Liam . . . and give her a hug too." With those words, Liam felt a warm touch to his forehead as his father vanished.

"Liam, are you awake?" Maggie spoke softly as she stood over the bed. "Sorry, hon, I hate to disturb you. You looked like you were having such a nice dream. You were grinning from ear to ear. But I thought you should take this call. I think it's important." Maggie handed him the phone. "It's Mr. Abrams. He says he has some phenomenally good news for you."

"I know, I know." He laughed out loud as he grabbed the phone and bounded out of bed.

Liam didn't wait for Frank's voice. "Frank, I just woke up from an incredible dream about my father! Hell, I'm not even sure it was a dream. He spoke to me about our investigation and had some advice for you on how you should proceed with the case. He told me to tell you 'Don't screw it up.'"

Right on cue, Frank let out a barrel laugh. "I'm glad to hear he still has his weird sense of humor. What else did he say?"

Liam provided every detail of the otherworldly visit in rapid-fire succession.

On the other end of the phone, Abrams could barely contain his exuberance. "Holy crap! I can't believe this. I spoke to Bob Anderson first thing this morning. It turns out that he and an agent friend of his, a guy by the name of Don Nelson, used to work together in the same counter-intelligence unit in Washington a few years back. As I recall, that's the name you lifted from that open file on Jones's desk the day we met with him. And didn't that strange guy Clyde Watson also mention the name Nelson?"

"I know, Frank. It looks like we've had most of this information all along. I think it's time we use it to our advantage and put some pressure on Canning. I'd say you might finally have enough detail to prepare your subpoenas, wouldn't you agree?"

"I was thinking the same thing, Liam."

"By the way, did Bob tell Nelson about the tape?"

"Yes. He told him everything. Apparently, Nelson never bought into the electrical-defect theory. He's been convinced that the government's official position has been wrong from the start. Bob said that he was ecstatic when he learned about the missile. Nelson wants to meet with both of us as soon as possible about the lawsuit. Do you realize what this means? I might be able to turn him into my star witness."

"If you can pull that off, Frank, we're home free."

"And get this. I also learned that the bureau recently placed a Middle Eastern informant in protective custody. This informant's story about the missile being fired off the deck of an oil tanker matches up exactly with what your father described on the tape. Nelson also reported that early this morning, a local lobsterman in Montauk pulled a body out of the water. Some guy who apparently had been shot got fouled up in one of his traplines. It sounds like Harley Mathers to me, Liam, just like your father said in your dream. The Suffolk County Medical Examiner is getting the body today to do the autopsy and investigate the death."

Liam cut off Abrams with the obvious question. "But what about the FBI investigation, Frank? Where does it go now?"

"Exactly where we want it to go. It sounds to me like they have no choice but to reopen it, just as we had hoped. Bob said that the bureau is filing an official request today asking the NTSB to expand the SONAR search of the wreckage field a couple of miles in another attempt to locate the missile and launch equipment.

"Liam, this is not over yet by a long shot, and we still have a long way to go. But as of this morning, we're in the middle of an entirely new ball game with a whole new powerful lineup. As soon as you and your mother give me the authority, I'll turn this case completely around and take it all the way to verdict. I can't wait to see the look on Canning's face when he realizes what we have and how we've changed our strategy 180 degrees on him. As far as the tape is concerned, as long as you've already made up your mind to publicize it, I don't see any reason why we can't do that as soon as possible."

Liam was still having trouble mentally digesting what had just happened in his eerie nocturnal meeting with his father and had not yet come down from his lofty level of exhilaration. He wondered quietly how his mother would react to his father's visit and whether anyone else had received any part of this ghostly message.

After a few quiet seconds, he spoke with a glowing confidence. "Frank, I want you to provide copies of the tape directly to defense counsel as soon as we get the OK from Mr. Jones. I'll handle the rest myself." He hung up the phone before Abrams had a chance to ask what he meant by that. Liam immediately dialed Mike Ketchum at the *New York Times*.

EAST MEETS WEST

The following morning, as Frank Abrams walked into his office, his secretary nervously whispered to him. "Frank, there's a man who's been seated in the conference room, waiting for you for the past forty-five minutes. He says he's with the FBI. When I asked him to tell me why he wanted to see you, he just handed me this card and said it was a personal matter and that you were expecting him."

Abrams looked at the card, which read, "DONALD M. NELSON, SPECIAL AGENT, FEDERAL BUREAU OF INVESTIGATION." Abrams could barely disguise his excitement as he rushed into the room and introduced himself to Agent Nelson, a tall, lanky middle-aged man with long gray hair that partially covered his ears and hung over the back of his starched white collar.

"I must say, you don't exactly look the role, Mr. Nelson. When I was in the bureau, the haircuts were high and tight. I guess things have slacked off a bit since then. Tell me, is it still the general rule of thumb that the farther away from SOG you are, the more relaxed the dress code and the longer the hairstyle?"

"Yes, sir, that's still pretty much the way it is. Working up here in New York, I can get away with a colored shirt and a blazer without a tie once in a while, but never when reporting directly to Washington. I can only imagine what the boys in Butte and Cripple Creek are wearing these days while on duty. Probably just camo shirts and rubber waders. Not that dress code matters that much these days anyway."

"So, Mr. Nelson, to what do I owe the honor of this visit? You told my secretary I was expecting you?"

"I don't know if you were expecting me. But I'll bet you were really hoping for someone like me to pay you a visit. Mr. Abrams, this could be your lucky day. I'm here as a personal favor to our mutual friend, Bob Anderson. He and I served together in counterintelligence for a few years in DC. He explained all about your lawsuit against TWA on behalf of the Mayfair family and the audiotape. Would you mind taking a little walk with me outside the building?"

Abrams chuckled and said, "Don't worry, Mr. Nelson. There are no bugs anywhere in these offices."

Nelson looked around the large room. "Probably not. But I'm a mountain boy from Northern California. I get a bit tense in tight quarters, especially lawyers' quarters. Let's take a walk over to the park and have ourselves a little chat. What do you say? And by the way, the name is Don."

"Lead the way, Don." Soon, both men were walking north toward Central Park in the bright morning sunshine.

"Look, Frank, I wouldn't normally throw my two cents into the middle of an active private litigation, but your lawsuit ain't exactly private anymore. It has the potential to impact national security in a big way, and real soon. I'm gonna be real careful here and limit our conversation to subjects and facts that are already generally known to the public about the Flight 800 explosion. But first let me be very blunt. I have never bought into the conclusion of the NTSB or the Bureau that Flight 800 was brought down by a rogue electrical spark that ignited overheated fuel vapors in the center fuel tank. Most everyone knows by now that we could never replicate that scenario under controlled lab or field conditions. I've always had a strong intuitive sense that a missile-type projectile struck that plane and somehow ignited that center tank. I personally interviewed most of those folks who claimed to be eyewitnesses. As a matter of fact, a few days before the crash, I also did an extensive interview with one of the passenger victims on that plane, a guy I'm sure you would have found very interesting. But I'll get to that in a minute."

Frank immediately thought of Hassad but kept quiet. "Please, Don, continue."

"Look, I realize that the eyewitnesses' stories weren't all exactly the same, but a lot of them had one common element . . . a missile plume *rising*, not falling to the ocean. And by the way, the latest theory about the fuselage rising into the air another three thousand feet in flames after the nose broke away is just plain bullshit. A Boeing 747, or any aircraft that big, just doesn't behave that way aerodynamically. Period.

"So let me get right to the point. When Bob Anderson told me what your former navy pilot recorded on that phone message cassette, I jumped up and down like a high school kid who just scored his first touchdown. Then and there I decided to do whatever I could to help Bob, and you, to get this investigation reopened and start looking for some more physical evidence. I just got a sworn statement from an informant who corroborates what your client, John Mayfair, said on that tape. I'll do whatever I can to help you get access to it for your case. Presuming, of course, that the Justice Department and bureau don't start waving around that bogus classified-secret, national-security flag. In which case I have no choice but to shut up."

Abrams decided to go for broke. "You mean the information from your Iranian informant, el-Kabir."

Nelson stopped dead in his tracks in the middle of the sidewalk and looked like he had been hit by a train. "Hold on there, Frank. I never mentioned the name el-Kabir to Anderson, or to anyone outside the bureau for that matter. You'd better tell me right now what you know about that name and how you know it!"

Abrams paused. "Don, I swear to you that his name did not come from a leak inside the bureau. I can't tell you right now how I got that information, but I promise that I will when the time is right. In the meanwhile, I know el-Kabir was on the forward deck of an oil freighter and that he saw his fellow crewmates fire that missile. I also know that you were stymied in pursuing those leads by the experts at NTSB. Correct?"

Nelson was still reeling from what he was hearing. He felt as though a thief had invaded the privacy of his home.

"I want you to understand something very important here, Frank. If you and I are ever subpoenaed to court and asked to repeat this conversation, I want you to remember that it was you, Frank Abrams, who mentioned el-Kabir and the ship, not me. Got it?"

"I understand."

"I have no idea how you got that information, Frank. But I know that without it, your case is going nowhere fast. You may not realize this fully yet, but it's very important for a lot of national-security reasons that you win this case."

Nelson stood on the sidewalk and looked around him. "Listen to me carefully, Frank. This is the only quasiclassified information I'm going to give you. And understand this, I will deny having told you any of it until hell freezes over. Everything you're looking for is contained in two separate informant files. One carries a single code name designation: 'Scimitar.' That's the folder on el-Kabir. The other is titled 'Hassad, PLO debriefing.' He's the dead passenger I mentioned before. When you serve your subpoenas for all of the aircraft accident investigation reports and exhibits and all the interviews, informant records, 302s, et cetera, you'll have to specify those two names. I can't promise that a federal judge will agree to turn them over to you or that the Department of Justice won't fight you for them. As I figure it, you can justify a subpoena of the Hassad file easily enough since his name is on the flight passenger list. On the Scimitar file, you'll come up with some plausible argument, I'm sure, based on the foreign registry and crew of the ship. What I can't and won't do right now is give you any particulars on the contents of those files. But I sure as hell won't hold back on any of those details once I'm sitting on the witness stand in court, under oath, and with a properly worded subpoena duces tecum in my hand. Understood?"

"Agent Nelson, please. I've been dying to find out the one thing that could make all the difference in my suit. Did you or anyone at the bureau ever issue a written or verbal warning to TWA of an imminent missile threat on Flight 800?"

"Let me answer your question with a question of my own, counselor. Do you really think that if I had developed information from a foreign informant, suggesting there was a foreign plot to fire a SAM missile from the deck of a ship at sea at a particular domestic flight, I wouldn't have issued a formal warning?"

"Is that a yes, then?"

"Well, Judas H. Priest, man! What the hell do you think it is, for Christsake? Look, just call me to the witness stand, Counselor. I promise you, all the pieces of the puzzle will come together in a real hurry . . . just like flies on a cow patty. Believe me, you won't be disappointed. What I have to say under oath will rock the good ole boys in the bureau and CIA intelligence community right down to the fallen arches of their flat feet. Even more importantly, when I get through prepping el-Kabir to testify, we might just begin to expose and break up support for Muslim terrorists coming from the ranks of those homegrown traitors who operate right here in our own backyard."

Frank was getting excited as he visualized the powerful and intimidating image of Nelson sitting on the witness stand in complete command of the rapt attention of the jury. He could almost hear his clear and unequivocal testimony buoyed by an impeccable credibility and childlike enthusiasm for the truth. He could picture the anguished, agonized look on the face of his nemesis, William Horace Canning III. "I can't wait to get you under oath in front of a jury, Don. If I thought I could get away with it, I would rent a white horse for you to ride into the courtroom."

Nelson stopped and pulled Frank by the arm away from the flow of pedestrian traffic. He spoke deliberately: "I'm no lawyer, but I'm guessin' that your case against TWA just became a whole lot easier to win than the one you had just one week ago. I'm sure it's not easy to prove that a major airline committed a wanton act of negligence, either in the faulty maintenance or design of an airplane. But now you have an entirely different set of facts to work with. This has got to be a trial attorney's dream come true. You have an airline that was given a detailed warning by the FBI that one of its flights was a precise target of terrorism. And even more important, we—I mean you—can now prove that they did absolutely nothing about it."

"Don, I need to ask you one last very important question. Why are you doing this? Why are you going out on a limb like this to help me and the Mayfair family?"

"It's not real complicated, Frank. Those passengers were murdered in cold blood, plain and simple. I'm a special agent of the finest criminal investigatory agency in the world. I'll be damned if I'll sit by and allow foreign jihadists to kill Americans with impunity and then watch them get away with it. I don't much care whether you get a big-money verdict for your clients or not. I want those sons of a bitch murderers identified and prosecuted and, in a more just world, publicly hanged.

"So, counselor, I'll wait for your personally hand-delivered subpoena calling for me and my files to appear in federal district court anytime you say. And don't forget, you owe me big-time."

"For what, agreeing to testify?"

"Hell, no. I'd never ignore a valid subpoena. You owe me an explanation as to how you got the name el-Kabir. And it had better be good."

Frank thought of Liam's inappropriate snooping around the desk of the New York SAC and of the ghostly words from his father. "Don, do you believe in the hereafter?"

"Ha! There'd better be something good beyond the grave, what with all the bullshit and evil we have to put up with every day of the week. Yeah, I do happen to believe in life after death. Why do you ask me that?"

"Good. Because then my explanation won't be so hard for you to accept. But that's for another day."

A WALK IN THE PARK

The sun was just setting behind a winding jogging path in Rock Creek Park as the two black SUVs slowly pulled up alongside one another. At first the FBI director thought of refusing the invitation of the White House chief of staff to meet away from their respective offices, especially in such a remote location. But he reconsidered when told that this meeting would be viewed as "a personal favor to the president."

The director got out first, telling his driver to stay inside the car. The chief of staff walked over to the director and slid his arm around his shoulder. "Thank you for meeting me here on such short notice, Lou. I hope I'm not taking you away from anything important. The president wants you to know how much he appreciates it."

The director did not return the smile and was all business. "What is this all about? And why all this secrecy, John?"

"Let's walk together for a few minutes, shall we? I'll explain everything."

"Come on, John, this is ridiculous. The only people who meet out here at night are spies and perverts. Make it quick. My wife and I have tickets to the Wolftrap tonight."

"OK, Lou. Calm down, for Pete's sake. This has to do with the strained conversation you had the other day with the president. He was very unhappy with the way everything was left hanging up in the air. He doesn't want you to get the wrong impression. You must know that he values your friendship very much and wouldn't want to do anything to jeopardize that."

"And just how am I supposed to respond to that, John? The president knows full well what was said. He and I were the only two in the Oval Office. As a matter of fact, he can listen to the tape of our conversation anytime he wants. And by the way, there was absolutely nothing left hanging in the air. I thought we both made our respective positions very clear."

"Yes, well, it seems another very important issue has come up, and the president would like to verify some information he learned of this morning."

"And he needs you to speak on his behalf? Doesn't he have my phone number? What exact information does he need verified?"

"It's come to my, excuse me, the president's attention that a very controversial audio cassette tape has just surfaced in the New York FBI office. On that tape is the voice message of a passenger on Flight 800, a former navy pilot, claiming to have seen a SAM missile fired from the ocean surface toward the plane. The president was wondering whether you've heard that tape."

"Why do you want to know that, John?"

"Lou, the national security ramifications are obvious, aren't they?"

"No, please enlighten me."

"Well, if that tape is somehow released to the public, it could cause a panic throughout the domestic airline industry and everyone who boards an airplane in this country. Especially now that the NTSB preliminary report has already officially concluded that there was no missile. That could create a serious lack of trust and confidence in the competency of our government and an even greater morale problem for all American travelers. Don't you see that?"

"John, in case you've forgotten what the proper role of the FBI is in this case, it isn't to bolster confidence in our airline industry or the NTSB. It's to determine what really happened to Flight 800 and whether there was a crime or act of terrorism committed."

"Of course, Lou. It's just that we need to have sufficient information to make a reasoned judgment on some urgent policy matters."

"A judgment? On what kind of matters?"

"There are so many broader factors this president has to consider in making foreign policy decisions. Many more than just whether a crime was committed."

"Really? Like what?"

"Well, for example, let's say, for the sake of argument that the NTSB report is wrong and there really was a missile, the timing now in releasing that tape couldn't be worse."

"What the hell does timing have to do with any of this?"

"Come on, Lou, do I have to draw it on a blackboard for you? I'm sure you know that the president is involved right now with very delicate preliminary negotiations with Israel and the PLO. He's trying to come up with a two-state solution for this mess in the Middle East. If Americans are told that the NTSB report is inaccurate and that this could have been a PLO-sponsored terrorist attack instead, what do you think would happen to their support for the president in bringing these two old enemies together? You must know that the polls show a high level of support right now for the president, but that will fall off dramatically if people think the PLO is back to their old tricks and can't be trusted. Especially now that Hamas is gaining prominence in their attempts to marginalize Arafat.

I'm sure you know what I'm trying to say. The lost opportunity could be devastating to the chances of achieving real peace."

The director paused for a few seconds. "May I be blunt, John?"

"Certainly."

The director turned and faced the chief of staff square in the face. "First of all, what makes you think the PLO is involved in this missile incident? As I understand it, there is no information on that audiotape that identifies who may have launched the missile, John. But let's just say, as a pure hypothetical, that this turns out to be a terrorist missile fired by the PLO with the support of the Iranian government and the president is successful in hiding those facts from the American people. The only thing lost will be the opportunity to finally end this charade our government has been playing in the name of peace. Not to mention the golden photo opportunity in having Netanyahu, Arafat, and the president smiling and shaking hands on yet another bargain with the devil."

"That's a very cynical view of the world, Lou, if I may say so."

"Look, John. Let's get right down to it, shall we? What exactly did you come all the way out here in the middle of nowhere to get from me anyway?"

"OK, Lou, here it is in a nutshell. The president would appreciate your letting him hear the tape so he can make some informed decisions as to how he manages the peace talks he's planning in the months ahead."

"And what else?"

"The president would like you to keep the tape away from the press and the public temporarily until the peace negotiations are concluded. Now, that's not asking for too much, is it?"

The director's smile was barely noticeable as the late-afternoon sunlight waned and filtered through the trees. "You know, John, like you, I read an occasional magazine or newspaper. Have you noticed that all the political wonks in Washington are talking about the president's very highly publicized peace initiative with Israel and the PLO? And are you aware that there is diplomatic scuttlebutt flying all around this town, especially among the UN effete, that he and Netanyahu and Arafat are all in the running for the Nobel Peace Prize? And that they all might even share in the prize together. Now, wouldn't that be something? That's what I would call the mother of all photo opportunities. Tell me something, John. Is the president still pissed that Arafat and Rabin got all the glory for their peace agreement in Oslo a few years back while he has nothing to show for his efforts? I'll bet he really wants that prize this time around, don't you think?"

"The president is interested only in hammering out a lasting peace in the Middle East, not photographs or Nobel prizes," John protested.

"Sure, whatever you say, John. Though I wonder if you see the same irony in all of this as I do."

"And what's that exactly?"

"Isn't it interesting that the prize this president wants so badly is named after a guy who invented dynamite as an explosive?"

John rolled his eyes. "Good grief! What's your point, Lou?"

"Well, think about it for a minute. Isn't it odd that the missile that took down Flight 800 probably never did what it was designed to do—actually explode? And yet that same defective missile has the real potential of symbolically blowing up in the face of both the PLO and the president. That's assuming, of course, that this tape winds up going public and our investigation shines the light of day on this whole sordid mess. Now, that would fall squarely under the category of true irony, don't you think?"

John glared at the director and exploded. "I've had just about enough of your bullshit! On behalf of the president of the United States, I'm directing you to turn that tape and all copies over to me immediately!"

The director laughed aloud. "First of all, how the hell do you think you have the authority to direct me to do anything? If the president really expected me to turn over the tape to him, he should have given me that order in person instead of through his weasel water boy. He sent you here tonight to do his dirty work because he already knows that he can't buy me off or intimidate me. He just wants to insulate himself. What's the term you guys use all the time? 'Plausible deniability'?

"Secondly, I haven't even heard the tape yet. In fact, I don't even have it. Even if I had custody, it's not mine to give to anyone. It doesn't belong to me. It's the private property of the Mayfair family. The last time I checked the US Constitution and the intent of the founding fathers, your king can no longer kick in a door and seize private property without due process of law. I believe you'll need to dig up somebody over at DOJ to find a pliant judge to issue a formal warrant for that. You know, one of those black-robed whores you keep in your back ass pocket. It seems to me, John, the more the president and you skulk around like this, the more exciting the nightly news could become in the weeks ahead."

The director paused and measured his words deliberately. "Here's my answer to your so-called directive. When, if at all, I'm given access to the Mayfair tape, I'll listen to it very carefully. While I'm at it, I'll probably also take a closer look at that PLO donor list we got from that Flight 800 passenger, Ahmed Hassad. You know, the guy who's been making your boss and his political cronies so nervous lately. Depending on what kind of intel comes to light, I'll probably reopen the investigation into the explosion and go hard after every new lead in both situations, wherever the hell they take me . . . even if they happen to point me in the direction of the Hill and the White House."

The director paused. "If the president really wants to hear the tape, John, why don't you suggest he call his other water boy over at the *New*

York Times. You know, that little shit who leaked the story to you about the tape in the first place. I'm sure he'll eventually be able to scrounge up a secondhand transcribed copy from one of the other news outlets. That is, if he still has a job by then."

"I don't know what you mean, Lou. We don't have that kind of relationship with the *Times.* We don't play favorites with the press. I'm sure the young man you're referring to, whoever he is, has a very reliable and trustworthy reputation."

"He has the reputation of a scorpion, John. Be careful. Someday he'll turn on you too, just like Aesop described."

"What the hell are you talking about?"

"I'm talking about Aesop's fables, John. Didn't you learn about them in grade school? One of them is the story of the scorpion who asked to be carried across the river on the frog's back. The frog, being your normal, rational frog, refuses at first, knowing that he could die if the scorpion decides to sting him while crossing the river. But the smooth-talking scorpion calms the frog's fear with the indisputable logic that his betrayal would result in both their deaths. The scorpion says, 'But, why would I ever poison you, Mr. Frog? I can't swim. If you die, we'll both drown and die.'

"Do you know what strikes me the most about this fable, John? It's the level of surprise and shock that everyone seems to have when they discover that they have been betrayed by people who have made a living doing just that over a lifetime. Surely you remember the ending. The scorpion stabs the frog. Realizing, in midriver, that he is dying from the scorpion's lethal sting, the frog becomes incredulous. He asks the scorpion, 'Why did you poison me? Now we'll both drown!' The scorpion calmly says, 'Because I am a scorpion. That's what I do!'"

"I resent your insinuation!" said the chief of staff.

"You'd better heed Aesop's warning, John. I wouldn't offer to carry anyone across the river, if you know what I mean. You're surrounded by scorpions, and you don't even realize it."

By now, the chief of staff was livid and could barely control his rage. Spittle flew from his mouth as he shouted, "What self-righteous drivel! Do I need to remind you that you serve entirely at the pleasure of the president? He put you in your office and can force you out of it in a heartbeat, and you know it! I'm warning you. If you make that donor list public, you'll be brought up on charges of violating national security and disclosing classified information and maybe even treason."

The director gritted his teeth. His voice was strangely repressed, as if ready to explode. "No, you don't need to remind me about the power of the president and how much he enjoys flaunting it in front of the whole world. But when you discuss our conversation with him later, while you're sucking up to him, why don't you remind your president that he also serves entirely at the pleasure of the American people who will be none too happy with him if he doesn't get off my back and let me do my job.

True enough, he can force me out of my job, but he's not going to make me to tiptoe through all the political dog shit and intrigue you guys love to roll around in. It ain't gonna happen, John. Not while my good name is still on the door of the J. Edgar Hoover Building. *Capisce?*

"And while you're at it, I want you to remind the president that he doesn't need to fire me publicly. You know, with all that usual, nasty innuendo and self-inflicted embarrassment. Ironically, he doesn't have the balls to do that anyway. So look, I'll make this really easy for him. As I've already told him, I'll resign immediately. Tonight, if he wants me to.

"And as far as that PLO donor list is concerned, all I can say is this. If the president and his political friends haven't been stupid and naive enough to give money to our jihadist enemies, then they have nothing to worry about. Do they? Look, John, let me put this into words even you can understand. If this is the way the president really wants to handle this situation, by suppressing evidence in a major air-disaster investigation, then make sure he understands one more thing."

The director leaned in even closer to the chief of staff's now flushed face. "Listen to me very carefully, John. My final official act as director of the FBI won't just be typing up a letter of resignation. My swan song will be sung on a big stage with lots of lights and an audience of hundreds of reporters when I publicly announce the exact reasons for my resignation. Are you getting all of this, John? And by the way, my staff tells me I tend to be way too long-winded at my press conferences. One of my shortcomings, I'm told. I really have to learn to be more concise and frugal with my words. As a matter of fact, I should probably never have even gotten out of the car when you pulled up. I should've just rolled down the window and told you to go fuck yourself. We're done here. You've already wasted too much of my time tonight."

The director turned abruptly and started to walk back to his car and his waiting driver.

"Now, if you'll excuse me, I have a date with my wife."

THIRD AND GOAL

Over the next three days, Abrams worked well into the night, eating his meals at his desk. He had felt a sudden and unexpected surge of energy. It was the once-familiar reserve of excitement he had not experienced since he was a young, cocky attorney preparing the very first case he ever took to trial. Frank had drafted an amended complaint, totally abandoning his negligent electrical-wiring-maintenance theory. In its place, he had put together new, alternative causes of action against TWA based on their willful and/or negligent failure to react to the official FBI warnings, which Agent Nelson would hopefully bring to light. He had also prepared detailed subpoenas for the explosive contents of the Scimitar and Hassad files. He could hardly contain the anticipation building in his gut.

Frank's secretary buzzed his intercom. "Mr. Abrams, I have Agent Jones on the line."

Abrams ran to his desk and picked up the phone. "Good morning, Merle."

"Good morning, Frank. I just wanted to tell you that our audio-lab folks have gone over the tape with a fine-toothed comb. Everything appears to be copasetic and authentic. Thank you for holding off on this. You and Liam are free to have that press conference, if you are so inclined."

"Thanks, Merle. We're in the process of setting it up here in my offices."

"Please accept a friendly word of caution, Frank. I'm sure I don't have to remind you that reporters can be a very devious and self-serving lot, especially over there at the *Times*. I wouldn't want any of them packing my parachute, if you know what I mean. If I were you, I would record everything said at this conference by all parties. As a matter of fact, I would only read from a prepared statement and not answer any questions, just to keep things uncomplicated."

"That's exactly what we plan to do. I understand how the system works. Thanks for everything, Merle. Wish me luck."

Jones laughed. "As I recently reminded our friend Bob Anderson, luck is not something you wish for, Frank. It's something you go out and make happen. Isn't it funny how the longer and harder you work at accomplishing something, the luckier you seem to get?"

STILL DANGEROUS

No sooner did Abrams get off the phone with Jones than his secretary buzzed his intercom again. "Frank, Lee Mayfair is on line one. She sounds really frightened. She says it's urgent."

Abrams grabbed the phone. "What's the matter, Lee?"

"Frank, I'm here in the condo with Liam. I'm very concerned about these two men who have been hanging out in the lobby of the building for the past twenty minutes or so. They followed me on the street for a couple of blocks from Lexington over to my building. When I went inside, I held the elevator door open long enough to see them go up to the doorman and show him what looked like some form of identification. When I got upstairs, I got a phone call from the doorman, who said that he was approached by one of the men in a dark jacket who claims he was an FBI agent and needed to confirm that I was living in the building. He swears that he didn't confirm anything. He said it was against management policy to do that. That was about five minutes ago."

Abrams immediately thought of the men Liam encountered in Montauk and asked, "Lee, did Liam manage to get a look at them? More importantly, were you alone when you were on the street and came into the building?"

"Yes, I was alone. Liam was already upstairs. And no, he hasn't seen them yet."

"OK. Sit tight. I'll call NYPD right now. Bob Anderson just happened to walk into my office this second for a lunch meeting today. We'll both be there in a few minutes. We're only a few blocks away. I want you to keep in touch with the doorman by phone and insist that he not let them in. Is that clear?"

"Yes, Frank."

"Lee, what are these guys wearing?"

"One of them is wearing a light-colored suit and a tie. The other has a short brown leather jacket. Frank, this is really nerve-racking. I'm really scared. Do you think they're looking for Liam?"

"It's possible. But as long as you both stay in the condo and dead bolt the door, you'll be fine. Call my cellular phone if anything develops. We'll be right over."

As Abrams and Anderson walked to the elevator, Abrams called 911 and relayed the Mayfair address and the information Lee had just given him to the dispatcher. Remembering the confusion that almost got one of his off-duty agent friends killed by a local town policeman a few years ago, Frank told the dispatcher, "Ma'am, I need you to tell the responding officers that I and a second man, a retired FBI agent, will be at the scene together. Both of us are in dark suits. Please tell them that one or more of the suspects is wearing a light-colored suit, not a dark-colored suit. Tell them also that my name is Frank Abrams. I'm six feet three inches tall, my head is shaved, and my partner has a white crew cut and horn-rimmed glasses. Please be very sure you emphasize that I am carrying a legally concealed weapon. Is that clear?"

The dispatcher was annoyingly curt. "I'll pass that information along, sir. But please stay out of the way and let our officers do their job."

"Ma'am, if by any chance I get there before New York's finest, please be aware that I won't be sitting by twiddling my thumbs. Do you understand what I'm saying? We may be facing a life-and-death situation here. Pass that information along to your officers as well, please."

As they rode down the elevator and ran to the street, Frank remained on the phone and insisted that the dispatcher write down both his and Bob's cell numbers.

By the time Abrams got off his cell phone, he and Anderson were already halfway to the Mayfair building, trotting, dodging, and weaving through the busy, noonday, sidewalk pedestrian traffic.

As they hurried into the building, Abrams noticed immediately that the doorman was not in the lobby. He and Anderson were the only two people in the expansive granite-enclosed room. No police, no tenants, and most importantly, no doorman. As Abrams walked to the elevator, Bob grabbed him by the elbow and pointed to a small, unlit janitor's room off to the side. The door was ajar. A man's foot was sticking over the sill.

Frank instinctively unholstered his 9 mm. Smith & Wesson and swung the door open. There, on the floor, was a middle-aged man in a doorman's uniform, unconscious, with a gash across his forehead. The concrete floor was covered with blood.

"This is not good," Bob said slowly.

"The cops aren't here yet, Frank. We have no choice but to get our asses upstairs and see what the hell's going on."

The old friends stepped into the elevator. As Frank reached for the button for the penthouse floor, his head was swimming in adrenaline and his breathing became difficult. Bob broke the silence. "Just like old times, huh, rookie?"

Suddenly, Frank changed his mind and pressed the door's hold button. "Look, Bob. Why don't you stay down here and wait for the police. Call them again to let them know what we have here. I'll go on up alone. You can follow in a few minutes. In the meanwhile, see if that guy is still breathing. If he comes to, maybe can tell us something useful."

Bob nodded in agreement. "I'll call 911 again and will be right up. Don't do anything stupid or dramatic, Frank. OK?"

Bob pulled out his cell phone as he stepped off the elevator. When Frank got to the top floor, the doors slid open and the elevator bell chimed. Frank had already squeezed up against the front corner of the lift with his gun drawn and was in a crouched position.

Frank looked around quickly. Nothing. No sound. No sign of life. He stepped forward, froze for a moment at the threshold, and then slowly pushed open the condo door, which was unlocked.

Suddenly, there was a blinding flash of light. Frank slumped to the ground like a sack of flour.

Back in the lobby, there was still no sign of police, not even the customary sound of sirens out on Lexington Avenue. Anderson couldn't revive the unconscious doorman, who was still breathing. Considering his limited options, he made a crucial decision to take the elevator to the floor beneath the penthouse and walk up the final flight of stairs. Knowing that the elevator would probably open directly in front of the entrance doorway to the condo, he wanted to make a little more discreet arrival without the obvious sounds of the elevator floor bell and the metal doors sliding open.

Bob sprinted up the long, final flight of stairs. By the time he reached the penthouse floor, he was out of breath and sucking wind. His heart pounded wildly in his chest with an extra surge of adrenaline coursing through his body. As he quietly opened the exit door into the hallway, he heard the faint sound of voices coming from the condo. His senses were so heightened, he could discern almost every other word. A man with a distinct foreign accent was angry and threatening someone. There was no sign of his partner.

As he approached the door, which was open about two feet, Bob's stomach tightened. He noticed Frank lying facedown near the threshold. As he stood motionless, he could hear the sound of a woman softly crying. He bent down to look though the doorway and immediately saw Liam and Lee Mayfair at the far end of the room, facing the door. Standing directly in front of them, with their backs to the door, were two midsized, heavyset men. One of them was pointing some kind of semiautomatic at Liam's chest. Bob spotted Liam's momentary eye recognition and quickly put his finger to his lips.

The man with the gun spoke again, in a strange, halting accent. "It would be very foolish of you to waste any more of our time. If you want your mother to live, you will turn over the tape to me immediately. Otherwise, she is a dead woman."

Liam kept the man preoccupied. "I told you, I don't have the tape. I gave it to the FBI. They know all about you."

"Perhaps you would like to watch as I rape your mother right here in front of you and then slit her throat?"

Liam flushed with a surge of anger. "You're not killing anyone, asshole!"

At that, the man raised his gun and pointed it at Lee's face. "Enough of your stupidity, you American pig!"

Suddenly, Liam heard a popping sound and watched in horror as a piece of white brain tissue flew forward through the air, hitting Liam in the face. Thinking that his mother had been shot, he tried to shield her with his body. The second man wheeled around and pulled his own weapon.

Two more cracks rang out as both men slumped to the floor. Both were killed instantly, each with deadly accurate head shots.

No more than thirty seconds later, the elevator doors opened and three uniformed New York City cops rushed into the room, their Glocks pointed at Bob Anderson, who was the only other person in the room holding a weapon. Bob lowered his gun and slowly put it down on the coffee table.

"My name is Bob Anderson, retired FBI. These two mutts are foreign operatives tied into one of our investigations. The man over there on the floor is my former partner, Frank Abrams, also retired FBI. Call an ambulance and get him some help, please, right away!"

As Bob reached for his identification, Frank moaned, sat up, and held the back of his head. He looked up at Anderson and, when he figured out what had just happened, said, "I thought you never carried your gun, Bob! Didn't you say they were too dangerous?"

"They're still very dangerous, rookie. Thirty-five years on the job and I never once fired my weapon on duty. I never told you this, Frank, but in my retirement, I've been going to the range at least twice a month. More out of boredom than anything else. Strange, isn't it? I think my skills today are probably better than they were when I was at the academy."

Anderson pointed at Frank's head. "But what about you? How's your head? We've got to get you checked out by EMS as soon as they get here. You probably have a concussion, Frank."

Frank took his hand away from his head and saw that there was no blood. "Well, at least I won't need stitches. But, man, do I have one hell of an egg shaping up."

As soon as the cobwebs cleared out of Frank's head, he got to his feet and looked down at the bodies on the floor. "Liam, do these guys look like the same two men who killed Mathers on the beach?"

"I'm not sure. I think so. They're about the same size, I guess."

Anderson leaned over and, without touching the weapon on the floor, said, "Well, well, what do you know? A Walther PPK! How 'bout that for a coincidence? Why do I get the feeling that the forensics on this gun and the slug from your car are going to match up like peas in a pod?"

Frank collected his thoughts. "Bob, you'd better get Jones's agents down here, pronto. We need to get these two identified right away. I'll give you two to one that they are hooked up with that tanker crew."

One of the police officers, a sergeant, finally spoke up. "Excuse me, gentlemen, we need to secure this room and conduct a crime scene investigation. You'll have to stand aside, but don't go anywhere. We'll need for you to give statements to the homicide detectives when they get here."

Frank smiled and looked at Bob. "Thank you, officer, but that won't be necessary. The FBI will take over at this point. This is all now under their jurisdiction."

"Sorry, sir, but I have NYPD procedures to follow. With all due respect, sir, you're in Manhattan, not Washington. We'll give the orders, if you don't mind. Nothing personal, of course."

Anderson stepped forward and smiled benevolently. "Maybe if you guys had gotten to this crime scene on time, you could have called dibs on controlling the scene investigation. Know what I mean? But you know how the old saying goes. 'He who hesitates is lost.' Right?"

The sergeant began to argue when Anderson's cell phone rang. Bob turned away, and after half a minute of muffled conversation, he handed his cell phone over to the sergeant. "I have your precinct commander on the phone, Sergeant. He would like to speak with you. He'll explain how federal and local jurisdictional issues work in airline-disaster cases. So now, if you don't mind, I'll ask you to please vacate the premises. Leave your names and badge numbers with my partner here, and try not to track around any of the blood on the carpet on your way out."

The young, paunchy Irish cop could only glare at his older counterpart as he reached out to take the phone.

"Not to worry, Sergeant. The FBI crime scene team is already on its way, as we speak. I know you may find it hard to believe, but they actually know how to do this. Too bad you boys won't be around to see how a crime scene is worked over in the big leagues. Nothing personal, of course."

Frank walked slowly over to Lee and put his arm around her. Her body was still trembling. "I'm sorry you had to witness all of this, Lee. Thank God my partner got up here and got the drop on these two."

"Frank, I know they came here to kill my son. Somehow I never thought they would get this far . . . to actually get into my home. This is all like a bad dream."

Lee took Anderson's hand. "But, Mr. Anderson, what a terrible trauma this must be for you! Are you OK?"

"Don't worry about me, Mrs. Mayfair. I'm doing all right, considering what just happened here. But I know that won't last for long. Based on past personal experience, I expect I'll be crashing from adrenaline withdrawal in an hour or two. That's when it'll hit me like a hammer between the eyes."

"Lee, you and your son are safe now," said Frank. "Liam, why don't you fix your mother a scotch and water and try to relax? Meanwhile, don't forget, we have the press conference planned for the day after tomorrow. Are you still up for it? Or would you rather I adjourn everything for a week or two so you can have some more time to prepare your statement and calm down a little bit?"

"No way, Frank. We've come this far. I'm not going to back out now that we have everyone's attention. The timing is perfect."

The following night, Liam sat at his mother's kitchen table, trying to frame the outline of a statement he insisted on giving at the next day's press conference. After an hour of writer's block, he threw down his pencil in frustration. "Mom, I need to clear my head. I'm going out for a walk. Will you be all right here by yourself?"

"I'll be fine, Liam. Please don't stay out too late, OK?"

Liam walked out of the empty lobby and turned up Lexington, breathing in the cold night air. After walking north a few blocks, he came upon a familiar corner bar that his father would occasionally haunt on his way home. Upon entering, he slid onto the nearest bar stool and ordered a Guinness stout.

About five minutes later, a middle-aged man in a black hooded sweatshirt walked through the front door. He looked briefly around the nearly empty bar and pulled up a stool right next to Liam without saying a word. The man stared ahead in silence for a moment before pointing to a faded photo hanging on the wall next to the register. It was a picture of the bar owner grinning and holding up a large fish. "Now, that's what I call a trophy!" he said aloud.

Liam followed his gaze to the wall and recognized the familiar photograph. He then turned to his left and looked at the man's face. He noticed it was pockmarked. Sweat lined the upper lip. "Are you a fisherman?" was all he could think to say in response.

"You might say that. Have you ever caught anything that big?"

"Yeah. That's one monster striped bass in that picture. I've caught a few of those out east."

Liam suddenly took notice of the accent. Not American. Subtle, but definitively foreign.

The man leaned in toward Liam and lowered his voice. "How did you do the last time you were out in Montauk, Liam? Catch anything exciting?"

Liam leaped off his stool, knocking it over. His eyes darted around the bar as panic gripped him by the throat. The man stood, slammed his hand down on the bar, and pushed Liam away forcefully. "Back away from this now while you still have your life!" he growled.

The bartender, who had witnessed the sudden explosion, assumed Liam had said something insulting to the stranger to provoke a fight. He started to come out from around the bar with a small baton in his hand when Liam suddenly landed a roundhouse punch, instantly breaking the man's nose, splitting his lip, and knocking him down. Blood spilled all over the floor.

The man quickly jumped to his feet and ran out the front door.

It was then that Liam noticed it. Lying on the bar next to his drink, in the spot where the man had slammed his hand, was a crumpled note.

The bartender was nearing the end of a long shift and was in no mood. "Say, aren't you one of JW's kids? Liam, right? Look, I don't want any trouble in here. Why don't you go home quietly and I won't report any of this to the cops? How 'bout it?"

Liam collected his composure, stuffed the note into his jeans pocket, and walked hurriedly out of the bar without saying a word. When he got to the street, he started running and didn't slow down until he got to the elevator of his mother's building about three blocks away.

When he reached the penthouse, his mother was still up. He grabbed the note out of his pocket and read it. His heart skipped a beat. There in bold, block letters were the words, "THERE ARE MANY MORE OF US THAN THE TWO MARTYRS YOU KILLED. STOP WHAT YOU ARE DOING NOW IF YOU WANT YOUR FAMILY TO LIVE."

Liam walked into the den and handed the note to his mother, explaining the entire incident. After reading it in silence, she put it down in her lap and began to cry. After a minute, she spoke. "Oh, God, I thought this nightmare was over. Liam, what are you going to do? Are you really going ahead with the press conference tomorrow with this still hanging over our heads?"

"I can't afford to stop now, Mom. First thing in the morning, I'm going to call Frank and fill him in. Then I'll call Mr. Jones. Maybe he can start to pick up this guy's trail by talking to the bartender. Then I'm going to live my life. Let them keep coming at me. I'm not going to let these scumbags intimidate or push me around anymore."

He walked into the kitchen, picked up his legal pad and pencil, and began writing with a newfound intensity and determination.

THE RED TAIL

Early the next morning, Abrams called Merle Jones to tell him about Liam's incident the night before. A few minutes later, Jones called him back. "Frank, I just spoke to the local precinct commander to bring him into the loop. I was shocked to find out that two of his foot patrolmen spotted this guy with blood all over his face as he was running across the street about a block away from the bar. When the cops tried to stop him, the idiot pulled a gun from his waistband. One of the cops drew his Glock and fired, hitting him in the upper leg. He gave up without any struggle and is now chained to a bed in St. Luke's Hospital. I have one of my agents on the way over there right now to interview him. We'll know more in a few hours, especially after we've contacted the bartender for a statement."

Jones paused. "You know, Frank, this puts a little different spin on the situation now. Apparently, this thing is not over. You realize that, right? Are you and Liam still going public with this?"

"Well, our press conference is scheduled to start in about an hour. And as far as I know, it's full steam ahead. I've already spoken to Liam. He won't back down."

"Does he understand the risks he's taking and that he might be looking over his shoulder for quite some time?"

"He doesn't care. Listen, Merle, is there anything you can do to protect him and his mother?"

"I'm one step ahead of you. I was able to convince the precinct commander, in spite of his objection, to assign round-the-clock monitoring of the Mayfair building and an escort for Mrs. Mayfair for the next couple of weeks. Don't worry about anything, Frank. I'll pick up the slack later with my own guys. Tell Liam he's covered."

"Thanks, Merle. That's a huge favor. We won't forget it."

Earlier that morning, Frank Abrams, as would any good trial attorney, had insisted that he act as the family's spokesman and that he alone speak to the press rather than his client. But Liam, with Lee's approval, had once again overruled his advice. After a short and heated debate, Liam had compromised with Abrams and allowed him to edit the statement that Liam, who was unable to sleep, had written out in longhand in the predawn hours of the morning.

The excitement from the night before had finally begun to fade when, at about 10:00 a.m., Abrams' conference room was opened for the press. As each reporter and cameraman filed into the spacious room, their credentials were screened by a big, burly man in a crumpled suit. The Mayfair boys knew him as a bouncer at a lower East Side bar. Liam had the foresight the day before to ask Colin to hire him specifically for the event. When Michael Ketchum and his crew arrived, Liam walked over to his enforcer friend and said to him, "Don't let these guys in, Joey. They're not real journalists."

Ketchum grew angry. "I have every right to be here, and you know it!"

Liam turned to the bouncer and said. "Where I come from, liars have no rights. Get him and his crew the hell out of here, right now."

"Come on, Liam, if you don't know how the game is played by now, you'll find out soon enough. Give me a break, will ya? Why don't you grow up and join the real world?"

Suddenly, Merle Jones pushed his way through the crowded room, winked at Liam, and grabbed Ketchum by the elbow. "Excuse me, Mr. Mayfair, I'd like to have a private word with Mr. Ketchum here if that's all right with you."

The bouncer looked at Liam. "What do you want me to do?"

"Leave him alone. The FBI will deal with him."

Jones, who towered over Ketchum, hustled the startled little reporter into an empty side office and grabbed him by the front of his shirt. "I know what you did, Mr. Ketchum. So does Liam and his attorney. You broke your word and ran like a puppy to your sleazy connection in the White House and told him about the tape. Unfortunately for you, now I may just have to name you as a co-conspirator and indict you for obstruction of justice and tampering with critical evidence in an ongoing federal investigation of foreign terrorism. You might as well hang around for the press conference to get a sneak preview of what's in store for you. Have a nice day, junior." Jones left Ketchum alone in the office, disheveled, frightened, and wondering what the hell just happened to him.

Liam, who had trailed Jones as he led Ketchum down the hallway, overheard Jones's threat. Taking Jones aside, he asked, "Are you really going to do that? Indict him?"

Jones grinned. "No. Of course not. But he doesn't know that for sure, does he? I've given him something to think about. Let him stew on that possibility for a while. I hope you don't mind, but I invited him to stay and imagine the mess he thinks he may have just gotten himself into."

Meanwhile, Ketchum flushed bright red, cursed under his breath, and stormed backed into the conference room, knocking over his assistant's camera equipment.

Liam looked at his watch. "Well, I've got a press conference to take care of. Are you staying, Mr. Jones?"

Jones put his hand on Liam's shoulder and, lowering his voice, spoke to him, almost as a father. "Son, give me a minute of your time first, if you don't mind."

Liam grew concerned. "Is there anything wrong? Have there been any more threats?"

"No, it's nothing like that. I just wanted to tell you privately how much I admire you for what you're doing here this morning. Especially knowing, as you must know, the danger you're still in. You're about to blow the lid off a major terrorist conspiracy, and there's no telling how much pressure you and your family may come under in the coming months. I know your attorney is focused on the lawsuit, but the biggest part of this story is the list of high-profile political names you are threatening to expose. Don't underestimate their ferocity and capacity for retribution."

"Mr. Jones, I'm really not afraid of any of them anymore. I just want my mother and siblings protected. Frank said you arranged to provide my mother with an escort and surveillance. Is that true?"

"Yes, it is. You don't have to worry about her while I'm in charge of this investigation. But there is one more thing I need to give you."

"Give me?"

"Liam, I hope you understand that you're a survivor. I want you to always remember that. And to help you remember, I want you to meet a real living survivor from Flight 800."

"Survivor? What are you talking about? There were no . . ."

Jones put a finger to his lips, reached into his briefcase, and pulled out a small plastic bag half-filled with water. "Do you remember the meeting we had with Abrams and Anderson in my office when I first heard your father's audiotape?"

"Sure, of course."

"Well, when I walked back into the office after that long phone call to my boss, I noticed you leaning over my little aquarium, probably wondering what the hell the man in charge of the largest FBI office in the country would be doing with two of these little guys."

With that, Jones handed Liam the bag. In it, Liam saw a small, green painted turtle, the kind sold in pet stores all across the country.

Liam smiled. "My father bought me one of these guys when I was a little kid. But why are you giving me this?"

"Liam, believe it or not, this little critter, along with hundreds of other turtles, somehow survived the disaster. They were being shipped from a pet dealer in Louisiana to a French businessman with a landscaping company outside of Paris. They were stowed away in the forward hold of the plane in steel boxes that held Styrofoam containers, which in turn held hundreds of water-filled bags. So far as we can tell, not one of the turtles was killed. Obviously, the containers broke open in the explosion. But we figured that the water in the bags insulated them from the concussion and heat. They were found alive, floating in the debris field. This little guy here was handed to me by Chief Petty Officer Steve Gross the first day I was out at the Moriches Coast Guard Station, right after I finished up a press interview. Pretty ironic, isn't it? There were almost as many survivors as there were deaths in that crash. I've kept two of them in my office for almost two years, as a symbol of hope and the incredible resilience of life. And more importantly, as a reminder to do everything in my power and ability to get to the unabridged truth about Flight 800, no matter where it takes me."

Liam was stunned at what he had just heard and fumbled for words. "I don't know how to thank you enough, Mr. Jones."

"It's I who should be thanking you, Liam. Your courageous role in all of this has been the kick in the pants I needed to complete my job. I'm afraid I've been a little lax in managing this investigation. But that's all about to change."

Liam looked up from the turtle and made direct eye contact with Jones. "I'm sorry it took me so long to come to my senses and build up enough guts to do this."

Pointing to the turtle, Jones smiled. "You don't need to apologize for anything, Liam. Remember, slow and steady wins the race."

Jones paused for a second and gently prodded Liam. "Now get in there and give 'em hell."

Liam looked down at his newfound reptilian friend and grinned ear to ear as he remembered that day long ago when his father handed him the same gift. He turned and strode into the conference room toward the podium and the waiting throng of reporters.

Liam Mayfair stood in front of dozens of TV cameras, microphones, klieg lights, and a host of reporters, all of whom filled every square inch of the large conference room in Abrams's offices. His primary mission now was to leave no doubt for the press as to who were the new and real targets in his search for justice.

His mind wandered as his eyes swept the room, trying to take in the import of what he was about to do. He delayed speaking for a few additional minutes as he watched a major TV network crew arrive late and hurry to set up. Liam suddenly came to the realization that he was about to take the first critical step in exposing multiple and deadly layers of human betrayal—from the lowly and the mundane to the highest and most profound levels of power in the world.

As he stepped up to the microphones, Liam spotted Bill Canning standing alone in the back of the room. He suddenly remembered a Latin phrase he had heard Frank use with his adversary. Those words instantly conjured up a mental image of that fearful moment when thousands of Caesar's tired and battle-worn soldiers crossed over the Rubicon from Gaul into the heart of the Roman Empire. Every one of Caesar's men understood the dire meaning and the consequences of their action. By merely crossing this small bridge, each of them would be forever considered an insurrectionist, subject to an automatically imposed death penalty. Julius Caesar, at the head of his feared, victorious legion, also understood that by marching on Rome to assume power over the Senate, he would forfeit, by law, not only his imperium but also any right he may have held as a Roman general and citizen. If he failed and yet somehow survived, he would be publicly executed.

Liam imagined the soldiers looking up toward the stone face of their Caesar, as if pleading for deliverance from the final battle and the uncertainty that awaited them.

He could visualize the general, mounted on a beautiful black stallion, in full battle gear, sun glinting off the Roman eagle emblazoned on his breastplate armor. He could almost hear the cold, stark words which echoed among his silent troops. "Alea jacta sunt!" the general shouted to his men. The words settled over them like a pall. They knew their deadly meaning all too well. They understood with every fiber of their being that, as with every empire created by mankind, theirs would rise or fall dependent on the level of each man's individual courage, integrity and especially loyalty—not to themselves, but to a cause greater than themselves. From this moment forward, there could be no turning back. He was all in. Indeed, the die had been cast.

Liam approached the bank of microphones and, without any introduction or hesitation, spoke in a voice filled with renewed confidence.

"What you are about to hear is the clear voice of a man who could not be silenced in death. I hope his words are as comforting and as definitive for all the families of those who were murdered on Flight 800 as they have been to me and my own family. These are the last words spoken by my father on this earth from an air phone aboard Flight 800 seconds before the plane exploded. His words are the only surviving eyewitness account of an actual passenger aboard that flight as to what really happened that night.

"But they are only the tip of the iceberg. There is much more to come to light. In the coming weeks and months, you will see even clearer and more convincing evidence from a host of reliable sources proving that the explosion that destroyed this plane was not caused, as our government has assured us, by a spark from an electrical-wiring defect. Flight 800 was brought down by a foreign terrorist missile, fired from the deck of a freighter."

A wave of low-level mumbling swept across the room as Liam continued without breaking stride. "When my family's lawsuit against TWA goes to trial in the Federal Courthouse of the Southern District of New York in the months to come, the world will hear the testimony of at least one living eyewitness who will describe the launch of that missile. We anticipate that, by then, we will finally be able to look at the physical evidence of the missile attack, including both the missile remnants and the launch equipment."

Another quick collective murmur rose up from the throng of TV and newspaper crews assembled in front of Liam as startled reporters and technicians lowered their cassette players and looked up wide-eyed from their notes and monitors.

Liam held up the tape in front of him and looked slowly across the room at all the hushed, surprised faces.

"My father's words are preserved here on this simple answering machine cassette tape. I only just recently learned about the existence of this tape, which had been virtually lost for nearly two years. I'll play it for you from start to finish in a moment. But before I do, I am also announcing that we have uncovered shocking evidence of an attempted massive government cover-up by certain members of Congress and the White

House to suppress this tape and the FBI's expansion of their Flight 800 investigation. We will identify everyone who took part in this conspiracy.

"The evidence that Frank Abrams will lay out to the jury will prove that the missile attack was part of a plan involving the PLO and the government of Iran to kill a PLO defector who was a passenger aboard that flight. It will also prove the more insidious role of several prominent American politicians who have funded PLO's terrorist activities for years, making then all equally complicit.

"More to the point of the lawsuit itself, my attorney, Mr. Abrams, will prove that TWA knowingly concealed and ignored a specific, official warning from the FBI of an impending terrorist missile attack directed at Flight 800. TWA could have prevented this attack. Instead, they chose to remain silent for reasons that were entirely self-serving. TWA is no less responsible for these murders than the jihadists who fired that missile from the deck of the freighter that night.

"You'll hear the entire, unedited tape. Most of what's on this tape is my father's deeply personal message to me. It and of itself, it has no direct bearing on the missile attack, but I am nevertheless proud to share it with you. His eyewitness account of the missile attack comes very suddenly and unexpectedly near the end of the tape."

Liam took a deep breath, paused, then continued. "There is one more very important note. At the risk of disappointing some of you, I must tell you now that after the tape has played, we will not take any questions or provide any interviews. The next time we speak publicly about this case will be at the post-trial press conference, announcing our successful jury verdict against TWA."

As Liam finished his prepared statement, Frank noticed a familiar face standing alone in the rear corner of the room with his jaw agape. It was Bill Canning, who could have sworn he had just witnessed a personal preview of Frank Abrams's opening statement to the jury. Just then, Frank Abrams caught the eye of his adversary. Smiling at him from over the cameras and klieg lights, Frank held up the formal, unsigned stipulation of discontinuance, which he had promised to give him that morning. Canning watched dumbfounded as Abrams slowly and dramatically ripped it in half, tossing it into the waste can. Without informing Liam or Lee, Frank had called Canning the night before to invite him to the press conference. He had assured his longtime nemesis that he would tender the white paper flag of surrender in the lawsuit against TWA and hand it over to him in person. At least that was the plan as of one short week ago. But that was before the case exploded wide open. *Such are the rare, exotic pleasures that more than compensate for the mindless drudgery and anxiety of litigation*, Frank happily thought to himself.

Liam backed away from the bank of microphones, inserted the tape into the cassette player, turned up the volume, and hit the play button. He folded his arms, put his head down, and focused once more on every syllable of every word of his father, as though hearing it for the first time.

As the tape played, he envisioned JW standing here in this very room where he had given so many interviews to the press for so many years.

An eerie silence enveloped the large room as the tape played through to its deadly finale. Finally, the harsh static, freezing the precise moment in time of his father's death, hissed through the speakers. Liam flinched reflexively and then once again as he spun away from the frenzied shouting that cascaded around him. He turned his back to the din of screaming reporters, their arms outstretched, firing their barrage of questions. He ignored the pandemonium as his eyes drifted upward through the large plate glass windows. There, high above him in a bright, cloudless sky, he saw the improbable yet unmistakable outline of a young red-tailed hawk soaring freely, riding the concrete thermals over the Manhattan skyline. Suddenly, he felt the fear, anxiety, and anger that had consumed and weighed upon every day of his brief life span being lifted up off his shoulders. He knew at that very moment that the emotional relief that now filled his mind and senses was real and permanent. The inner peace he felt was palpable. He was sure that while he would finally be liberated from his own personal nightmares and demons, there were others, soon to be exposed to the entire world, whose nightmares were just about to begin. As for Liam Mayfair, he had slain his dragon. He had kept his promise.

ABOUT THE AUTHOR

John F. Picciano was born in Newport News, Virginia, and grew up on Long Island, NY where he is currently the Senior Partner of the civil defense law firm Picciano and Scahill P.C.

Mr. Picciano has served as a Special Agent for the F.B.I. and as Deputy Nassau County Attorney.

The author spends his leisure time with his grandchildren, golfing, and fishing the waters of Long Island.

CPSIA information can be obtained
at www.ICGtesting.com
Printed in the USA
BVHW08s1030110818
523999BV00001B/11/P

9 781628 383454